FOOLS' PARADISE

MICHELLE BAILEY

Smiffy Publishing

Smiffy Publishing

ISBN 978-1-3999-7343-4

This novel is entirely a work of fiction. The names, characters and incidents portrayed in it are the work of the author's imagination. Any resemblance to actual persons, living or dead, events or localities is entirely coincidental.

Michelle Bailey asserts the moral right to be identified as the author of this work.

First edition

Smiffy
Publishing

Fools' Paradise

FOOLS' PARADISE is a compelling narrative following the tumultuous journey of Ashley, a young woman with the unique ability to perceive the world even before birth. Silently witnessing her mother take pokes for money, shapes her perceptions about the world she is soon to inhabit.

Abandoned at birth, Ashley is raised by her strict and highly religious grandparents, where beatings and being locked in the cellar become an everyday occurrence. Her life changes drastically when the family move to a rough inner-city estate. Induction to her new life is harsh, but she survives thanks to the help of Paul.

At sixteen, Paul introduces Ashley to Reggie, one of the biggest drug dealers on the estate. She thinks her new life will lead to riches, but she couldn't be more wrong. It quickly descends into a living hell. Reggie regulary beats her and forces her to be his drugs mule, only escaping when he is sent to prison. Alone and addicted to drugs, she discovers she is pregnant and gives birth to her daughter on the floor of a hostel.

Through determination and a bit of luck she secures a job at a prestigious property firm, offering a glimmer of hope for a better future. However, her happiness is short lived as she faces heartbreak once again, this time at the hands of her boss.

Just when it seems all hope is lost, Paul resurfaces, offering a chance for love and redemption. But as Ashley navigates the complexities of her past and present, she must confront the possibility that all is not what it seems.

"Fools' Paradise" is a gripping tale of survival, love and betrayal, showcasing the resilience of the human spirit in the face of adversity.

To my son Kai and beautiful granddaughter A'mei,
you are my source of strength.

What If....

*A husband and wife bring their newborn baby home from
the hospital, where their five-year-old son is waiting,
eager to meet his little sister.*

'Can I ask her a question?' he asks his parents.

'Yes,' they reply.

'In private,' he says.

*Slightly perplexed, they honour his request and leave the
room, ears peeled firmly against the door.*

*'Tell me how it all began,' he whispers into her tiny ears,
'I'm beginning to forget.'*

*What if we are born knowing where we come from,
but over time forget? What if?*

UNKNOWN

Contents

1

Unborn Witness

A FEW FACTS YOU should know about my mother, Eve:
One, the only thing she loves more than money is Ernie.
Two, if dictionaries had pictures, her face would probably
be found beside, scared and broken.

Dear God, I pray if you are real, please make the sticks
stop poking me. I know she wishes I would die; she tells
me this every day. Is this why she makes them poke me?
First, it was Ernie's stick, then all the others. I sway in her
tummy while they push something hard inside her. I fear
they will break into my home, but they always fall short,
stopping inches away from my sac. Until the day George
poked her, I had been a secret. No one, not even her
mother Mary, knew I lay hidden under her loose clothes.

'Six months, and you're still my dirty little secret,' she
whispered that morning as she tightened the band that
helped hide me away from the world.

'Get down on your knees,' the voices always say, but
today is different.

'Turn around; Big George wants to see your pretty little face.'

The force of Big George moved me so far into her back that I heard her bone crack, and I kicked out in pain.

'What the fuck is this?' he shouted. 'You're fucking pregnant, you little whore,'

'Please don't tell Ernie,' She begged. But it was too late. I felt her arms wrap around me as Ernie entered the room. 'I promise, I was going to tell you,' she cried.

'Eve, Eve, Eve, you really are a piece of work.'

'It's yours,' she lied.

I felt the quiver of fear in her words. The truth is, she doesn't know whose sperm conquered her egg but has already claimed Ernie as the victor.

'Get dressed and get the fuck out of my house,' he said, shoving us back onto the bed.

The tremble of her hands vibrated into my bones as I clenched my fists in readiness for her to feel his. My head throbbed as Eve pounded at me with her fists.

'It's all your fault!'

I knew what was coming next. She would get on her knees and pray for me to disappear, tell me I was a bastard baby, and that she would throw me away as soon as I was born. Since that day, I've tried my best to make her love me, curling myself up, hoping she will forget I am growing inside her, but mostly, I wish she would tell me she loves me the same as she loves Ernie.

We were about to leave when Ernie came back into the room. 'I've been thinking, I know plenty of men who will pay even more now you're pregnant,' he said, leaning in so close to her face the fumes of his tobacco breath wafted through her lungs and down into mine. 'Do as I say, and I'll take care of you.'

Take care of her, of us, of me? Something in my tummy swirled, the way it does when Eve spins in the playground, and for the first time since I could hear, I smiled. Eve was wrong; I will have a daddy and a mummy too. I wiggled my ears closer to her tummy as I listened to my daddy's voice.

He promised that once I was out, he would help her make more money than she could ever spend. 'When you've had the baby, you can come and live with me, but you can't bring it with you,' he said. 'Leave it outside a church or in a phone box; trust me, someone will find it.'

I lay silently, listening to their every word.

* * *

Most adults think babies are born pure, untarnished by the unknown world we suddenly inhabit. They believe we learn as we grow. This is not true.

I was a thirty-week-old foetus when an all-knowing in-sight, usually reserved only for the most sacred of shamans, emerged from within me, and like a princess awakened from a deep slumber, my senses tingled to life. Not only can I hear, I understand the words of everyone around me.

3

Some may think this a gift, and others a curse, as not only can I feel joy, pain, love and contempt, Eve and I also share a maternal bond real only to me. Her bitter emotions slam constantly into my growing cortex like Ernie's fists against her back.

'I want to love you, but I don't know how.'

These, her first words to me, stung like the bush Ernie had pushed us into last week. We were sitting in her bedroom, hiding from Mary, who was on the warpath because the school had informed her that Eve had not been in school for the past three days.

'You're sixteen and until you turn eighteen, you is still my child and you will go to school.' Mary said as she chased Eve out of the kitchen with her belt.

I enjoy going to school and learning new words every day. Eve's English teacher says she should stop daydreaming and pay more attention in class. 'Your young brain is like a sponge; it adsorbs everything,' she says.

My brain must be like ten sponges because I remember more words than Eve does. But I learn better from the voices around us. Even when Eve is sleeping, I hear lots of different voices; someone asks questions and when another answers, they win money or a new car. My favourite voices are game shows. Mary and Eve listen to the same ones every day—Chain Letters, Wordsy, Who Wants to be a Millionaire, Word Class, and Scrabble—but they never guess the right answers. I answer the questions in my head and mostly get them all right.

'What is a shaman?' the voice asks. This was question number five on Who Wants to be a Millionaire. 'A, B, C, or all of the above?'

'A, you stupid woman, A,' Mary shouts.

'Do you want to phone a friend, use a lifeline, or ask the audience?'

'Phone a friend', the lady says, calling her best friend Jill, who is an expert in all things spiritual. Jill studied the ancient Shaman tribe for many years and knows for a fact they begin to hear and understand the world around them before they are even born. She says that research suggests that most foetuses awaken to this mystical power at just six weeks.

'What nonsense,' Mary mutters.

'So, the answer is definitely A, Jill?' the lady confirms.

'Yes, defiantly.'

'You've just won £5,000!' The man screams, and the lady begins to cry.

When I learn all the answers, I will win lots of money for Eve and show her she's wrong; we don't need Ernie or the others for their money. This will make her want me. I'm sure it will.

The news at ten scares me the most. Ernie isn't the only one who hits. On yesterday's news, the woman speaking said a man had beaten, shot, and killed his pregnant wife. I pray some more and ask God not to let anyone shoot or kill Eve.

Eve has two sisters and one brother. I hear Mary hit them sometimes, too, but I think she likes hitting Eve the most. One, two, three, four—she counts every whip, and Eve always gets the most. Once she counted to fifty, I think she only stopped because she ran out of numbers and air in her breath. Sometimes Eve's bottom is so sore she can't sit down and so lies on her side or tummy, pushing me backwards. Once, whilst beating Eve, Mary hit me on the side of my bottom with her flogger. Now, it hurts me every day; I think it hurts Eve, too, because, since then, she's always rubbing it.

I hope whoever finds me in the phone box never hits me. Eve cries hardest when Mary hits her; when Ernie does, she whimpers quietly. I wonder why she keeps going back for more hits, but then I remember the money she gets for pokes.

'Soon I'll have so much money I will run away, and Mary will never see me again,' she laughed.

'Eeny, meeny, miny, moe,' Eve sings this song every time she's about to make a decision. 'Phone box or church? Phone box or church?' She is trying to decide where to leave me. I will try hard to stay in her tummy forever.

I am the unborn witness to Eve's secrets, learning more about her each day. I'm sure if she knew I could hear, she would never talk to me, but the more I learn from our time locked in her room, the more I enjoy the sound of her voice.

'When I first met Ernie, he promised me the world,' she said. 'I was waiting at the bus stop after school when he pulled up in his black BMW.'

'You want a ride?' he asked me.

'I jumped right in his car—didn't even know his name.'

'How old are you?' he asked me afterwards, his trousers still on the back seat.'

'Old enough, almost eighteen' I lied. He was twenty-five but said it didn't matter because age was just a number.

'Those young boys can't do anything for you. I'm a man, I can take care of you,' he told her.

The moment she saw his car, she knew he could. He was as dark as tar and his nose spread so wide across his face she thought she might see inside his head. He was the meanest looking man she had ever seen, but his car, diamond studded gold teeth, and rope chains that hung from his neck transformed him into her saviour.

'He's my way out,' she told me. Way out of what, I wonder. 'For your sake, I hope you're a boy. Boys do bad things, and girls pay the price,' she says. 'People who do bad things never face the consequences.' I remember this word from the Wordsy game show—Consequence: *a result or effect, typically one that is unwelcome or unpleasant.* If I am a boy, I don't want to do bad things, and if I'm a girl, I don't want bad things to happen to me.

'Whatever you do, wherever you end up, make sure you find a man with money. Being piss poor is no fun.' She said this after another beating from Mary.

'I never come all the way from Jamaica to London to raise no wayward pickney!' Mary shouted. This time, she'd beaten Eve because she declared she didn't believe in God.

'At church today, the minister said all gay people should be shot and will burn in hell. What kind of wicked God is that?' Eve had asked.

Eve went to sleep covered in welts, waking early the next day to change her bed sheets, which were covered in blood and loose skin that split during her beating. Ernie is her only hope, and as soon as she can, she will leave. Even me growing in her tummy won't stop her.

When she first met Ernie, he appeared gentle and kind. He loved her pretty toes and spent hours rubbing them. He gave her money and even let her wear his gold rope chain that she hid beneath her shirt. But things changed when he began to invite his friends over to his house. 'Just do it for me, babe. I'll give you £30 if you do.' First, it was Chris, then Karl, then Simon, and before long, they were lining up, ready to take their turn with Ernie's 'ting. 'I love you babe, and as soon as we get enough money, you won't have to do this anymore.' Ernie tells her every time his friends leave.

Scorching water runs over her body as she washes away the shame, scrubbing hard between her legs, eager to rid herself of the scent that lingers for days—sometimes weeks—later. Over and over, she tells herself it's worth it. Anything is better than a life with Mary.

'Sometimes we need to do things we don't want to do, especially for love, sex, and money,' she repeats as the water pours over her skin. 'Ernie is the only person who has ever told me he loves me,' So what if she has to share herself to earn it? As she always tells me: 'Some love is better than no love at all.' I pray every day she will find some love for me; I want her to be as afraid of losing me as she is of losing Ernie.

We spend all our Saturdays at Ernie's now, and we sit in Eve's room counting the money every Sunday evening. She keeps it hidden in an old metal biscuit tin. She tells me that when I'm born, she will squeeze me into it and leave a note and fifty pounds inside, asking whoever finds me to please take care of me. But then she changes her mind and decides not to leave anything because they might take the money and still leave me behind. Anyway, fifty pounds, she thinks, is a lot more than I am worth. Now Ernie gives her ten pounds every time she takes pokes, and so far, she has counted her tens to five hundred. Most of his friends come back again and again; I can tell by the smell of their slime.

It's a man called Kane who finally bursts into my home. He pokes Eve so hard she screams the whole time he's inside her. 'Please stop,' she begs him, but the more she cries, the harder he pokes until the mineral-rich fluid that taught me to breathe underwater begins to disappear from around me.

'Oh, shit.' Kane says as he withdraws his stick.

Eve lets out a shrill so loud it temporarily deafens my ears.

'I told you not to do it hard! Now I want one hundred!' Ernie demands when I can hear again. Eve's screams grow louder, and I feel my head squeeze tightly. 'You ain't having that thing in my house. I'll call you a cab,' Ernie says.

'Please come with me!' she begs as pain grips a temporary hold of her stomach, forcing me closer to the outside. But I'm not ready; I enjoy living in my home, and I don't want to be left in a phone box or outside a church.

2

Labour of Hate

MY ENTRY INTO THIS world is tenderly painful for Eve and equally traumatizing for me. I relish being wrapped in the safety of my warm cocoon and fight hard not to leave it, but Eve's contractions, determined to push me out, are much stronger than me. It's birthtime. I listen as she lay panting on the hospital bed, imagining her legs ripped apart, hanging loosely in mid-air by a pair of metal stirrups that weigh heavily on her ankles like a pair of shackles, the type she once told me was used to restrain her ancestors during gang rapes and childbirths. She shakes, screeching in agony, as a lightning bolt of pain rips through her ever-expanding pelvic bone. 'I want Mum! I want my mum!' she screams. I sense beads of sweat rushing to cool her reddening pores.

'What you screaming for? You wasn't screaming when you was tekking man between your legs,' Irene, the Jamaican midwife, huffs. 'If you was studying your books and not opening up your legs to man, you wouldn't be in dis position; you get what you deserve, now, push!'

Through deep wails, Eve pushes hard as I kick and fight with her womb. Irene is so busy cursing that I don't think she notices me emerging feet first until the sole of my left foot pushes through Eve's bloodied gateway. Her youthful vagina tears open as blood haemorrhages from her body, bursting free from her once-tight riverbank. Irene's hands tug at my body, determined to draw me out from between Eve's limp legs. Irene calls the doctor, who rushes into the room. Not to Eve, but to me. Born with the umbilical cord wrapped around my neck, he quickly unravels the twine life giver that had fed me for nine months yet now threatens to take my life away.

Irene is the first person I see. Against her dark, leathery skin, the whites of her eyes and her chipped-enamel tooth shine as bright as the lights that hang from the ceiling. I cry as another nurse wraps me in a blanket and takes me away from Eve. 'Stitch her up,' are the last instructions I hear the doctor give to Irene. Eve has lost a lot of blood, so I sleep in a special room with other babies.

The next day, I hear Eve pleading with Irene to let her stay another day.

'This is not a hotel. We need de bed space; there'll be another one just like you along in a minute.'

As the taxi stops outside Mary's house, I sense the swirl of fear and regret in the tears that stream down Eve's face. She slowly approaches the front door and rings the bell. Mary stands boldly, like a giant looking down into an ant's nest. 'Here's the baby, Mum,' Eve says as she hands me over.

Mary stands motionless in the doorway, her eyes widening as though the fog lingering in her head for months has now lifted, revealing the truth that had been trying to break through. Eve had fooled her; she had been pregnant right under her nose. Once her temporary paralysis allows, she asks, 'What's her name?'

'Ashley,' Eve says before turning to walk away.

'Please don't leave me here!' I wail, but my pleas are deaf to all ears but mine. She walks away, never looking back, and I wonder if I will ever see her again and how long I can keep a lock on her secrets.

'You're my bastard baby now,' Mary whispers as she brings me into the house.

3

Cotton Wool Girl

Mary calls me her wash belly. 'At home in Jamaica, that's what we call the last child,' she tells me as she changes my nappy. 'You're nasty, just like your mother. She never liked getting her nappy changed.' I'm not nasty, I just hate the feel of slimly poo on my skin. I'm crying because I miss Eve. My tummy jumps whenever the doorbell rings, and I listed closely, hoping to hear her voice, but it's always the postman or one of Mary's other children. By my third birthday, I'm using the big toilet by myself and even clean myself too. Auntie Pauline is the only one who lives with us now. I think the others got tired of being hit, so, like Eve, decided to live somewhere else. I've never seen Mary hit Pauline. 'You're my only decent child, all the others are worthless,' Mary always says, telling her how proud she is that she listened to her and became a secretary.

Grandad Johnny, who is usually so quiet I forget he lives with us, agrees. 'You are the only one of our children who will amount to anything,' he says. He always smells of smoke and likes to sit hidden under his cap buried in his special green chair.

I wish Pauline would leave too. Sometimes, when Mary works late, she collects me from Mrs Brown, my child minder. 'Pick her up, give her dinner, a bath, read her a story, and then bed,' Mary always instructs.

'Hurry up and eat your food!' Pauline shouts.

I try to eat faster, but the spoon always has too much food on it, and there is no space left in my mouth. She taps her heels on the floor, shaking her legs as she waits for me to 'hurry up and swallow.' Once, the food slipped out of my mouth and she pushed it back in, hurting my new teeth. I cried a lot then, mainly because the grey ash from Johnny's cigar stuck to the food.

At bath time, I watch as clouds rise from the water and cover the mirror until it disappears. 'Hot!' I scream as the water turns my brown skin red.

'You're nasty, just like your mother. She never liked getting a bath, either.'

Before sleep, she always tells me the same story. 'There was once a girl named Ashley. She was the bastard baby of a whore named Eve. Eve hated her baby so much she gave her away. Ashley will grow up to be a dirty little whore, just like her mother. The End. Goodnight, Ashley. Don't let the bedbugs bite,' she says before turning off the lights and leaving me in darkness with the bedbugs.

I am happy when Pauline leaves forever, and I go to Mrs Brown's all day. I play with my new friends until

Mary comes to collect me. Mrs Brown always smiles and gives me more hugs than anyone ever has. 'Ashley, you are the most beautiful child.' she always tells me before engulfing my head in her chest. Mrs Brown's breasts are larger than the red watermelons she feeds us in the summertime. Her short frame and cylindrical stomach make it impossible to determine where her neck begins and her torso ends. Her course hair reminds me of the special pads Mary uses to scrub pots that have become blackened by burnt oil. Every Friday, Mrs Brown straightens what she calls her unruly mane. I sit in my chair and watch as she lights the stove and places a heavy flat piece of rusting iron into the flickering flames. Once hot, she removes it with a cloth and allows it to cool slightly. Struggling, she then attempts to part her thick hair with her short stubby fingers, applying heaps of jelly grease onto it before ironing out her tight black, grey curls. I watch as her hair sizzles and smokes the way it does when Mary burns the hairs off a chicken. The end result is a high, stiff, badger-like crown that becomes unruly as soon as she starts to sweat.

Mrs Brown is the first person to tell me she loves me. Her words are as warm as milk, her hands as soft as my silk ribbons, and they make me happy. I play and sing and laugh, never worrying that I might get hit for a mistake I never knew I made. Sometimes I wish she were my mother.

Mary's heart is as soft as her knitting balls, but her hands are as hard as rock. Mostly, I feel warm when she looks at me, but when she's angry, her eyes make me shivery cold. Unlike Mrs Brown, Mary's hair is soft and straight and reaches past her shoulders, sitting halfway down her back. Her skin is as smooth and brown as mine. She hides her chest under loose clothes and long skirts, saying women should never wear trousers and anyone who wears skirts above the knee are ungodly hussies. Our neighbour, Mrs Malone, wears what Mary calls "skimpy underwear". 'She should be ashamed to hang them on the line,' Mary says. I like Mrs Malone's underwear, especially her red frilly knickers. Mary's knickers look like tea cloths and are so big she sometimes holds them up with pins.

It is the weekend of my fourth birthday when I first feel the force that had lain dormant within her ever since Eve left. I was lifting a spoon full of rice to my mouth when her hand struck my face as fast as lightning. Stars danced in my eyes and fire burnt my cheek as tears rushed to cool my burning face. My audacity is about to ask what I did wrong, but as the heat settles and my welts rise, it quickly becomes clear.

'Don't you ever raise a spoon to your mouth without thanking the Lord first.'

The Lord's Prayer was the first words Mary taught me. Every night she prays, her voice filled with thunder as she talks to her maker, desperately adding a mixture of pleads at the end, asking God to save me from the sins of my mother.

'*Dear Lord and Saviour, save Eve, bring her back to the comfort of your bosom, show her the error of her ways. And I pray for Ashley, oh, Lord, may you wrap her in your blood and shield her from evil, save her. Oh, Lord, I beg, don't make her turn out like her mother. Thank you, in Jesus' name, Amen.*'

Mary doesn't realise that prayers don't work. I know they don't; I listened to Eve pray for months and her Lord didn't answer a single one of them. He didn't answer mine either.

'You must thank God for everything. Without him, I wouldn't be here,' she says. Mary was an only child whose mother died when she was five years old. She lived with her father, Bill, but was raised by her aunt Enid. 'I will never forget the first time I attended church with Aunt Enid.' Hall of Hope was the largest church in Maroon Town that stood at the top of a steep hill. 'It was a scorching morning. I watched as the powder Aunt Enid had applied earlier slid slowly off her face. The sun grew hotter as we ascended the hill, and Aunt Enid dabbed her cheeks, leaving bits of the white tissue stuck to her face,' Mary laughed. 'The sound of clapping and singing grew louder as we approached.' Having never climbed the hill, Mary had only ever seen the tip of the black metal cross that sat atop the church steeple. I wanted to run, eager for the church to reveal itself and all who sang in it.

'Walk, young lady,' Aunt Enid said as she struggled for air.

'The brightness of the building temporarily blinded me as the sun shone from its freshly painted white walls, causing it to almost glow.' Mary wondered how long it took to clean its many windows. 'I held tightly onto Aunt Enid's gloved hands as we approached. Two ushers greeted us; one handed a hymn book to Aunt Enid, and the other directed us to our seats. I stood right by a little window. I was sure God was looking down on me from the cross at the front of the church. I could almost feel him inside me,' she said. And for the first time since her mother died, Mary felt a sense of peace and belonging.

Spasmodically, members of the congregation would tremble uncontrollably, gripping their Bibles, holding them up towards heaven, and speak in a strange voice that sounded like someone had pinched their throats, causing their words to become a jumbled-up mess.

'Dis is what we call talking in tongues, Mary. It happens when people are filled with the Holy Spirit,' Aunt Enid explained.

That day after church, Mary went straight to her room and began to shake her body, willing the tongue spirits to enter her. But they never did. That day, Mary decided to become a Christian and promised God she would never miss a Sunday service.

'It was God's grace and blessings that brought me to this country. Without him, I wouldn't be here,' she said.

For my fourth birthday, Mary gives me my first Bible. It is filled with words and colourful pictures. The front cover is painted with a picture of a large brown wooden boat, lots of animals, and a rainbow.

'By the time you are five, I expect you to have learnt every book of the Bible. There are seventy-three of them,' she says.

I open the book and stare at the letters dancing around the page like flies, wondering how I would learn them, especially as I couldn't read. 'Can you help me?' I ask her.

'Ask your teacher, that's what school is for.' she says.

I learnt lots of words before I was born but can never read them from books. Whenever I ask Mary for help, she says that's why she sends me to school. I don't think Johnny can read; he has the same Topsy and Tim books we read at school. I watch him silently as he tries to read the words. 'C-c-cat,-s-sat.' Then I remember when I was two, and Mary was telling me she and Johnny came to England from Jamaica with nothing.

'Miss, can you teach me the books of the Bible?' I asked Mrs Patterson the following day.

'You'll have to learn that at church or perhaps Sunday school, Ashley,' she laughed. I wonder how I will ever learn the books of the Bible if I have no one to help me read them. I love going to school, but playing is my favourite thing to do.

Every Sunday, Mary irons my clothes and plaits my hair ready for the week ahead. 'You look just like my mother and have soft hair like she did.' I listen, and for the first time, hear Mary's voice soften as she rummages through a drawer and hands me a picture of her mother. I stare at the picture and intuitively know her name; we say it every time before we eat. Grace. She was of Taino descent and was one of the most beautiful women in the district. She had dimples as deep as wells and eyes that shone like crystals. Every man wanted her, and every woman wanted to be her. 'You're lucky you take after my side of the family, that's where we get our long hair and caramel skin from,' she says.

The last memory Mary has of her mother was at her funeral. She had taken ill two weeks earlier. 'It was as if something was eating her from the insides and the doctors couldn't figure out what it was.' Mary remembers standing outside her room, listening to her painful cries. 'She sounded like a chicken pleading for its life, knowing it is about to get its head cut off.' She says she never forgave her father for not allowing her to enter the room and see her before she died. 'I was convinced if I saw her, hugged and kissed her, she would feel better.'

The next time Mary saw her she was lying in a white silk-lined coffin. 'I kissed her cold hard cheeks, screaming at her to wake up. I wanted to get in the coffin with her.' Her father dragged her away as her tears smudged Grace's makeup. 'Where are her shoes? She won't get into heaven without shoes!' she pleaded. I can feel the heaving in Mary's chest and look up to see tears fall from her eyes. For the first time, I feel sad for her. I try to hug her, but she conks me on the head with the sharp teeth of the comb. 'Turn around and keep your head still,' she says. I'm crying too, and I don't feel sad for her anymore. I miss Eve and want to be with her and Ernie.

4

Peter Rabbit

'ASHLEY, THANK GOD YOU'RE pretty. You'll have to use your looks to get anywhere in life because there isn't much going on up there, is there?' Mrs Patterson says, tapping my head with the top of her ring. She tells me that all I do is daydream. I'm six now and still can't read very well. When I tell her the words won't keep still, she says it's because I'm not getting enough sleep and that Mary must be feeding me lots of junk. She says I have the reading age of a five-year-old. I don't daydream; I just wonder where Eve is, how much money she has, and if she will ever come back for me.

'I'm not daydreaming, Miss. I'm contemplating,' I tell her.

She laughs so loudly the entire class turns to face me. I feel heat rise to the surface of my cheeks, and I sit at my desk, staring at my shoes, hoping their beady eyes will have averted when I look up. They haven't; they stare at me and then at Mrs Hall as she approaches my desk. 'Peter Rabbit,' she says, placing the book on my desk. 'You know more big words than I do, God knows how,' she says so that only I can hear her. I once told Maggie I could hear before I was born, but she just laughed and called me cuckoo, so I will never tell anyone my secret again. 'If you can say the words, you should be able to read the words.' Mrs Patterson declared. I stare up at her, my eyes begging her not to make me read in front of the class. 'Come on, Miss-I-swallowed-a-dictionary-but-can-barely-read-or-write. Stand up.' I rise slowly from my seat, and she ushers me towards her desk at the front of the room. 'Ashley is going to read Peter Rabbit for us all,' she announces.

I swallow my spit, trying desperately to wet my throat, which feels as dry as dirt. I wipe my hands on my skirt, now sticky from the moisture that seeps from them, and suddenly, I'm absent again. Have my wet palms left a mark on my skirt, and will it dry before Mary sees it?

'Is anybody there?' I break free from my daydream to see Mrs Patterson clicking her fingers in front of my eyes, her spit spraying my nose as she leans into my face. Again, my eyes plead, *please don't make me read*, but again, she doesn't hear me. 'Get on with it. We haven't got all day,' she says. I open the book. 'It's upside down, for heavens' sake,' she says. Grabbing it from between my fingers, she turns it around, opens it to the first page, and hands it back to me. I stare hard at the words, willing my brain to understand them, but they won't keep still and move around the page like the butterflies dancing in my tummy. I feel the glare of a million eyes and want to shirk myself, to disappear like melting ice, hide in the cellar and never come out again.

I begin, 'P-p-p-Peter Rabbit.' Mrs Patterson lets out a sign so huge she blows my hair to the front of my face. 'Lit-lit-little-p-pet-peter-ra-rab-rabbit,'

'She can't read,' Jayne, the girl with the long red hair and shoes, shouts. The entire class erupts into fits of laughter so loud the headmaster, Mr Jenkins, enters the room.

'Go back to your seat. I'm going to have to speak to your mother,' Mrs Patterson says.

'I don't have a mother, you silly cow. She doesn't want me—nobody does!' I shout and immediately wish I could swallow my words. The class falls silent, and Mrs Patterson stares at me with her mouth open as if trying to catch flies. I look up and see Ben staring at me. His blonde hair looks like someone put a bowl over his head and cut it, but not short enough, as it still covers his eyes, causing him to constantly flick his head to the side. I give him a hateful stare, but he just smiles at me, the kind of smile I wish Mary or Jayne would give me. I smile back.

The look on Mary's face tells me I'm not only going to get a beating, I'm going to be locked in the cellar tonight, too.

'I just don't know what's wrong with her. She has a vocabulary to rival an eleven-year-old, but she has the reading age of, well, a child half her age.'

Mary looks down at me as if in shock. 'Well, if you could read, then maybe I would be able to as well,' I want to say, but I know this would be asking for a beating that will leave me unable to sit for a week.

'Is everything okay at home?' Mrs Patterson asks. I stare up at Mary and watch as her breast rises. She crosses her arms around her chest, as if doing this will quieten her breath, which is now suddenly heavy and fast. Her smile fades from agreeable to angry distortion. 'I'm, I'm just saying,' Mrs Patterson stutters. 'She clearly has a gift with words, but, well, it cannot be fully nurtured if she can't read them.' If looks could kill, Mrs Patterson would be lying dead on the classroom floor. She rocks unsteadily from left to right, her eyes searching towards the door for help that won't come. I stare at Mary; her eyes stare at a painting on the wall as if searching for an answer lost in the paint. Finally, she breaks her silence and speaks in her best Jamaican-English accent she only uses when answering the phone.

"Mrs Patterson, Ashley, as you say, is a bright child, and you are her teacher. If she cannot read, is it not your fault?' Before she can respond, Mary grabs my hand, and we stand to leave.

'I'm sure if we work together, we can come up with a solution,' are the last words Mrs Patterson says before Mary drags me out of the room. I hope this is the last time Mrs Patterson asks me to read in front of the class. Every day, I creep into class and sit silently at the back. Even if I'm certain I know the answers, I sit still as a statue and hope she never speaks to me again.

'Le-lear-learn your books!' Mary shouts that night. Her beatings are always filled with angry commentary and remind me of the men who ride the horses that Grandad cheers at. 'I've sacrificed everything for you!' she says as she locks the cellar door behind her. 'Do you know how often I don't eat and instead watch you fill your tummy?'

I know it's a lot of times. Sometimes, I am still hungry but don't eat all my food; I leave it for her to eat. When she had two jobs, she would eat with me and save Grandad's dinner in the oven until he got home from work, but now she mostly eats what's left on my plate. I wonder why she doesn't eat some of Grandad's. I used to wonder if Grandad disliked me for eating his food, but the first time I got locked in the cellar, he told Mary to let me out. That was on my fifth birthday.

'How is she supposed to learn the books of the Bible if we can't teach her?'

'Exactly, Grandad!' I wanted to say. He is now on level three of the Topsy and Tim books. I like to sit and watch him trying to read, hoping to learn too, but whenever he sees me looking, he fidgets in his seat and moves to another room.

I love the smell of the cellar; its dampness smells like a mixture of rotting wood and musty dust that I long to taste. I rub my hands over the hard brick surface, collecting dust with my fingers, sniffing them as I curl the dust into a tiny ball between my fingertips. Once, Johnny caught me licking the wall and, for the first time, slapped me hard on the side of my face. I never ate dust again after that.

'Sorry for not learning the books of the Bible.' I say and walk towards her. I reach for the hem of her skirt, about to hug her legs, but she pushes me away. I see the glint from Grandad's glasses and turn to look at him, but as quick as a fly, he turns his head back towards the TV. Mary says Grandad is as quiet as a church mouse. I'm usually in bed by the time he gets in from work, and when he is at home, he sits in his chair trying to read, or he watches cowboys on TV. They're worse than Mary's game shows because I can't learn anything from them. They just kill people and ride horses.

'Here you go, Ashley.' Every Friday, Grandad brings me a sweet.

'They'll rot out her teeth,' Mary always says.

'Thanks, Grandad.' I hug him. He never hugs me back, but he doesn't push me away, either. I think he likes my hugs but is too scared of Mary to touch me. Grandad sometimes smells like metal, and his short, fat fingers are always full of dirt as if he plays in the mud all day. Mary makes him wash them as soon as he walks through the door. Sometimes, if I'm locked in the cellar, he will give me a piece of bread when Mary isn't looking. Once, she caught him giving me a guinep.

'How will she learn if you spoil her? It's the same thing you did to her mother, and look at how she turned out.' Mary is determined I won't turn out like Eve, but I want to be pretty when I grow up, too.

After my reading attempt of Peter Rabbit, only Maggie will still be my friend. She is from Ireland and lives with her mum, dad, and older sister. 'Would you like to come and play at my house?' she asks me one Friday afternoon.

I have never visited anyone's house before except one of Mary's church sisters. We stood in the hallway while she collected the bottle of white rum she had brought back from Jamaica so Mary could make her famous rum cakes.

'Come in and have a cup of tea,' Sister Thomas said.

'Thanks, but I've left the peas on the stove.'

Mary had strict rules: never eat from anyone, never eat in public, and never buy takeaways—except for the occasional fish and chips on a Friday.

'Not even if I were really hungry?' I asked.

She answered with the back of her hand against the side of my head—slap! 'Not even if you're starving.'

'Would you like a drink?' Sister Thomas asked me. My throat was so dry I felt the air lodge in my lungs as I inhaled, imagining her fridge filled with every flavoured fizzy drink in the world. I lifted my eyes to meet Mary's, standing silently as Sister Thomas waited for my reply.

'If you say yes, I will beat you so hard when we get home.' Mary's eyes said.

'No, thank you,' I lied.

At the end of school, I run to Mary with Maggie. 'Can I play at Maggie's house?'

'Please, please, please,' Maggie adds. We hold hands and jump around like a pair of grasshoppers.

'Not today, dear,' Mary says, squeezing my fingers so hard I let out an unintentional ouch. I walk home in silence, but Mary won't shut up. 'You're just like your mother! She loved going to people's houses, and now look at her; she is a street rat.'

The voice in my head responds, 'No, she's not. She doesn't have to work two jobs, and she has lots of money that Ernie gives her. I'd rather be Eve than you.'

Eve gets money for pokes, but so does Mary. Every Friday, Grandad comes home and gives her a brown envelope stuffed with money. 'Twenty, forty, sixty,' Mary counts it out, takes most of it, and hands the rest back to Grandad. When he returns from the pub, Mary lets him sleep in her room.

'Take that bloody nighty off,' I hear him say. The headboard bangs against my bedroom wall, and I know he's poking her; I hear the noises, so she takes money for pokes too.

5

Eve

'Would you like a piece of chocolate?' Ben asks. He has kind eyes, and I think I like him. He snaps it in two and hands me the bigger half.

'Thank you,' I smile.

'I think you're really pretty. Will you be my girlfriend?'

'Do you have any money?' I ask.

He reaches into the back pocket of his grey trousers with a black patch stitched into the left knee and pulls out a shiny fifty pence coin. 'Here,' he says, holding it up in front of my eyes. 'If I give it to you, can I kiss you?'

I close my eyes and try not to move whilst he kisses my cheek. If I make him kiss me every day, I will be rich soon. The next day, he wants another kiss but only has twenty pence. 'I'll only kiss you for fifty pence'.

'I'll bring it tomorrow,' he promises. I let him kiss me, but this time, without his tongue.

Sitting in my room, I count my coins. So far, I have ten pounds. That's more than Mary has in her money jar. I keep it hidden inside my pillow, where Mary will never find it. She made my pillow out of old jumpers, skirts, tatty knickers, and other scraps of clothing. I try hard to remember before I was born, but I think the hits Mary gives me make my memories fade into the back of my brain.

Sometimes I lay my head on the pillow and then onto the Bible. God's book is softer than my pillow; I open it in half and lay on its soft pages. The more I sleep on it, the more pages I find on the floor the next morning. Mary will beat me and lock me in the cellar for days if she sees even one page of Psalms is missing. I try to stick them back with Sellotape from Grandad's toolbox, but it's black and too obvious. I decide that if Mary ever asks me to read Psalm 22, I will read Psalm 27. She can barely read anyway, so hopefully, she will never notice the difference.

I lay awake on my Bible, thinking about Ben. I will be seven soon, and he is the only person ever to have kissed me. I don't think I like it, but I like feeling wanted and loved. The warmth from his body feels as warm as the heat that surrounds me when I sit between Mary's legs when she combs my hair. The feel of her soft hands on my face as she parts my scalp and slushes a finger full of green grease between the partings. This is the closest we ever get to affection, and I wish we could stay here forever. I hold on to her legs, wrap my arms around them, and rest my head against her brown laddered tights. She smells like a mixture of onions and currants. It's only August, but today, she started soaking berries in preparation for her Christmas rum cake.

'Cherries, dates, and currents,' she told me as she covered the dried fruit in the white rum.

A berry dropped onto the floor, and I picked it up and popped it into my mouth before Mary noticed. But the taste went up my nose, and my eyes streamed as I coughed. I tried hard to swallow it but had to spit it out before it burnt a hole in my stomach.

Whack

'What on earth are you doing? This is full of rum!' Mary said, causing me to spit the fruit onto the floor. My head hurt, but my stomach felt nice and warm. When she went into the living room to watch Wordplay, I licked the bowl and slurped up the remaining liquid that burnt and lit up my tummy.

That night, I dream of my great-grandmother Grace and Eve. I feel the pokes and fear they may break into my home. I picture Eve on her knees as Ernie, Paul, and Big George break into my home.

'Wake up, Ashley!' Mary shouts. 'Did you wet the bed? You're lazy, just like your mother. She could never be bothered to go to the toilet and always wet the bed.' She pushes me so hard towards the bathroom my head hits the door handle, and blood pours from my nose onto the purple carpet. I hope she doesn't see it. I grab some tissue, pinch the bridge of my nose, and tilt my head back just like Mrs Patterson does whenever Kenny has a nosebleed. I pull my knickers down; they are dry, but my nighty and hair are dripping with water. 'If you're too lazy to go to the toilet, you can sleep in your wet nightie.' Mary says as she turns out the lights.

Today is Saturday, and I'm glad I don't have to go to school. Slowly, I unravel myself from the dry corner of my bed and remove the coat I slept under last night. I try to lift my head, but it feels as heavy as Grandad's toolbox, and I feel something inside my head beating against my forehead. It thuds harder than Mary's fists, and I squeeze it, hoping it stops.

'Get up, you lazy girl,' Mary enters my room and opens the curtains. The light hits my eyes, and I fall back onto my bed, unsteadied by the assaulting rays. 'Nasty girl still wetting the bed at your age, same as your mother did.' Mary rips the cover from under me, causing me to slide to the floor. I jump to grab my pillow, but it's too late. My money jar, now full of coins, falls out of my pillowcase, landing on Mary's feet. Her eyes tighten in pain as she clutches her little toe covered in corn plasters. I run into the bathroom faster than a chained dog now free of its leash. My stomach churns, and my head bangs. I want to wee, but before I can lift the lid, the contents of my stomach force my mouth open. Bits of potato mixed with fish and cake mix cover my feet and drip from the corners of my mouth. Mary follows closely behind me, my money jar firmly in her hand. 'Where you get dis money from, you little thief?'

'It's my mon-' But before I can get the words out, the back of her hand slaps them back in.

'Take off your clothes, get in the bath, and don't move!' she shouts.

I do as I'm told, pulling my nighty over my head, and I look in the mirror. Great, now I have yesterday's food in my hair, too. I wrap my arms around myself, rubbing them up and down my body, stepping from one foot to the other, trying to quell the cold creeping into my bones from the enamelled bath that seems determined to steal my body heat. The smell of last night's dinner rises and seeps up into my nostrils. I gag, but there is nothing left in my tummy except liquid. I lean over to the sink and am about to spit when Mary walks back into the room with a mop, bucket, and leather belt.

'Please, Mum. Please, I beg you, I didn't steal the money.' This is the first time I have ever called her mum, and I do so hoping she will loosen the grip on her belt. Upon hearing my pleas, she lifts the belt, lowers it slightly, and then raises it again, high above my back.

'You think you're smart? Well, you is a ginal, just like your mudda.' are the last words she says before striking, counting to fifty as she does—one strike for every coin in my money jar. The pain in my head subsides, but my back feels like it's been stung by a swarm of angry bees. Slowly, I lay on my bed. At least I can sleep on my left side; Mary missed that part.

* * *

I know she is at the door before the bell rings. I've only ever felt this once, and that was over seven years ago, before I was born. That all-knowing presence only reserved for shamans, a distant memory buried in the crevices of my brain, unfolds and finds its way to the forefront.

'Hi, Mum,' her voice says.

I knew she would come back for me! It's been years, and I still jump whenever the doorbell rings. I run to the door so fast I don't see Mary's shoes in the hallway. Tripping over them, I fall clumsily at her feet. 'Sorry,' I say and wipe her black shiny boots with the cuff of my red jumper. An action I regret the minute I see the transfer of dirt and feel the rays from Mary's eyes burn a hole in the back of my neck. I look up at her, but she doesn't lower her head. Instead, she shakes me off her boot like she's just stepped in a muddy puddle. Seven years, but the smell of her skin and the black spot in the middle of her nose are exactly the same.

'What are you doing here?' Mary asks, shoving me back inside the house.

I stand stiffly behind the door, listening in hope. I knew she would come back for me; I just knew it. Finally, I'm going to have a real mum like the other girls at school. One who waits at the school gate and hugs me like Maggie's mum hugs her, handing me sweets and a carton of juice. A mum who can help me with my homework, who can read, who will give me a hug so big I will get lost in her arms and have to fight my way out for breath.

'What do you want?' Mary asks.

'I want what's mine,' Eve says.

'Over my dead body will I let you take her.'

Eve laughs. 'Two hundred pounds, and you can keep her. I'll never come back for her again.' Mary pleads with her. She doesn't have that kind of money but promises she will get it and asks Eve to come back in a few days. Her heels clink, and I run into the living room and watch her get into a car; I can't be sure, but I think it's a black BMW.

Two days later, I wait by the window. This time, I want to get a longer look at her.

'If I catch you at that window again, watch what I'm going to do with you, you ungrateful little child!' Mary shouts. Wanting to cry, I swallow my tears in my mouth. If Mary locks me in the cellar, I won't be able to see her.

The next morning, I brush my teeth for six whole minutes, rub my face with extra Vaseline, and tie two blue ribbons in my hair. I will look so pretty, Eve will want to take me with her. Staring out the window, I watch as she walks up the pathway. This time, her eyes look darker, as if she's been crying. And then I notice it, something hiding under her jumper, something where I was. The pristine boots she wore yesterday now look dirty, and one of her feet lean to the side, making her wobble. She stares at the door before knocking, looking back at the car behind her. I think I can see water in her eyes. Her fingernails are covered in red patches and are black underneath. I think she is wearing lipstick like Mrs

Patterson, but one side of her bottom lip sticks out and looks extra red. Her hands shake as she rings the bell.

'Ashley!' Mary calls. I try to move away from the window, but it's too late. 'What did I tell you about staring out the window? You wait till later; I'm going to give you what for,' she says as she slaps me across my bottom.

6

And Then There Were Three

IT'S THE WEEK AFTER my eighth birthday when the phone rings. I watch Mary's face screw up like a ball of paper, then slowly unravel as she bites on her bottom lip, frantically scribbling words legible only to herself onto an old envelope. I struggle to intercept the voice on the other end of the receiver that faintly sounds like my headmaster, Mr Jenkins. 'Get your coat! We need to go out,' she shouts. So, it isn't Mr Jenkins. She would almost certainly have hit me if it was. Her eyes almost glistened as a puddle of water surrounded them. Mary never cries, but whatever she's just heard makes her hand shake. What if something bad has happened to Eve? A strange feeling whirls in my stomach, and I know this is going to be a bad day for me.

As Mary holds my hand, I feel like I'm floating on air. My feet hover over the pavement, landing only to be lifted again by the tug of her arm. We take the train to Paddington Station—now I know something is really wrong. We only ever take buses unless we're going to Dalston market. Buses are much cheaper, Mary always says. I stare out the window as gardens fly by. One has a climbing frame ten times bigger than the one in our park. Some have bikes and sheds like we have in ours. One even has a swimming pool full of blue water. The yellow sun beams through the window from a blue cloudless sky, and people pour onto the train like they do at church. Mary pulls me closer to her when a man whose holes in his shoes are so large, I can see his socks as he sits beside me. Most of his face is hidden behind thick grey hair; his forehead is creased like a dried-up leaf. I lift my eyes to meet his. His smile reveals a single brown tooth, and his breath smells like the toilet after Grandad does a number two. Mary hits me across the back of my head before we move to another seat further along the train.

'If you ever talk to strangers again.'

'But I didn't.' Before the words could leave my mouth, Mary's hand hits them back in again.

'Don't answer back,' she says. The lady sitting opposite gives me the same look our neighbour always does. A look that says, 'I feel sorry for you.' Mary gives her a look that says, 'It's none of your business how I raise my child.'

'Paddington Station,' the invisible man announces as we exit the train.

Mary asks a lady for directions to Portland Street, and I begin to fly again. Mary stops abruptly when she sees two police officers standing outside a house.

'Mary?' the officer stretches his hand out to meet hers. My feet fall to the ground, and my arm aches with relief. 'I'm Officer Thomas, and this is Officer Barnes.'

The lady officer points towards stairs that lead to the bottom of the house. 'It's the basement flat,' she says.

'Following her arrest this morning, Eve asked us to contact you,' Officer Thomas explains as we walk down the steps. I search Mary's face for clues, but it revealed none.

'How long has your daughter and her children lived here?' Officer Barnes asks.

Mary stared blankly at the blue door. 'I'm not sure,' she finally answers. 'I know about the children, but I have never met them.'

Thoughts bounce around in my head, crashing into each other as my mind searches to make sense of this information. I knew Eve was hiding a baby under her tummy, but not two. Officer Thomas asks if Mary has a key, to which she replies with an exhaustive, 'Of course not.'

They eye the two large windows and attempt to find a way in.

'Shut solid,' Officer Barnes says.

I follow Mary's eyes up to a small window, but it is too small for them to fit into. Mary turns to me and, for the first time, holds my hands gently in hers and kneels in front of me. 'Ashley, you are going to have to be a brave girl and climb through that window.' The window is taller than Mary and the officers, so I don't know how she thinks I can reach it.

'I'm not sure I'm comfortable with this idea,' Officer Barnes says.

Officer Thomas says he understands her concerns, but as the children have been left alone for God knows how long, time is of the essence. If they wait for a locksmith, it could take hours, and they need to get them out before nightfall. He says they will lower me through the window so I can open the door for them. 'You're a brave girl, aren't you?' Officer Thomas asks me.

I think of Wonder Woman saving the world and smile. 'Yes, I can be like Wonder Woman and save the children.'

They laugh, but not as much as I want them to. Mary cuts her eyes at me like she does when she calls me a dunce.

'We don't have time to dillydally,' Mary tells them.

'Listen, Ashley.' This time, Officer Thomas kneels in front of me. 'We will lift you up, then lower you down through the window,' he says.

They lift me up so I can have a look through the glass. As I poke my head inside the window, a smell rises to meet my nose, and my eyes water as the sting of wee clings to my lashes. My head shakes involuntarily from side to side. 'I'm not Wonder Woman. I'm not Wonder Woman. I'm not Wonder Woman.' I tell myself as I retreat, Officer Thomas catching me in his arms. I imagine being flushed down the toilet into the sea of brown poo, never to be seen again. 'The toilet is open; it will swallow me up,' I say.

41

'Don't be stupid,' Mary says. Officer Barnes shoots her a look.

'I promise we won't make you fall into the toilet. Even Wonder Woman gets scared sometimes.' Officer Thomas reassures me. 'Just place your feet on either side of the seat and jump onto the floor,' he says.

Officer Thomas holds one of my arms, and Officer Barnes grips the other as they slowly lower me down through the window. As soon as my feet touch the seat, I jump quickly onto the floor. It sticks like chewing gum to my shiny black shoes. The house is dark, but a beam from the window casts a shadow of light into the hallway. My fingers search the wall for a light, and I tiptoe to reach it. *Click, click, click,* it doesn't work. Ever since Pauline told me about bed bugs and Mary started locking me in the cellar, I've been afraid of the dark, and now I am in an entire house almost alone. What if monsters are in here? The bathroom door leads to a long hallway. I can just about see what I think is the front door at the end of it.

'Aaaah!' I scream as something resembling a small cat with long whiskers runs past me towards the back of the house. Then I hear Officer Barnes calling through the letterbox, temporarily shining slivers of light onto the floor.

'Ashley, walk towards my voice and open the door,' she says. I rock back and forth, willing myself to move, but my feet feel heavy. I think they're stuck to the chewing gum on the floor. 'Come on, Wonder Woman. You can do it.'

I peel my feet off the floor and walk slowly towards the door, my hands feeling their way through the partial darkness. I am almost at the front door when I trip over something. I'm falling backwards now and hit my bottom hard as I land by the entrance of a large room. And there they are. Two figures huddled together on a mattress in the middle of the floor, their shadows so thin they almost seem like one person with two heads. The light shining through the gaps of torn curtains that hang from a tall window reveals empty crisp packets, old newspapers, and a box of cereal. Four eyes filled with sadness stare into mine, and I feel their sorrow as if it is my own. The smell inside the room makes my eyes water again.

'Ashley, are you okay in there?' Officer Thomas shouts, breaking us from our geneal trance. I search the door, running my hands up and down its wooden frame until I find the lock. I stretch myself, pointing my fingers high above my head as I grip the latch. 'Turn the knob to the right,' Officer Thomas says.

'Don't you mean left?' Officer Barnes corrects him.

Mrs Patterson's face pops into my head. 'The cat is on the left. The dog is on the right.' I hear her say. I listen to Officer Barnes and turn it to the left.

Officer Thomas tries turning the lights on before taking a torch out of his big belt. It is so bright it lights up the entire hallway. 'They're in there,' I say, pointing towards the room. I can't tell if they are boys or girls. They sit still and silent, two half-naked children on the mattress, their noses barely visible, hidden by slimy green goo.

43

'Don't be afraid, we won't hurt you.' Officer Barnes says. I like her voice. It reminds me of Eve's. 'I'm Officer Barnes, and this is Officer Thomas, like Thomas the Tank Engine. And this is your grandmother Mary; she's come to take you home.' With this, they retreat to the furthest corner of the mattress and start to snivel.

'Don't worry; I'll take you home and give you lots of cake. Would you like that?' Mary asked. The last time I heard this tone in her voice was when Eve first handed me to her. I watch as Officer Thomas helps Mary lift them off the mattress while Officer Barnes searches for their clothes. He can only find some towels. 'These will have to do,' Mary says as she wraps them around the children.

The taller one has funny legs; they stick out at the knees like a monkey. At first, the smaller one looks like she doesn't have any knees at all, but then Officer Thomas points his torch towards them, and I see she does. Officer Barnes stretches out her hands, careful not to touch them with anything other than her gloved hands. I think she thinks they have leprosy, like the man in the Bible that Jesus cured.

As we drive home in the police car, their smell grows stronger. I make myself as small as I can, holding my breath, trying my best not to touch them, and let out a large breath of air when Officer Thomas finally opens all the windows. I eye these two strangers and watch silently as they eat the bowl of cereal Mary has given them.

'Ashley, these are your sisters, Donna and Marcia. Donna and Marcia, this is your older sister, Ashley.' They look at each other as though reading thoughts through their eyes and then look at me. I offer a slight but friendly smile, but they stare into their milk as though they might find my face there. I always wished I had sisters or even a brother, but now I am twice as happy there are two extra bottoms for Mary to slap.

From the corners of my eyes, I watch my two sisters. Marcia, the tall, darker one, hugs the bowl and shovels the cereal into her mouth so fast Mary gives her another helping. She eats every flake, then holds the bowl above her mouth until the last drop of milk falls into her throat. I watch, waiting for her to lick the bowl, but she looks up at Mary with eyes that say, 'Please, can I have some more?' I know better than to ever ask for more and wait for Mary's hand to come down on the back of her head or the side of her cheek. But instead, she rests her hand on her shoulder and squeezes it. Not a hard squeeze she gives me when I embarrass her in church, and she doesn't want to shout, but a squeeze so gentle, I don't think Marcia even feels it. I search Mary's eyes; they have a kindness in them she only reserves for special occasions. I felt that kindness when I first came home from the hospital and also when Mary speaks to the minister at church or Pauline. She then refills the bowl until it's almost overflowing and hands it back to Marcia.

'Eat up, you poor thing, eat up,' she says.

Donna, the fairer one, eats as if her last meal is still stuck in her throat, leaving no room for the food sitting in front of her. Her cheeks are large, her skin the same colour as the red Jamaican dirt in the picture on the fridge of Grandad's farm. Her nose is as small as the button on my skirt, her tiny nostrils almost invisible under the dried goo that sticks to them like blue tac to my drawings. She looks up at me, and I look away. Mary asks if I want any cereal, but I can't eat with them; their smell makes me want to vomit. I turn to go to my room. *Slap!* My head jerks forward, and I feel blood rush to my cheeks as I look up to see my sisters staring at each other—again, saying nothing, but saying something, communicating with their eyes, not their tongues. I stare back; I don't think I like them.

Marcia was born a year after I was, and Donna a year after that. Eight, seven, six. June, July, August.

'Get two towels from my bedroom,' Mary says as they climb into the bath.

'It stings,' are the first words I hear Donna say as Mary peels the dried goo from around her nose that cracks and falls into the now murky water.

'Oh, you're nasty, just like your mother,' Mary tells her.

They speak with their eyes again, and I realise I understand every blink. Donna sucks on her thumb like it's a strawberry lollipop. Her two front teeth remind me of the long white ones Bugs Bunny has. Her head is full of soft brown curls. Her nose is as flat as the wonky Mr. Potato Head I made at school. Her legs are so short it looks like she walks on her knees. If she didn't have nails, I would have thought someone had cut her fingers in half.

Even though I am the eldest, Marcia is much taller than I am. Her long, skinny frame exposes her sharp bones that threaten to poke through her dark skin. Her chin is as sharp as an icicle, and her face is as flat as a piece of paper. Her eyes are as small as a penny and lay close to her ears that stick out like the side mirrors on Grandad's car.

Mary slathers their ashy skin with cocoa butter. She rubs and rubs until the cream disappears, and they shine so brightly I can almost see my face in their skin. Silent tears fall down Marcia's cheeks as Mary fights to pull the comb through her hair. When she gets fed up with trying, she sends me to fetch her dressmaker scissors and cuts the tough bits out. This makes Marcia cry loudly now, but she quickly falls silent again when Mary conks her head with the comb. I pick the clumps off the floor; they feel like the hay in Jesus' manger on display in the church hall. She looks nicer now, even with patches on her head. Mary says Donna is lucky; her hair is so soft she can glide her fingers through it. I like them much better after their bath. The smell of wee has now left my nose but still lingers on their clothes that Mary places into a plastic bag and throws into the outside bin. She never throws anything away except actual rubbish. I guess the yellow and brown stains are too ingrained even for her scrubbing brush and blue soap to remove.

I peer through the crack of the living room door and listen as Mary tells Grandad about my new sisters. Mary has seen Eve since I was born and knew about Donna and Marcia, but I still don't think she knows about the one I saw hiding in her tummy. 'What will I tell the people at church?' Children or no children, Mary will not miss a Sunday service for anyone.

'Just tell them they are your eldest son's children. No one will ever know,' he says.

'I can't lie in the house of the Lord; God will strike me down.'

He takes a long glug of his Guinness, eases his feet deep into his checkered slippers, and turns to watch the horse racing. 'Tell them the truth then,' he says.

'It's a disgrace that she has three children with three different fathers,' Mary says.

Without taking his eyes off the moving horses, Johnny says, 'In the eyes of God, we are all sisters because we all come from the same womb.'

Mary calls him an idiot, and I move away from the door as her footsteps approach. Now I know why we all have different coloured eyes. Mine are the colour of the soft brown sugar Mary puts in her tea, whilst Donna's and Marcia's are as dark as Johnny's coffee. I wonder who my father is, if I look like him, and why he doesn't come to see me. Probably the same reason as Eve's—he doesn't want me.

'That bloody daughter of mine does nothing but bring shame on me.' I hear Mary wail.

I thought having new sisters would be fun, but now I have to share everything with them, and I don't want to. I have four dolls and give one to Marcia and one to Donna. The two with blue eyes and blonde hair are my favourites, so I keep them for myself. A week after they arrive, I catch Marcia in my room, holding one of my dolls. 'Give it back,' I say, snatching it from her hand. She pushes me so hard I fall backwards onto the bed.

'Make me,' she says.

I stand up, but she pushes me back down with her chest. I want to cry but hold the tears behind my eyes. I stand up again, but this time, she lifts my doll above her head and forcefully brings it down to meet mine.

'She won't give me my doll back,' I tell Mary.

Suddenly, Marcia appeared with my doll in her hand. 'She hit me,' she cries, tears streaming down her blue-black cheeks. She hands me my doll, who is now naked with her head missing.

'She broke my doll,' But before I can say another word, Mary sends me for her belt. This is the first beating I received because of Marcia's lies. Mary always says that whatever is hidden under the floorboards will always come to light and shine from the rooftops. One day, I will make Marcia pay for my scars.

The worst part of having two new sisters is sharing my bed with them. Donna took my space at the top-left, even though I chose that space first. So, now I sleep at the top-right side, and Donna is in the middle at the bottom. Marcia hit me when Donna told her I kicked her in the face, but I was asleep, and it was an accident.

'Be like a statue and don't move,' Donna says, pulling my hair.

Now, I sleep touching the wall and try to be as still as a dead person. Now I don't really like Donna, either. She sneaks around quietly and only really speaks to Marcia, staring at the wall as if watching a TV screen only she can see, only speaking when she wants something and when Mary says no—she cries as easily as a rain cloud with snot and everything. One minute, she's smiling; the next, tears stream down her face like a tap that won't switch off until she is given a piece of cake or whatever it is she wants. I copied her once. Mary made vanilla sponge cake we ate with tea. Donna had almost finished hers before purposely dropping the last bite onto the floor and started crying as she quickly leaned down to pick it up, throwing it into the bin. She then switched on her tap of tears, and Mary swiftly handed her an even bigger slice, even though she only dropped a tiny piece. So, I dropped my last bite, too, which was actually bigger than the piece she dropped, and switched on my tap of tears. As I bent down to pick it up, Mary looked down at me.

'Stop your crocodile tears, you ginal, just like yuh mudda. Clean up the floor, and get out the kitchen.'

Donna's eyes smirk at mine. 'I can get what I want, but you can't,' they said. And this is how she gets more: more cake, more juice, more rice. She milks her tears like a maid milks a cow—tears, tears, and more snotty tears.

Mary and Grandad, when he's around, raise Donna and Marcia like their own, and Mary gets a second job as a dinner lady at a nursery near our school. My disdain for Marcia grows as her dominance takes over my life.

'Blessed are the peacemakers,' Mary tells me every time we have a fight.

'I am the peacemaker. She's the bully,' I want to say, but I know better. I thought them living with us would mean a share of the beatings, but with Marcia's bully tactics and Donna's ability to pull the wool over the eyes of Sherlock Holmes, my scars only increase. I envy Donna and Marcia's relationship and secretly long to be a part of their sisterhood, so when Donna asked me to bring their towels into the bathroom, I jumped at the chance to share in their bathtime fun and wished I could get in with them. But Mary won't let me.

Donna is standing in the bath with Mary's false teeth in her mouth. 'If you do that again, dog nyam your suppa,' she says, pretending to be Mary.

'My turn!' Marcia says, placing the teeth into her mouth.

'Wanti, wanti, can't get it,' she says.

I laugh so hard, my stomach hurts; we haven't had so much fun since they arrived. 'Okay, my turn,' I say, rinsing the teeth out under the tap before placing them in my mouth.

'Blessed are the peacemakers. You is lazy, just like yuh mudda. What sweet nanny goat a go run yuh belly, when Eskimo have money him buy fridge.' I'm on a roll, laughing so hard, until I notice Marcia and Donna are as still as statues, staring at me like I'm sharing a private joke with myself. I feel her breath on my neck before I see her. Slowly, I reach into my mouth and pull the teeth

51

from my gums. As I lower my hand, they slip from my grasp. *Splash!* I look down to see a gold tooth shining up at me from the bottom of the toilet. Heat rises from my neck as Mary's shadow engulfs me.

'A wah de braces,' are the last words I hear before her hand deafens my ear with a slap so hard, I fall to the floor. 'You know how hard mi afi work fi get dem teeth? How much pain mi go through!' Mary had never visited a dentist until she came to England in 1963. She had been working as a cleaner in an Italian restaurant and was in so much pain her boss Maria insisted she see a dentist. 'Him pull out nine teeth and tell me fi come back in six weeks fi mi dentures.' She says all these years later, she can still smell the stench of rotting flesh, hear the sound of cracking enamel, and taste the blood in her mouth. Severe tooth decay, he told her. Her teeth cost over one month's wages and are now sitting at the bottom of a bleach-filled toilet.

7

Boomerang

MY SISTERS HAVE BEEN living with us for five months when, as we approach the school gate, I notice a lady standing with Mary. She is wearing a purple leather coat, a furry hat, bright pink lipstick, and black shiny boots. I have never forgotten those boots that shoved me away a year earlier. Her pink lips smile as we approach.

'Hello, Mummy,' Marcia and Donna say as she kneels to kiss them. She turns towards me, but Mary pulls me away, shielding me with her legs. Eve holds their hands as we walk home in silence. We sit at the kitchen table, drinking milk and eating digestive biscuits as Mary and Eve talk in the living room.

'They are my children, and I've come to take them back,' Eve says.

'Take them where?' asked Mary. 'You don't live anywhere; you don't really care about those girls. You can't just come and go as you please. It's not fair on them.'

'I'm their mother, and I have rights. I don't need Ashley; you can keep her, but I need the other two. Without them, the council won't give me a place.'

For the second time in my life, I watch Mary weep silently as she packs Donna's and Marcia's belongings. 'How have I raised such a selfish, heartless daughter who loves herself more than her own children?' Mary says.

I stare at my sisters and remember how I'd found them cold, wet, and dirty. Feelings of guilt, relief, and sadness wash over me. Relief because I am glad to get my bed back and no longer have to worry about Marcia hitting me or pulling my hair, guilt because, secretly, I wish I'd never met them, and sadness because Eve doesn't want to take me with her. I run to my room to get the dolls for them but see my favourite doll without her head and decide to give that one to Marcia instead.

'Look after those girls,' Mary warns.

The house is still now, woken hourly by the grandfather clock hanging on the living room wall. A part of me wishes they would return. I continue to sleep by the wall, the double bed now a lonely place for one, and my fear of bedbugs, which I forgot I had, has now returned.

They have been gone three months, and I am adjusting to life as an only child again when the phone rings. The look on Mary's face speaks words I cannot hear but feel in the pit of my stomach, and I know they are coming back. I don't enjoy fighting with Marcia or sharing my toys, and even Mary's beatings have become less frequent since they aren't around to prompt her hand to my bottom.

When we arrive at their school, they are sitting in the headmaster's office. I refuse to look at either of them. This time, things will be different. It's my room, my house, my toys, and if they want to share them, they will have to be nice to me. And it's payback time for Donna. When Mary hits her, it's going to be ten times worse than when she hits me. Only Marcia is glad to be back and tells Mary about their life with Eve. The day she took them, Eve didn't have anywhere to live. So, that night, they slept on her friend's sofa. 'Was his name Ernie?' I want to ask but decide not to.

The next morning, tired and hungry, they walk for miles to the housing office. 'I have two children and nowhere to live,' Eve tells the lady behind the counter. The lady tells Eve to come back next week as they have no accommodation available. 'I'm not leaving here until you find us somewhere,' Eve shouts.

'I will have to call the police if you don't calm down, Miss Benjamin.'

'Call the police! In fact, I've got a better idea; why don't you bloody keep them?' Eve said and turned to leave. Marcia was about to follow her. 'Sit back down!' she shouted.

'Please, Miss Benjamin,' the lady pleaded.

'We can't sleep on the streets. Either you find us somewhere to stay, or you keep them.'

That night, they were placed in a hostel where they stayed together in one room for two months before they gave Eve a three-bedroom house. They never attended school during their time at the hostel and rarely left the room. Eve usually left them alone during the day and returned only at night. They ate mostly cereal and jam sandwiches that Marcia made. Their new house was the biggest they had ever lived in, but the lack of furniture made it almost impossible for them to play hide and seek, with the bath being the only suitable hiding place. The garden belonged to the neighbour, so they weren't allowed to use it. They each had a room to themselves, but all slept in Eve's room as there was only one bed. And now, they are back to sharing mine.

I eavesdrop as Mary talks to Grandad. 'She's been sentenced to one year in prison for fraud.' Mary said.

I am nine now, so Mary says we are old enough to stay on our own. I hold the door key, and we let ourselves in and make cereal or bread with peanut butter until Mary gets in and gives us our dinner. 'Come straight home from school, look left and right when you cross the roads, and hold hands.' I refuse to follow this order; I'm not holding their hands. 'Take your clothes off as soon as you get home, have something to eat, and do your homework before switching on the TV.' These are our daily instructions.

We are playing hide and seek when I find it. Since the day Mary took it from me, I have searched the entire house and never discovered where she'd hidden it. The only place I never thought to look was on the back shelf in the tall kitchen cupboard.

'Ready or not!' Donna shouts.

I am about to squeeze myself into the cupboard when it falls—my money jar full of the coins Ben had given me. Quickly, I place it on the kitchen table and hide under it, curling into a ball as Donna's feet approach. I hear the coins jingle as she takes the jar and runs out of the room. I count to one hundred before leaving the table and returning to my room.

'1,2,3,4,5-' I hear them counting my money.

'What's that?' I say as I enter the room.

'None of your business,' Marcia says.

'I'll tell if you don't show me.'

Marcia stands up and closes the door. 'If you tell Mary, you're dead.' she says.

Donna holds the jar up. 'Let's all go to the shop. If we take a few coins, Mary will never notice.' Marcia says.

'No, you two go. I'll stay here in case Mary calls,' I say.

They return with two bags of sweets. Sharing them out, Marcia takes ten for herself, ten for Donna, and gives five to me before placing the jar back on the kitchen table. They eat half of their sweets and hide the rest in their school bags. I eat all of mine, hide the wrappers in a piece of tissue, and bury it in the rubbish bin. I hear Mary push her key into the lock of the front door. 'Who took the money from the jar?' she shouts from the bottom of the stairs.

Marcia's and Donna's eyes widen in disbelief. 'How does she know already?' Donna whispers.

We stand at the top of the stairs. Mary's eyes look as heavy as the four bags of shopping she was carrying. 'Just wait till tomorrow. When I get home from work, I'm going to give you all a good beating.'

Later that evening, whilst Donna and Marcia are in their bath, I go downstairs into the kitchen. 'Mary, it was Marcia and Donna who took the money. They brought sweets and hid them in their school bags.'

They emerge from their bath to find Mary holding the sweets in her hand. 'So, you two are thieves, just like your mudda,' she says before going back downstairs.

The next day, we walk slowly home from school, half knowing what fate awaits us. 'The best trick is to put on lots of jumpers,' I tell them as we undress out of our uniforms. 'That way, you won't feel the pain as much.' They both think this is such a good idea and take all my jumpers, leaving me with just one. Marcia chews her nails like she hasn't eaten in weeks, and Donna jumps every time the clock chimes as we wait for Mary to return home. She calls us down into the kitchen. My stomach churns when she tells me to step forward.

'But, I didn't do anything, remember?' I whisper, hoping Donna and Marcia can't hear.

'That's exactly why you're getting beaten first. You're the eldest, and if you see them doing something wrong, you should have stopped them.' Great, so now I'm being punished for their stuff, too. She wraps the top of my skipping rope around her hand. I close my eyes and grit my teeth as the rope skims across my skin.

Next, it's Donna's turn. 'One, don't be a thief like your mudda! Two, three, four, five.' Mary hit Donna until she stopped flinching. Grabbing the back of her neck, Mary lifts her jumper, revealing several layers beneath it. 'You tink you smart? Take off all your clothes down to your knickers.' If the tears that streamed down her face evoked sympathy in Mary, she wasn't showing it. Once Donna finally removes her knickers, my rope comes down on her back like the whip of a jockey close to the finishing line.

She screams and pleads, 'Please, Mummy! I'm sorry, Mummy! Please, Mummy! I'm sorry, Mummy! Please, Mummy! I'm sorry, Mummy! Please, Mummy! I'm sorry, Mummy!' Her cries fall on deaf ears. I flinch with every whip, feeling her pain as if it were my own, but I am glad my turn is over. Sweating and panting, Mary finally stops—exhausted, unable to count another number. I can't believe Marcia has escaped a beating. They look at each other, then stare at me, and I know they will make me pay for telling on them.

It is a month after my tenth birthday. Marcia, Donna, and I are playing in the front garden when a group of people pull up in a blue car with no roof. Loud music blares from its speakers that grows louder as the two front passenger doors open. The driver is our mother, Eve.

'She's come back for us!' Donna shouts. The frown on Marcia's face tells me she isn't as happy to see her.

Eve lifts the boot of the car and pulls out several large bags. As she approaches the gate, Mary walks out of the house. 'Get inside!' she shouts to us. We go to the living room and watch from the open window.

'Hi, Mum,' Eve says.

'What do you want?' Mary asks.

'I've served my time, sorted myself out, and have come back for the girls. Look, I've even brought them new clothes and toys.'

'Is where you get de money from fi buy dees tings and a who fi car dat?' Mary always switches from her posh English-Jamaican accent to a strong Jamaican-Jamaican one when she's angry.

'It's my car, Mum,' Eve says.

'Where yuh get de money from?'

'I worked for it,' Eve replies sarcastically.

'Well, yuh can tek it all back. I don't want your devil tings inna my house.'

'Oh, Mum, don't be silly,' Eve retorts and pushes her way past Mary into the house.

'Girls, Mummy's back.' Donna runs so fast into her arms that she almost knocks her over. Marcia and I stand silently beside Mary. 'Ain't you gonna give your mum a hug then?' Eve asks as she approaches us. Marcia reluctantly reaches her arms out, but before I get a chance, Mary jumps in front of her.

'Leave her alone!' she yells, grabbing my arm.

'They're my kids, Mum.'

'You gave up your rights to Ashley the day you gave her to me.'

'Well, you can't stop me taking Donna and Marcia,' she says.

'Take them where? You don't want them. You're just using them for your own benefit.'

'I've got a house, Mum. I've got a car, and I've got money. I can look after them now.'

'And what have you done fi get dat money?' Mary asks.

Eve ignores this question and turns to face us. 'Let's ask the girls what they want. Do you want to come and live with me, girls?'

Donna looks at Mary before lowering her head and whispers, 'Yes.'

Marcia is silent, but her grip on Mary's hand says she isn't going anywhere. Eve shrugged her shoulders. 'Oh well, pack your bags, Don. In fact, pack nothing. You've got all these new clothes and toys,' she says, staring at Marcia with disdain. 'I'm going to take you shopping, and you can buy whatever you want.' Donna seems sad she is leaving us, but she's always asking why Eve left her, so I'm not surprised that she wants to go with her. When Eve leaves, she doesn't leave us any of the new toys or clothes she came with. 'If they're not coming with me, I'm not giving them a thing,' she tells Mary.

'Good, I don't want them getting used to expensive clothes and toys, and I certainly don't want your ungodly things in this house.' Eve offers Mary a handful of scrunched-up notes. 'A devil money, dat. You never earned it honestly, and anything dat is not earned honestly will

61

never last; you mark my words.' Mary says, closing the door behind her.

Marcia and I peer out the front room window as we watch Eve put the bags back into the car. One of Eve's friends lifts Donna up, puts her into the back seat, and hands her the pair of sunglasses she had been wearing. She smiles and pushes them over her button nose. She turns, staring towards the front room window. I hope she can't see us watching her from behind the curtains. A part of me is glad she's gone; her whiny tears were getting on my nerves, and at least there'll be more room in the bed now. I stare and wonder what her new life will be like; I wish I had nice clothes, new toys, and a new mother. I wish I could drive in the back of a nice car. I wish I could go with her. I wish, I wish, I wish.

8

Summoning the Devil

MARY HAS MADE ALL but one of my church dresses, and that's the only one I really like. Sister Thomas gave it to me as a gift for my ninth birthday. Made of red cotton, it is covered in colourful butterflies that dance every time I spin around. It is the best gift I have ever received. I would wear it every day if Mary would allow it. But on Saturday evenings, Mary always decides what I will wear to church. We were on the last leg of our travel through Dalston market when she spotted it—a stall covered in lace curtains.

'Bargain bag! Bargain bag!' the man in the long white dress shouted.

Mary has an eye for a bargain, like a magpie does for shiny things. 'How much?' she asks, fighting her way to the front of the stall table.

He holds the large black bag in his hands. 'Five pounds for everything, Mummy. You can make nice dress for pretty daughter,' he says, smiling at me with teeth that look like they have only been brushed twice since they grew in his mouth. Mary hands him a crisp five-pound note, grabs the bag, and spends the next three hours sewing on her machine, calling me every half hour to 'stand still' while she places a piece of curtain against my back.

When Donna and Marcia moved in, I carefully folded my red dress and hid it in a bag under my bed. The week they arrived, Mary searched my wardrobe for clothes they could wear to church. 'Where's your red dress?' she asks.

I am prepared to take a beating rather than let either of them wear it. She always told me it was too short and that I looked like a hussy, just like my mother, so I don't see why she would want either of them to wear it. I looked in my wardrobe and handed her the two lace creations I most disliked. Blue poly silk with white lace trim and frog lace green poly silk with red lace trim at the hem—the latter was my least favourite of her creations and made my skin itch the moment it touched me. 'For Marcia,' I said and handed the dress to her.

She eyed it up and down, examining the back and then the front as if seeing it for the first time. Pressing it against Marcia's back, she looked at the hem that fell just above her knee. 'It's too short for her; you wear it.' she said, handing me back the froggy green dress. 'Make sure you find your red dress by the time we get back from church. It will fit Donna perfectly,' she said. I pray she will forget all about it by then.

On Sundays, the gospel music blares from Mary's radio and wakes us up earlier than on a school day. Grandad never attends church with us; instead, he makes his Sunday-only special breakfast. It's called 'mix up, mix up' and is made from bits of every meal he's had over the past week and whatever is left in the fridge. Chicken skins that, once fried, turn sweet and crispy, pieces of boiled yam, breadfruit, potatoes, dumplings, bits of ham Mary brings home from her dinner lady job, and an egg—there's always an egg thrown in at the last minute, scrambled into everything in the pan. 'One pan cooking at its best,' he always says. It's my favourite part of Sundays. I don't enjoy Johnny's 'mix up, mix up' as much as I usually do. Having to share it means I get a large slice of hard-dough bread but only a little of the mix up. Now I have to share everything, including my shoes. For church, I have one black shiny pair, but Mary keeps everything and finds my old ones for the girls. My oldest pair fit Donna perfectly, but none fit Marcia.

'Take your shoes off,' Mary says.

'What?' I don't mean to say it out loud; the word just jumps from my brain and out of my mouth. I cover it, trying quickly to push the words back in, but it's too late.

'What did you say?' I duck as Mary's hand swings towards my face, causing her to hit the side of the door. The crash of her hand sends the door flying into Donna's forehead, and she bursts into tears. 'Wait till you get back from church,' she says as she soothes Donna in her arms— great, now I have two beatings to look forward to! I don't understand; seeing her on her knees holding Donna, I want to tear her arms off and wrap them around me. My eyes catch Donna's; she smiles slyly and cries harder, squeezing Mary tighter. A wave of heat engulfs me, and I run to the bathroom. My skin feels like it's being pricked by a thousand of Mary's dressmaker pins. Red blotches rise to the surface of my legs as the hard lace rubs against them. Desperate to stop the itch, I claw my nails deep into my skin until flakes fall like fish scales and my legs bleed. I place the green poly silk over my legs and watch as it sucks up the red droplets like a kitchen towel. My skin begins to cool until I hear Mary's footsteps approach the bathroom.

'How you dutty up your dress? God help me tame dis child,' she repeats until beads of sweat threaten to dampen the rim of her hat. Mary's ring finger catches the side of my face, and an angry bruise now resides on the bottom left side of my cheek. This is the only Sunday, apart from when I had chicken pox, I didn't go to church.

'When I was young, I only had one dress. I had to wash it every evening, so it was dry for the next day,' she said. I secretly rolled my eyes. She tells me this story whenever she makes me one of her hideous creations. 'My father was a man of means.' He refused to send her to school and forced her to work the family land at the age of five instead.

'Girls don't need no education,' he would say.

She could rear chickens and plant yams and crops, but she couldn't spell her own name. She was so scared of her father, who only ever smiled when he counted or received money. 'Spare the rod, spoil the child,' was his motto, and hardly a day went by without Mary feeling the tip of his cane.

I stand over the sink, washing the blood out of my dress, watching as my salty tears mix with the soapy water. I don't want to hate my sisters; I enjoy playing with them, and I love Mary—she saved me from the phone box—but today, for the first time, I pray they never come back. 'I hate this dress! I hate Mary, and I hate you, God,' I scream as suds wash the blood away. 'Why did you let Eve leave me? Why don't you ever answer prayers? You're not even real! Mary is praying to the sky!' I scream. I try to hang my dress on the line when the lace brushes against a smear of my bloodied leg. I feel my eyes turn as red as the blood that now boils within me as I rip the lace away from the poly silk, revealing the white threads I watched Mary painstakingly sew together. Buoyed by my new-found rebellion, I run into the house and grab Mary's dressmaker scissors from their basket. Grandad sits so still in his chair that I wonder if he's watching TV, asleep or dead. Carefully holding the heavy metal cutters, I cut and cut and cut until only the zip remains. I dip a strip of the poly silk sleeve into the bucket of water and bandage my wound. 'If she ever hits me again, I'll run away,' I tell myself. I scrape the fragments into a heap and place them inside a plastic bag, tie it securely, and bury it in the compost bin at the back of the garden. I dance happily in the garden, knowing I will never have to wear that froggy green dress again.

I hear singing. 'Jesus is Lord,' Mary's home. The happy birds in my stomach stop dancing, crushed by the weight of my anxiety. 'Where's your dress?'

'It's soaking in the bathroom,' I say. I don't know why, but lately, lies seem to roll off my tongue like a ball down a hill. They come to me quick and easy without me even thinking. Mary is about to go back into the kitchen when I see her eyes spot the bandage on my leg. I am about to lie again and say I found an old piece of fabric inside my pillow, but before I can speak, she drags my half-naked body through the dirt out of sight of the neighbours and picks up a piece of wood that had recently fallen off the garden fence. I cower into a bush as she raises the wood above my back.

'I will beat the devil out of you and ram God into you if it kills me,' she says.

That day, under the bush, I decide that no matter how much Mary beats me, I will never cry again. I grow immune to her buckled belt, whip, rope, and even the flogger she brought from Jamaica. I learn to close myself off from the pain, imagining myself anywhere but standing in front of her. I refuse to make a sound, and I stand firm, planting myself as strong as a boulder, never flinching. She tries her best to jerk tears from my eyes, but my silent protests remain. I will not make a sound. I repeat this silent mantra in my head, silently meditating through the pain. She thinks she's beating the devil out of me, but she's driving him further in.

9

Growing Pains

Marcia is smarter than I am. She is Mary's pet who obeys the 'be good, be seen, and not heard' rule like a nun. I think she just wants to be Mary's favourite so does exactly as she's told. I stay out of her way, and she stays out of mine. I fill my daydreams with thoughts of Eve and Donna. Wondering where they live and if Donna has a large wardrobe full of beautiful dresses. Does Eve hit her? I imagine the wind blowing through her hair as music blares from the car speakers. I see an advert for McDonald's and wonder if Eve will buy her a Big Mac with fries and a Coke. Mary says we can't afford takeaways, so she makes us burgers and chips she cuts from potatoes, but it never looks as nice as the McDonald's ones.

Most days, I stare out of the window into the front garden, hoping the blue car will reappear and, this time, Eve will take me with her. I want new shoes and dresses that don't make me want to itch my skin to the bone. I never really liked Donna, but I miss her now she's gone. Even though she doesn't want me, I love Eve. But I love Mary more. I am eleven now, and she hasn't hit me in nearly six months; I think she's tired of trying to make me cry. Anyway, we only talk when she's teaching me how to cook rice and peas, curry chicken, mutton, or run down, which is a really difficult dish to master. The first time she told me to clean the chicken, it didn't go very well.

'Where the bloody hell is the chicken?' She said.

I threw most of it in the bin; it all looked like fat to me. Mary fished it out of the bin and told me to finish cleaning it with fresh lime and vinegar. Bloody hell is the only swear word she says. God doesn't mind that one, apparently, but she doesn't like the other words they say in the movies Grandad watches. She always tells me to cover my ears, as if she thinks the words will pass through them without lodging in my brain or instructs me to leave the room when a man and woman are kissing. I still remember some of the swear words Ernie's friends used to call Eve—bitch, slut, whore—but I never heard them again until Simon said them to me.

At almost six and a half feet, Simon is the tallest boy in my class. His mum is white, and his dad, whom he has never met, is black. His skin is the colour of milk after cornflakes have sat in the bowl for hours, rich and creamy. He is the only person in our year who is allowed to wear Nike Air Jordans to school. His mum sent a letter to our headmaster, Mr McInally, explaining she couldn't find any suitable shoe that would fit his size eleven feet—which I think is a dumb excuse because McInally is almost as tall as Simon, and he wears black shoes.

'Ashley, you do know you're the prettiest girl in this school, don't you?' I feel my cheeks burn as he looks into my eyes. I turn to stare at the pieces of chewing gum stuck to the floor until he holds my chin, tilting my head back until our eyes meet again. 'I love how you're so shy. You're beautiful, and you don't even know it.' I wonder why he likes me; I'm nowhere near as pretty as the girls in Year Ten. They wear black mascara and short skirts. My skirt sits just above my ankles. I try to fold the waist until it reaches my knees, but then I'm left with large folds around my stomach and look stupid, so I let them out. He is the only boy who talks to me; he even offered to pay for my lunch once. 'Let me touch your tits,' he asked me one day after PE. My breasts seem to have grown even bigger than Mary's, and I wish they would disappear.

The week before I started secondary school, Mary brought me my first bra from Dalston Market. It is so small it squeezes into the sides of my rib cage and makes my back ache. My breasts fall out as soon as I put my hand up or start running. Simon was always kind to me, offering to share his crisps or sweets. He enjoyed watching me play netball or rounders and always waited for me after school. But when he asked to touch my tits, I said only if he gave me £5. I could tell he was desperate. I could hear the hunger in his voice. 'Please let me touch them. I promise I won't tell anyone.' he begged. I knew there, and then he would pay. 'You can be my girlfriend, but we have to keep it a secret,' he said. Then he tried to get me down to £3, saying he had to take the money out of his mum's purse.

'Then there will be no next time,' I told him. Since then, he's stopped watching me during PE and has told his friends I made him touch other private parts, which is not true. I would never make him touch me there for just £5. I know it's worth much more than that. So now, I'm a slapper. Simon tells his friends he felt me up but forgets to mention he paid me for the privilege.

My first week of secondary school is full of inductions. Year Eleven pupils show us around the school in small groups of seven. English, mathematics, business studies, Science, PE, cooking—there is so much to remember. But I blend in easily, falling behind the group. My plan is to remain as invisible as possible, to be as Mary always says children should be, 'seen and not heard.' By Thursday, I already know my least favourite teacher is Miss Sion-Daley.

'My job is to teach; yours is to learn,' she says. Her glasses sit so far down her nose, I wonder how she breathes and why she bothers to wear them. She is from Trinidad and came to England to teach twenty years ago. 'I already have my education. If you want to learn, I will teach. If you don't, leave this class now.' She reminds me of Mary, and I want to leave immediately.

On the last day of induction week, we sit a maths

and English test. 'This will determine which set you will be placed in,' Mr Humphries, the English teacher, says. I stare at the sheet and run my fingers over the words, urging them to keep still. Like green frogs, they jump around the page. Sometimes, if I close my eyes and count to ten, they stop moving, but now they won't keep still at all. I close my eyes again and, this time, count to twenty. When I open them, Mr Humphries is standing in front of me. 'Wake up, girl! Didn't you get any sleep last night?' he shouts. The other students lift their heads and are now staring in my direction. I wish I could dissolve like an ice cube in the sun, but I can't, so instead, I lift my pen, bury my chin in my chest, and begin to write. Yes, no, no, yes are my answers to every question I don't know the answer to. When the words do decide to keep still, I read them—*which, king, prime minister, empire, arrived?* I just wish the stupid words would stay still long enough for me to take them in.

The following Monday, my form tutor, Mrs Kennedy, hands me a timetable. My first lesson is English with Mr Humphries. 'Well, you're in this class, which means you're at the bottom of the barrel, and it's my job to get you out!' he shouts above the thirty-odd voices all talking at once. They met his pleas for silence with eyes that say, 'We hear you but don't care,' and mouths that refuse to remain closed.

'Ashley, can you please hand the books out,' Mr Humphries says. How does he remember my name, and why is he asking me when I am sitting silently at the back of the room? Taking the books off his desk, I distribute them to the class. 'A Tale of Two Cities by Charles Dickens.' I stare at the title as I walk towards the first desk. For the first time, the words don't jump, and I can read them clearly. I sit back at my desk and eagerly open the first page. The words start to fly again. I close the page and stare at the front cover. I know what the words say; I read them only minutes earlier, so why won't they keep still now? 'Ashley, please read page number one,' Mr Humphries calls from the front of the class. Remnants of this morning's breakfast leave my stomach and push their way into my mouth. I swallow hard, sending them back down where they belong and sit staring at the page. 'Stand up when you read, Ashley, and speak up. We don't have bionic hearing.' Some pupils laugh, others stare at me with eyes that seem glad he picked me instead of them. Silently, I beg the words to keep still, but they disobey and fly like a flock of migrating birds in a David Attenborough documentary.

'Charles Dickens, A Tale of Two Cities,' I say before turning to page one. As I walk, the words stop dancing. 'It was the best of times, it was the worst of times.'

'What are you doing, Ashley? Stop walking around and keep still; you're not in bloody drama class.'

I want to explain that unless I walk around while reading, the words won't keep still, but even as this thought enters my head, it doesn't make sense. It should be the opposite. Words keep still when I am still and move around when I'm not. So, I do the only thing I can think of. I shout, 'I'm not bloody reading!' and throw the book onto the floor.

'Get out of my class!' Mr Humphries shouts back. Just the words I want to hear; I grab my bag and head towards the door.

It is the beginning of my third school year, and I am a master of avoidance. I know every poster on almost every corridor of the entire school. 'Get out, wait for me outside the headmaster's office! One hundred lines, young lady, will amount to nothing; one-hour detention!' These are my daily reminders from my not-so-favourite teachers. I hate all the lessons except art. I am currently working on a sculpture of the human form. The feeling of the clay between my fingers makes me so happy; I wish I could stay in the studio forever. I don't like PE; running in a cold, muddy field isn't my idea of fun. Today is the first and last day I will ever do another swimming lesson.

Mary hasn't been paid yet, so I have to wait until the end of the month before she can buy me a swimming costume. 'You'll have to wear my girdle until I can buy you a costume,' she tells me. I want to ask her why we are so piss poor, but I already know the answer, so don't bother.

Square, cream tiles surround the pool, and the potent smell of chlorine irritates my eyes. There are two large changing rooms, one for boys and one for girls. I change out of my uniform and nervously walk out into the cold swimming hall. I cover myself with my hand towel, trying my best to hide Mary's girdle from the class. 'What are you wearing, your granny's knickers?' It's the class bully, Patricia. I turn to walk back into the changing rooms but feel a palm nudge the middle of my back. I will my body to fall backwards, but it's too late; the hand pushes me forward into the cold blue water, its sharp edges cut into my skin as I hit the surface. Water fills my lungs, my body sinks to the bottom of the pool before it rises, and my head bobbles to the surface. I grab the metal rail that surrounds the pool as echoes of laughter drown my near-death experience.

'You have tested my patience to the limit!' Mr McInally shouts. He says I am one of a group he calls 'disruptors' who spend more time out of the classroom than in it. 'You've left me with no choice but to suspend you for a week. Hopefully, this will give you time to reflect, and you'll be ready to make a fresh start once you return.' He tells me I just need to apply myself and that if I work hard, I can achieve great things. 'Ashley, you have so much potential. Someone with a vocabulary like yours can go far.' He's just saying this to get me to stay in class.

I just hate that Patricia and the others laugh at me when I get a question wrong. I'd rather sit in silence or make people laugh than have them laugh at me. The class clown is what Mrs Sion-Daley says I am. Anyway, how can I have potential when I'm so rubbish at everything? I know what it means; I heard it on the dictionary game show years ago but never thought I had it.

Potential – adjective: *having or showing the capacity to develop into something in the future.*

For the first time, I go to the school library and look through the P section until I find it. My memory does serve me; it means what I think it does. I loan the book for fourteen days. Words and their meanings jump out at me like grasshoppers in a field. The urge to string the words into long sentences makes my hands itch. I buy a notepad for a pound and write. Words flow from my mind, through my hand, and onto the paper like bullets from a machine gun. I write until the ink runs dry and stare at the pages, eager to make sense of the words heaped in the pile, and I think I've just written my first story.

Mr McInally's words ring in my ears, 'Potential lies in all of us, if we are only willing to nurture it,' I promise myself I will try to nurture mine when I return to school.

'You're bad just like your mother; she used to do the same thing. Get the belt.'

'Your belt; are you mad? I'm almost fourteen! There's no way you're hitting me,' my mind says before I pull the belt from the battered leather chest in her bedroom. She snatches the belt out of my hand so quickly that the prong slides across the surface of my skin, slicing it open. I hold my bloodied palm up to my face; my chest is now as hot as my blood. Like a boxer, I close my fists as blood drips onto the brown lino. 'Hit me,' I dare her silently, knowing she can read my eyes. I stand, fists clenched, my feet planted firmly on the floor. At five foot eight inches,

I am taller than she is and now look down on her the way only months earlier, she looked down on me. I stand so close to her face, I can smell the ginger tea she boiled and drank earlier. My fists clench tighter, and I inhale heavily, my chest rising to meet hers as she raises the belt above my head. But then something strange happens. She lowers her hand, dropping the belt to the floor as if it suddenly weighs ten tons. Stumbling back onto the kitchen table, she falls exhausted into the chair, her breath heaving like a person in need of an asthma pump. I stare, wanting to hold her, but I don't know how. Then, like a baby, she lets out a whale so loud that, if I were a passer-by, I would have thought someone was being killed or had just been told their entire family had been. The sound that rises from her throat sends shivers down my back and up into my heart, and for the first time in what feels like an eternity, we cry together. Falling to my knees, I hold her ankles as we cry a million tears. I cry away the pain I kept buried deep within me. Holding my head in her hands, she squeezes it tightly between her palms as her tears soak my hair and run gently down my cheeks. They say I am sorry; I love you; please forgive me, and my heart says yes. Yes, I forgive you, and I, too, am sorry. Then she reveals more about her life than ever before, and now I finally understand why she hits so hard.

'All I ever wanted was for my children to have a better life than I did, to get a good education and make something of themselves.' She had taught herself to read and write since arriving in England. 'I know you think

I'm hard on you, Ashley, but it's for a good reason. I don't want you turning out like your mother.' Why does she always have to compare me to her? She's always saying how worthless she is, then tells me I am the same. 'You're not stupid, Ashley. You see how hard I work to put food on the table and keep a roof over your head.' I see this and love her despite the beatings. 'I love you more than any of my own children. I didn't get it right with them, but I'm trying to get it right with you.'

I listen as she tells me she would have given anything to have been sent to school, telling me I must get an education and become a secretary or a nurse. I don't know what I want to be, but I know I don't want to be poor. Mary's father, Bill, could have sent her to school but chose not as he believed 'girls don't need an education; they should just stay at home and have babies.' He took out all his frustrations on Mary, especially after her mother died.

'He would beat me till I was black and blue,' she said. He even broke her nose twice. 'The beatings I give you are for your own good. You will thank me one day.' Looking at my bloodied palm, I find this hard to believe. Following her mother's death, he forbade her from mentioning her mother's name again. When she did a year later, on the eve of her memorial, Bill left a scar on her leg. He beat her with a sugar cane, leaving her with a permanent reminder never to say her mother's name again. 'I named the scar Grace after my mother,' she says, running her fingers across a raised scar below her knee.

This is the first time she has said her name since that day over forty years ago. I clasp her legs as I feel more tears begin to flow.

Now that we're being open, I decide to take a chance and ask Mary a question I have longed to know the answer to since I was a little girl. 'Can I ask you a question?' I hold my breath until she answers, fearful this new Mary will revert to the old one.

'Yes,' she replies.

My lips quiver, and I stutter before asking, 'What happened to my mother? Why is she the way she is?' I lift my head out of her lap, fearful she may feel my heart thumping through my chest, and watch as she calculates a response.

'Your mother was always the worst of my children. If I told her to go left, she'd go right. If I'd say go up, she'd go down.'

'But why?' I press.

'She got worse after we caught her with her brother, Matthew.' I am unsure what she means but am too afraid to ask. 'After that, we had to send her away for a few years to a children's home until they said she was out of control and sent her back.'

'Why didn't you send Matthew away instead? He is much older than she is.' I ask.

She stares out the kitchen window as if the answers are hiding in the bushes. Her eyes glaze over and fill with a sadness that makes me want to hug her again. 'I didn't want her to go, but Johnny insists.' I want to shake her now. I stand to leave the room, but she grabs my arm. 'She was so bad, Ashley. I couldn't put a penny down without her stealing it. She even tek my wedding ring.' I can't look at her. It's no wonder Eve is the way she is. I saw a programme about a children's home, and the things that happened to some children were horrific.

I spend the rest of the week mostly in my room, only leaving to eat or use the bathroom. Mary barely talks, either, but our silence speaks volumes. I think she knows I blame her for ruining Eve.

'You're my chance to make things right,' she says.

For the first time since we last spoke, I look her in the eye. 'Well, you've failed,' I say.

My first day back at school is a blur; I just can't stop thinking about Eve and wish I could find her. When I return home, Mary is waiting for me in the kitchen. 'I need to speak to you about something,' she says. Dread fills my stomach as I wait for her to deliver the news. If anything has happened to Eve, I will run away and never come back.

Johnny has decided he is ready to return to Jamaica.

'I begged him to wait for you girls to finish school, but him tell me he is going back with or without me.' Mary doesn't want to go back, but Johnny is selling the house, so she has no choice. 'I tell him to wait another five years, that the value of the house will double, but he will not listen.' I think all men are users. All they do is take and give nothing unless they receive something first. Mary works two, sometimes three, jobs and still has nothing to show for it. 'In a year's time, I will receive a bonus from

81

work. Twenty years, I have worked at the Heinz factory, and I'm not leaving until I receive it. First, Johnny will return to Jamaica, and we will follow him a year later.'

'But what about the house? Where will we live?' I ask. Our family home is to be sold, and we will move into a flat on a nearby housing estate. I can't believe that, after more than thirty years of marriage, Johnny is prepared just to pick up and leave his wife if she doesn't follow him like a lapdog back to Jamaica. He's always saying how bad the economy is there, so why does he want to return anyway? I think Mary is a fool; for years, she has paid half of the mortgage and doesn't even have her name on the deeds, so Johnny can just sell up and leave us homeless. She says Eve lives an ungodly life, but where is God in Mary's life now? At least Eve has money and nice things. When I'm older, I hope I meet a rich man to take me far away from this life. Now everything Mary has worked so hard for is being sold, and the entire contents of our home will soon be on a ship, sailing its way to Jamaica. This will never happen to me; I'm never getting married.

We will move in the next four months, but we won't have to change schools. Marcia doesn't mind; she likes school and doesn't mind where we live as long as it's not with Eve. She even wants to go to Jamaica with Johnny, but Mary says she has to wait for us.

'I know Johnny can be stubborn, but he is a good, hardworking man. I made my vows and will honour them till death us do part.'

My intuition races ahead again, and I have a bad feeling about this move, a really bad feeling.

10

Ghetto Life Ain't Nice

I AM THIRTEEN. I have never visited an estate but am now suddenly living in one of the largest in London. Conleigh estate, probably named so because they built it using huge grey concrete slabs. It's very dull; even the play area is made from concrete. There is a playground with four swings, a roundabout, a slide, a climbing frame, and a concrete maze in the middle of the estate. Dirt cleverly disguises itself in its grey walls, partly hidden beneath the colourful graffiti that brings life to the otherwise dreary park—a melancholy wafts throughout the cramped space filled with over two thousand flats.

Our flat is on the fourth floor of a high-rise block where we can see the maze and a phone box from our bedroom window. Suddenly, we have gone from living in a family home with a front and back garden to a small flat on the fourth floor of a ten-story tower block. The neighbours to our left appear deaf as they play music so loud it thumps through the thin walls, causing the books on our shelves to vibrate as if dancing to the reggae beat. Mrs Abola, the neighbour to our right, is from Ghana. She lives alone with her two children after her husband went on holiday to Ghana, took a second wife, and never returned. She diligently informs Mary that the neighbours to her right are constantly in trouble with the police.

'Their youngest daughter is only fifteen, and she is pregnant with her first child. Keep your girls locked up and away from the boys in the neighbourhood; they are no good.' she advises.

Our flat is so small we can't pass each other in the hallway without brushing shoulders, so we have to wait until the other has passed just to go to the bathroom. The nice furnishings Mary had collected over the years are now in a trailer sailing the Atlantic on their way to the Kingston wharf, where Johnny will be waiting, ready to dress his dream forever home in the parish of St Elizabeth with its contents. By contrast, we purchased our new furniture from what looked to me like a brick-a-brack shop on Monclife High Street.

'I give you good deal, Mummy,' the Indian man bargained. Mary purchased two white wardrobes and a chest of drawers. My attempt to open the wardrobe door nearly resulted in me being flattened by the flimsy chipboard frame. If it were not for the quick reflexes of the shop owner, it would have flattened me. 'Once it is full, this will not happen,' he reassures us. I don't believe this for a second. We also purchased four chairs, a table, and two beds. Everything, including two double beds—without headboards—costs £300.00.

Mary decides not to buy furniture for the living room as she would never have guests over. She has always been very house-proud, and our new flat is nothing to be proud of. She will never allow friends to visit our new temporary home. The floors are covered with a thin, dark blue cord carpet that, once lifted, reveals cold black tiles with white veins. The walls are painted the colour of custard. It's obvious a smoker used to live here, as they have permeated the walls and ceiling with yellow nicotine stains, and the smell of tobacco hangs in the stale air. The bed makes my back ache. Its springs poke irritatingly into my bones like the tickles Johnny once gave me, even when I asked him to stop. I resort to laying extra blankets over the mattress to help soften the pokes. Our private outside space comes in the form of a balcony that is about the same size as my headmaster's desk but is now home to a family of pigeons. Just looking at them makes my veins itch. Our bedroom window overlooks the balcony, so until it's cleaned, we can't open the window and rid the room of the urine smell that seemed to have soaked into the walls. At night, the coos of the pigeons become a part of my dreams. I try to secure the corner of the bed furthest away from the window, but when I get out of bed to use the toilet, Marcia jumps into my space and marks it as hers, forcing me to sleep by the wall next to the pigeon's nest. Their sound reminds me of our visit with the church to Leicester Square, but now, rather than shooing them away, I feel as though I am sleeping with them.

Once we've settled in after a week, Mary, Marcia, and I put on our rubber gloves and facemasks made out of an old shirt and chase off the pigeons with a mop and broomstick. We leave their unhatched eggs on a small piece of concrete by the phone box. Mary pays a man to put up a net to prevent them from coming back. After a long bath and a good scrub, my veins stop inching.

'I hate it here. Why did we have to move *here*?' I moan.

'We won't be here for long; we'll be going back to Jamaica soon.' But I know this is a lie. I heard Mary discuss her plans with her church sister, Aunt Vee. She is adamant we will be educated in England, so she has contrived to prolong returning to Jamaica for the next few years until we finish school. She plans to visit Johnny in Jamaica to keep him happy and will keep making excuses until she is ready to return for good.

On our first day on the estate, we help Mary unpack, and then she sends us to the local shop on the ground floor of a tower block opposite ours. 'Buy yourselves some sweets,' she said, trying to cheer us up. 'Go to the shop and come straight back.' The disapproving look she gave a group of children we saw standing on the street corner as we drove into the estate speaks volumes, and I know we won't be allowed out to play here. I'll be a prisoner in a prison inside a prison. I wonder if Mary thinks she's made a mistake by moving us here. 'Don't worry, we won't be here for long, girls,' she says as if reading my thoughts.

There are two passenger lifts in the block. The call buttons look as though someone had attempted to set them alight as the plastic rim of one button is slightly singed. I use a coin to press the button; I do *not* touch it with my fingers. The lift makes a loud rumbling noise as it makes its way from the ground floor, and the doors screech irritatingly as they struggle to open. There is a puddle in the lift's corner of what I assume is piss; its pungent stench makes both Marcia and I cough.

'Shall we take the stairs?' she suggests.

'We're here now. Let's just get in,' I reply, stepping into the lift and covering my mouth with the sleeve of my jumper, trying to mask the smell. Marcia follows closely behind me and presses the button to the ground floor. As the lift makes its descent, it gives a violent shudder before coming to a halt. We breathe a sigh of relief as the doors open. 'Never again.' I exhale. 'On the way back, we're taking the stairs.'

As we make our way across the block, a group of girls approach us. They seem older than Marcia and I and stand in front of us, blocking our path. They look as though someone has dragged them through the mud with their tatty clothes and ungroomed hair. Those shoes have seen better days, I think as I look down at their feet. Mary takes great pride in our appearance and always makes sure we are immaculately groomed. For as long as I can remember, she taught me the importance of a well-groomed appearance; our hair is often decorated with colourful beads.

'Always look respectable. First impressions mean everything,' she always says. She pays a lady from church to cornrow our hair every two weeks. We even have a special headscarf to wear at night that keeps our hair in place. Mary herself dresses conservatively. She never wears trousers, make-up, or nail varnish. 'God doesn't want me to pretty up myself with things that are not sent by him' is her attitude. She will use her clothes as adornment as long as they cover almost every inch of her body. 'Showing too much flesh is a sin,' she says. Her collection of church hats from Walthamstow and Dalston Market has taken up almost every surface in her bedroom. She is a member of the church choir and never wears the same hat twice in the same month. My job every Sunday is to starch Mary's choir collar, and if it has so much as the tiniest crease in it, I get beaten for not doing a good job. I hate that choir outfit with its white collar, long purple gown, and shiny white gloves. Mary often forgets a piece of her ensemble at home, so we get halfway to church, and she says, 'Oh dear, I forgot my gloves,' or 'Oh dear, I forgot my collar. Ashley, go back and get it for me.' So, I have to run back home and get to church before it starts or face a beating later.

It's obvious we are not from the estate and stand out like polar bears in a desert.

'Where you going?' asks the tallest of the four girls blocking our path.

'None of your business,' Marcia replies, folding her

hands in defiance.

'Oh, you think you're tough, do you?' she says as she shoves Marcia's shoulder.

'Come on, let's go.' I grab her hand. But before I can move, one girl pushes me to the ground and punches me. My head feels like it has been thumped by a football as I hit the concrete. After the fourth blow, my eye begins to swell, and the light around me fades as it closes in defeat. Marcia jumps on one girl, throwing her to the ground and hitting her repeatedly. The girls quickly turn their attention away from me onto her.

'Who the hell do you think you are?' one shouts. Holding her down, they rip the shoes off her feet, plunge their hands into her pockets, take her money, and run off. The taste of blood trickles from my nose into my mouth, and I peer out of my good eye. Marcia is furious and wants to run after them.

'Don't be stupid, there's four of them and only two of us,' I say, quelling the flow of blood from my nose with the cuff of her jumper.

We take the stairs on the way back, which are even worse than the lift. The smell of piss is comfortably at home here and soaks into the corners of the grey concrete steps, the graffiti-sprayed light fittings giving the stairwell the feel of a dungeon. A group of boys stand smoking by the stairwell entrance. I see them and immediately want to turn back, but it's too late; they've spotted us.

'What's your name?' one of them asked.

'Ashley and Marcia,' I answer.

'Why are you telling them our names?' Marcia shouts at me. 'You're so naïve, even with strangers,' she says.

There are three boys. One is tall and muscly. He wears a white vest that shows off his smooth brown chest. His hair is cut to precision with patterns etched into each side of his head. Another is slightly darker and chubby. He wears a T-shirt with the words 'Black Power' printed on it and a cap with the letters 'NWA'. From what I can see out of my remaining good eye, I think the guy wearing the black power T-shirt is the cutest. He is wearing black tracksuit bottoms with three white stripes down the sides of each leg and the cleanest, whitest trainers I have ever seen. He looks at us and smiles, and a gold tooth glistens from the corner of his mouth. I have never seen or met anyone like him before and feel embarrassed. Why now, why do I have to meet him now, when I'm looking a mess and have just been beaten up?

'What happened to you lot, and where are your shoes? You can't walk up these dirty stairs with no shoes,' the cute one says.

'We just got jumped by a group of girls,' Marcia explains.

He tries his best not to laugh, hiding his smile behind his hands. 'What do they look like?'

'You'll know who they are when you see one of them wearing a pair of black trainers with a white tick,' Marcia says sarcastically.

'Just chill, man; I'm trying to help you. You better

take the lift; come, follow me. No one will touch you if you're with me. My name's Paul.'

Marcia seemed intrigued by the piece of jewellery fitted neatly into his gums. 'Why do you have a gold tooth in your mouth?'

What a stupid question, I think. 'Because it looks good, and I want one.'

As they escort us to the lift, we spot the girls who just beat us up. Paul turns to Marcia. 'Is that them?'

'Yes! She's wearing my trainers, and I'm getting them back!' Marcia shouts. All the beatings Marcia has received from Mary over the years seem to have toughened her up, but I hate violence and fighting. We follow quickly behind Marcia as she hurries towards the girls. 'Give me back my shoes!' she demands.

'Come and get them.'

'You cow!' Marcia screams and lunges forward. The girl wearing her trainers is stunned as Marcia's fists connect with her jaw, and the glasses she is wearing fly off her face, cracking as they hit the pavement. Her friends are about to jump in, but Paul stops them.

'Let them fight one-to-one,' he says, raising his hand.

I stand beside him; I want to help but am too afraid. I already have one black eye and really don't want another. Anyway, it's no contest. Marcia hits the girl until she begs her to stop. 'Now, give me my trainers.' The girl wearily unties the laces and thrusts the trainers into Marcia's outstretched arms.

'They're shit trainers anyway,' she mutters under her

breath as she hangs her head down in embarrassment and shame.

'Touch me or my sister again, and you're dead,' Marcia says before walking away.

'Wow, you can fight! Touch me.' Paul holds his fist out.

Marcia looks at him in confusion. 'What do you mean?'

The boys laughed, shaking their heads in amusement. 'Where you girls from, anyway? We know you ain't from round here; you girls are different.' And that was our first introduction to life on the Conleigh estate: meeting a gang, being robbed, and getting beaten up. I think we are going to have to toughen up and adapt quickly if we're going to survive life in this ghetto.

Mary is shocked when we return an hour later, looking as though we've just returned from war. 'What the devil happened to your eye?' Marcia explains our unfortunate encounter. 'Right, that's it; neither of you are to leave this house unless you're going to school or church. You is not allowed to play outside,' and she means every word.

We are on summer holidays and have three weeks left before the start of the new school term and can only leave the house for church on Sundays. 'Genisis, Exodus, Leviticus, and numbers…' During this time, we revise our Bible verses again! We are so bored, and for the first time, I long to return to school. Staring out over the balcony and watching children play in the concrete maze below becomes the highlight of our day. We are like spies. We see who kisses who, who slaps who, who sells drugs, and who takes them. I even learn the words to several reggae songs, courtesy of our left neighbour's speaker box.

Mary has a full-time and part-time job, working most evenings and weekends. Johnny is happy being 'back home' and immediately starts about renovating our house. It has stood empty for a long time and needs everything from a new roof to a new kitchen and bathrooms. He employs a group of men who help bring the house back to its Colonial splendour, adding an extension and one additional floor that is filled with original furnishings from England, things he says his mother would be proud of.

* * *

It has been a year since Johnny returned to Jamaica, and with Mary working every hour God sends, she has less time to keep an eye on us. Every month, she calls him with an excuse explaining why she can't return yet. He is becoming increasingly impatient, and I suspect from her anxious tone she fears for her marriage.

'Go home to your husband.' Mrs Abola tells her. 'Back home, they now consider him a wealthy man. Those young girls will throw themselves at him.' Her words seem to have shaken Mary, as later that evening, she calls Johnny and promises to be home within a year.

I am becoming restless and bored with the routine of

school, home, and church and decide I will do anything to avoid going to Jamaica. I stare out the window, watching the excitement that I now want so much to be a part of. Marcia likes her own company, and as long as she has food and a book, she is content. I hate school but have improved, especially in English. My teacher, Mr Humphries, has predicted that if I continue to work hard, I can pass most of my exams. I have been taking extra lessons with him twice a week after school. I think he and Mr McInally are the only teachers who don't think I'm stupid. I am still bullied, but Marcia often comes to my rescue and saves me from the playground bullies. I dread the walk home through the estate after school. Although, since that day Marcia fought the ringleader of the girl gang and earned Paul's respect, we are no longer everyday targets.

Most days, Mary leaves for work before we even wake up, returning late in the evening. I am sixteen now and have had enough of school, and I really don't want to go back. My failure to learn basic skills in primary school has followed me into my secondary school life. Marcia keeps trying to convince me not to drop out, but I've made my mind up. Compared to many of the girls in my class, I am not what Mrs Kennedy calls 'naturally academic', and Mary's constant criticism of me, although unintentional, has massively dented my confidence. 'You're too lazy. Why can't you do well at school? Why can't you be like the girls at church?' These words have long changed from a slight nag and are now Mary's everyday mantra, second only to her daily prayers. So, when I decide I'm not going back to school, I mean it. Mary works long hours, so she'll be none the wiser. I can easily intercept any letters the school sends home.

I spend the first week bunking off school inside the flat, standing on the other side of the net curtains and peeking out the window, looking down onto the estate, careful not to be seen. Except for children going to school or adults heading to the station for work, everything is relatively quiet until around noon when the phone box starts ringing. Paul or his friends always answer it as if they have been expecting the calls. I've timed them, and they never talk for longer than fifteen seconds. I wonder what they are doing, but by day three, I figure it out when a man comes to meet Paul. He gives him a handful of what looks like money, and Paul gives him something too small for me to see, but I know it's drugs. I remember Mrs Abola warning Mary about this, saying the estate is in the midst of a drug pandemic the world has turned a blind eye to. I've thought about Paul a lot since we moved here. I still remember the way he smelt when we first met, his smooth chocolate skin shiny and smelling of coconut oil. I'm getting bored and want to talk to him, but I don't know what to say, so I decide to get dressed and wait until I see him, then pretend I need to use the phone.

'Are you going to be long? It's just that I'm expecting a call,' he says as I lift the receiver.

'No,' I say, inserting a coin and dialling an imaginary

number. I feel his eyes creeping up and down my body. 'No answer,' I say and turn to walk away. He asks why I'm not in school, and I tell him I've quit.

'A girl as beautiful as you should be in school or modelling,' he says. I feel the heat rise in my cheeks and stare at the ground, hoping it will open up and take me away. He smiles and asks me to sit with him on the swings. His teeth are as white as snow, his gold tooth as bright as a light. When he laughs loudly, I notice a few gasps at the back of his mouth. We sit and chat on the swings until the phone rings again. This time, he tells one of his friends to answer it. 'They work for me,' he says.

'Doing what?' I ask.

'This and that,' he says, grinning those white teeth again. My heart flutters, and I hope he can't hear it beating.

We hang out all the time now; he comes up to the flat, leaving before Marcia gets home from school. I went to his house once. We played on his PlayStation, but when his mum saw me, she told him that until he has his own roof over his head, he cannot bring girls into the house. I've never been back since. We talk about who runs things on the estate or who has beef with who. I never let him smoke inside the flat, so we hang around outside on the stairwells or communal landings, rolling spliffs and smoking weed, making sure Mrs (nosy)Abola never sees us. He hasn't said so yet, but I think he likes me, and I like him too—a lot.

11

Money Moves

THE MORE TIME WE spend together, the more Paul trusts me. Okay, so he's a drug dealer, but he's not a bad guy. Anyway, living in the hood means his chances of getting a decent job are slim, so what if he took the easy way out to work for Reggie, one of the biggest dealers in the area? I've never met him, but I try to hide the light behind my eyes whenever Paul mentions his name. Recently, I casually dropped it into conversation that I'd like to meet him; Paul ignores this comment but, days later, tells me he wants to meet me too. He spotted me one day when Paul and I were chilling by the maze.

I know Paul likes me, and I thought I liked him too until I heard about Reggie. Paul says he liked me from the day we first met and that, even with a black eye and bloody nose, my beauty couldn't be disguised. Sometimes, I purposely brush my hair against the side of his face or arms and imagine him running his fingers through it. But when Paul says Reggie wants to meet me, I momentarily stop breathing. 'Bring her to meet me,' he told Paul. I can see he feels uncomfortable about this and probably hates the thought of Reggie smothering me with his lips. He's already told me that Reggie is a gallis who uses girls only for sex and to help him make money. 'Girls are only good for two things: fucking and sucking.' Apparently, this is his favourite line. Paul says he has a frost-bitten heart and doesn't care for anyone besides himself. He thinks I'm a young, naïve sixteen-year-old and that, at twenty-six, Reggie is too old for me.

'Guys like him can smell your type of innocence in a room full of shit and know how to manipulate you,' he says. I think he's just jealous; he knows he can't compete with Reggie, but I'm sure he won't dare get in his way. 'All girls get like that about him; they're attracted to his money and power. Is that why you want to meet him, Ash?' The more he tries to convince me not to meet him, the more I want to.

So, why has he now decided to tell me how he feels about me? That he's been dying to kiss my soft lips, hold my slender waist, and caress what he calls my perfect breasts. He's had countless dreams about me and is now about to introduce me to who he calls the devil's brother. The truth is, I've dreamt about him too. I've wondered what it would feel like for him to make love to me. I so wanted to give myself to him, but I still remember Eve's words whispered to me just before she handed me to Mary, 'Your virginity is the most precious commodity. Use it wisely.'

'Now you're going overboard,' I laugh.

'Seriously, I will never forgive him if anything happens to you.' I ignore him again.

'When does he want to meet me?' I ask, trying to contain my excitement. He looks at me with annoyance.

'Don't you want to know why he wants to meet you?'

'Because I'm your friend, and he wants to be my friend as well?'

He shakes his head, 'You're so gullible.'

'Get ready, and I'll meet you downstairs in an hour.'

I can hardly contain myself. I have so longed to meet the mysterious Reggie Paul so often talks about. I know he doesn't understand why, telling me I have been raised in a good Christian home and wonders why I am drawn to the ghetto lifestyle. He has no idea what my life was like growing up. Just because a family goes to church doesn't mean their sin is any cleaner than his or Reggie's.

I'm fascinated by Paul's stories about his life on the streets. I sometimes ask if I can follow him on his moves, but he refuses to take me, saying he doesn't want me getting mixed up in his lifestyle, that I'm like a little sister to him, and that he feels protective towards me. Yeah, right; a little sister he wants to have sex with.

I wear a black catsuit with white pearls that hang in a row from my shoulders. Jamie, the local thief, gave it to me. He travels into central London almost every day and steals clothes, perfume, or anything he can get his hands on. It clings to every inch of my five-foot-eight-inch frame, accentuating my curvaceous figure. Paul says

I have the body men dream of, and the shape girls envy. I first met Jamie a year after moving to the estate, and apart from Paul, he is the only person I really speak to. 'Girl, you have the body of a goddess but the wardrobe of a pauper,' he commented one afternoon as I walked to the sweet shop. 'Don't worry, I'm gay, so I won't try to jump into your knickers like every guy around here is probably trying to do.' I think he's so brave. A few days ago, I watched from the kitchen as a group of them chased him out of the playground. But the next day, he strutted right past them again with a busted lip, waving his hand in the air like royalty. He walks like Naomi Campbell as if the streets are his runway and everyone else is his subject. I tell him I envy his wardrobe; he says he feels sorry for mine. 'Not you, but your actual wardrobe. Having clothes like yours hanging inside must make it really miserable,' he laughs. I give him a sideways smirk. 'No, but seriously,' he waves his long, slim royal hand up and down my body, 'You 're really pretty, but where do you get your clothes from, Walthamstow market?' I want to defend myself but can't. My clothes are from every market within a fifty-mile radius of our home. 'Don't worry, babes; I'm gonna kit you out,' he says. We laugh and sit chatting for hours until the same group of boys who chased him approach.

'What you doing back here, batty boy? The beating you got the other day wasn't enough? You want another one?' The chubby, one with skin so bumpy, it resembles Mary's fake brown crocodile skin handbag steps forward and pushes Jamie, causing him to fall backwards onto the concrete floor.

'Leave him alone!' I say.

'Your Paul's ting, init. Why you hanging around with this faggot?'

I want to say, 'Thou doth protest too much,' but I am sure readings from Mr Humphries Shakespeare's lessons will be wasted on him, so I don't bother. 'I'm not Paul's ting. Just piss off and leave us alone.' I don't know where this new-found bravery is coming from, but realising I'm surrounded by a group of ten guys, I want to put it quickly back inside its box. Then I hear Paul; I have never been so relieved to hear his voice.

'What's going on?' he asks.

'They keep picking on my friend and won't leave us alone,' I say. Paul tells them that if they ever trouble Jamie again or even look at me sideways, they will have him to deal with. They try to apologise, but Paul tells them to fuck off; well, not before he makes them say sorry to me first. 'And Jamie,' I say, my new-found bravery raises its head again. They look at Paul with pleading eyes that say, 'Please don't make us apologise to this batty man.'

'You heard the girl,' Paul says. Crocodile man looks at me, and my bravery smirks back.

'Sorry,' they finally mutter almost mutely before turning to walk away. That's one of the things I like about Paul. Unlike many, he doesn't judge Jamie for being gay.

'Live and let live,' he says.

Since then, Jamie calls himself my gay BFF and never comes back from a spree without at least one item for me. I tell him he has to keep some at his house because I'm running out of space to hide them.

'Thanks, Ash. You've got my back, and I've got yours for life,' he says, twirling like a ballerina in Swan Lake.

I style my hair into a ponytail, ensuring my long mane falls over my left breast. I wear a pair of black ankle boots and gold hooped earrings and spray myself in an expensive perfume, all courtesy of my gay BFF. The tightness of my catsuit highlights my recently developed curves in a way I've never noticed before. My ample breasts and nipples appear unusually large pressed against the velvet fabric, and the thickness of my vagina protrudes as though it wants to escape. I remember a dream I had about Paul. We were on the swings, and he told me he wanted to take me upstairs, lay me on my bed, peel my clothes off, and lick me slowly until I begged him to enter me. But I'm not interested in him anymore; he's a bit too quiet for me. I want excitement, a fast life filled with money, clothes, and glamour. I want the top man; I want Reggie.

Reggie lives about a twenty-minute walk from my house on the east side of the estate. As we make our way there, I notice people staring at me. They look at me as though I'm from another planet. 'Why are they staring at me?' I asked Paul nervously.

'Because you're hot, Ash. Don't you know that?'

As we walk across the estate, I notice deprivation screaming from the atmosphere. We come to a precinct with a variety of shops, a laundrette, a betting shop, a takeaway, a convenience store, a doctor's surgery, and an old dentist. My eyes dart around as I survey my surroundings. A lady leaves the laundrette with a pushchair, but in place of a baby sits a large black bin liner stuffed with clothes. Two children trail behind her, a boy carrying a large box of soap powder and a girl carrying a half-empty container of blue fabric softener. An old man grips a cigarette butt between his yellow fingernails, swaying carelessly outside the betting shop, shouting animatedly at the air while tightly gripping a brown paper bag that failed to disguise a can of Special Brew. A group of boys shout to Paul as we walked past Roosers, the chicken shop. I love Rooosters chicken and am always asking Paul to buy me a portion with some chips and a can of Coke. I glance at the dentist's building; slabs of wood cover the broken glass windows that have been smashed but are now boarded up.

'They closed this surgery down a few months ago. The dentist was pulling people's teeth out for money. Nothing was wrong with their teeth; he was pulling them out. Fucking bastard pulled two of mine out. It was the worst pain I'd ever felt. I thought he was going to pull my mouth out of my fucking head the way he put his knee up on the arm of the chair and yanked my teeth out with his pliers.' I wince as he tells me about the horror of his extractions. His story is interrupted when a woman approaches us. She is as thin as a bamboo cane.

103

Her bones look as though they want to jump out from under her skin, and she has two missing front teeth.

'I beg you, fifty pence,' she says, holding out her hands in front of me. Her fingernails are long and dirty with remnants of red nail varnish that looked like it was applied months ago.

Paul pushes her away, 'Get the fuck outta here, you crackhead.' I feel sorry for her and give her a pound. 'Never talk to those people, Ash. They're fucking thieving junkies.'

Next door to the dentist is the doctor's surgery, where a long queue has formed outside. Mothers wait in line with their crying children planted on their hips; junkies queue twitching, waiting for the methadone clinic to open again. I stare at a baby in a pram sucking on her empty bottle and want to buy her some milk.

We go into a sweet shop. The sign on the door reads, '*Only two schoolchildren allowed at one time*'. The shop-keeper stands behind the counter, and another watches us while we select our sweets. As we leave the shop, we are confronted by two women in the midst of a heated argument.

'If you come near mi babyfada again, watch what will happen to you!' One shouts.

'It's not my fault you can't keep your man. Me have de good hole, and him love it, so g'way!' She turns to walk away, but her love rival runs up behind her, tugging at her hair, pulling her to the ground. They grab at each other's locks, rolling around on the ground like a pair of wild wolves until the subject of their disagreement intervenes and prizes them apart.

'I don't want any of you! Look at you behaving like dutty rats!' he shouts.

One woman collects her weave off the floor before trying to neaten the remaining strands left on her head, stroking her hair as she walks away, looking as if she wishes she could take her dignity with her, but that has long gone. This place is crazy. Fuck this poverty shit; I'm getting out of here. Now I feel more determined than ever to hook Reggie.

As we approach the house, I catch Paul staring at me. I think he knows that once I meet Reggie, any chance he had with me will be gone. It's his fault. He should have told me how he felt sooner—not that I'm sure it would have made much difference. Mary is getting ready to go back to Jamaica soon. She doesn't know it yet, but there's no way I'm going with her. I'm sixteen and legally never have to spend another day in school or under her roof. Paul stops and turns to me with the saddest eyes I have ever seen. 'Ashley, I'm genuinely worried for you.' He reminds me that Reggie is ten years older than me, that I'm not like most of his girlfriends; I'm too young and naïve. I don't know why he's telling me this; he knows I want to leave home before Mary goes back to Jamaica, and as far as I see it, this is the only way I can. 'Once you meet him, your life will change forever, for better or for worse,' he says. I smile, and I think it's a chance worth taking.

12

Maybe There is a God

As we approach Reggie's house, my stomach churns like a cement mixer. The east side of the estate looks pretty much like the west side, decorated with the same dull grey concrete cladding. I often stare out my bedroom window and wonder whether the architects purposely designed the estate to keep its residents in a permanent state of depression and angst. A group of guys resembling bouncers at a nightclub stand side by side outside Reggie's house, chests lifted; they stare as if inviting me to compare their iron-pumped pecs. Reggie lives alone in one of a row of fifty houses next to a twelve-storey tower block. All the houses are covered in cream cladding, white plastic framed windows, and blue wooden doors with a peephole in the centre. The house three doors away had been caught on fire but still stands firm. Black soot covers the cream exterior; its melted windows buckled and charred from the heat of the flames. Reggie's foot soldiers step aside, allowing Paul and I to enter the house.

As we walk in, the smell of marijuana and sweet-smelling incense hits my nose. I hold my stomach and lean my hand against the wall; the smell makes me dizzy and nauseous. I'm already nervous, and the strong smell isn't helping. An NWA song, *Gangsta Gangsta,* is blaring from a speaker box—since hanging out with Paul, I know all the latest hip-hop songs. Paul leads the way along the corridor to a room at the back of the house. A long shoe rack spanning almost the entire length of the hallway is filled with white Adidas trainers. Most of them have sunken backs, as though they've been worn as slippers rather than training shoes. 'These are the only trainers Reggie wears,' Paul says as we walk past the gleaming display of neatly stacked shoes.

The door ahead is slightly ajar, and as we enter, all conversation stops, and everyone turns to look at me. Marijuana smoke melts into the black check wallpaper. Two red leather sofas face each other, separated by a low, hand-smudged, black-lacquered coffee table. Reggie sits on the sofa surrounded by two girls. One sits close to him, carefully rolling a joint between her long pink acrylic nails. Another stands behind him, massaging his thick, muscular shoulders. They both wear long weaves that trail down their backs. Reggie shifts his head, signalling for them to leave the room. As they do, they look me up and down like I'm covered in shit. The girl with the extra-long nails bounces past me with such force she almost pushes me backwards.

'So, who do we have here?' Reggie asks. His eyes fix firmly as he stares into mine. He is wearing dark blue tracksuit bottoms and a white vest top that clings to his body, proudly displaying the cuts of his muscly chest. His white Adidas trainers are laced neatly with black and white rope. He must work out every day, I think, glancing at the bench press and weights in the corner of the room. His jewellery looks so heavy, I wonder how he holds his neck up. His thick gold chain resembles marine rope, and his gold bracelets hang weightily from each wrist. The darkened knuckles on his hands are barely visible under the gold sovereigns that adorn his fingers. His dark-molasses skin and short frame remind me of Wesley Snipes. I notice his hair has started to recede and wonder why he doesn't just shave it off completely. 'So, you're the famous Ashley,' he says, slowly sliding his bottom lip between his teeth. 'I always hear Paul and the others talking about you, and now I see why.' I lower my head, hoping to hide the redness in my cheeks. His eyes slowly survey my body as if he is imagining what I look like naked. They linger over my breasts, and my chest heaves, hoping they will soon be in his mouth. I imagine myself groaning as he eases himself gently inside me.

'I'll leave you to it,' Paul says, obviously feeling slightly awkward. The attraction between us is so tangible you can almost reach out and touch it.

'Come, sit down.' Reggie motions me to the red sofa. I try to hide the wave of nerves that wash through me, but my nervous, deep breath and rising chest won't allow it. He stands up and holds out his hand to meet mine. As I place my hand in his, he brings it up to meet his mouth and kisses it gently. His enormous smile, revealing two gold teeth, immediately makes me feel at ease. 'Can I get you anything to drink?' he asks. I am way too nervous and politely decline. He walks over to the kitchen area and pours himself a drink before returning to join me on the sofa. 'Why are you so nervous? Take a sip of this; it will help you relax.' I take a huge gulp of the brown liquid that makes my chest light up as it hits the back of my throat and creeps slowly down my chest, burning my stomach.

'What is this?' I say, coughing violently.

'Hennessy,' he says, laughing. 'You ain't never drank brandy before?'

'No,' I say, 'Can I get some water?'

He pours himself another drink and hands me a glass before rolling a joint. I don't smoke, but I have watched Paul and his friends, intrigued by how they can roll a joint with one hand and hold a drink in the other. Reggie rolls one of the fattest joints I have ever seen. Unlike Paul, he doesn't add any tobacco; instead, he rolls it with almost the entire contents of his weed bag. 'You smoke?' he asks. I shake my head. 'Wow, you really aren't from round here. You don't smoke. You don't drink. What do you like to do?'

I smile; the Hennessy is beginning to take control of my senses, giving rise to a weird relaxing sensation that makes me want to giggle. 'May I?' I ask as I take Reggie's glass and hold it up to my lips.

'Of course,' he says, watching me.

Smoke fills the room as he pulls on his spliff, and I become more and more relaxed. I watch him from the corner of my eye, intrigued by the way his biceps expand every time he holds his spliff to his thick brown lips. He licks his lips every time he speaks to me, and my dream of Paul resurfaces as I imagine him licking me, kissing my neck and the space between my legs. I reach for his spliff. 'You don't smoke,' he says, pushing my hand away.

'I just want to try it,' Reluctantly, he hands it to me. I inhale the smoke and begin coughing ferociously. He shakes his head and laughs, attempting to take it back. 'No, wait.' I push him away and reach for his glass, taking another pull on the spliff and a sip of brandy before handing them back to him. I rest my head on the back of the sofa, and the room begins to spin. 'I feel good. I feel nice,' I drawl.

The weed is doing something to me; it's giving me a feeling I've never felt before, and my body becomes hot and starts to tingle. I close my eyes and imagine Reggie unzipping my catsuit, removing my boots, and leaving me in nothing but my black lace bra and knickers. As the room spins, I imagine lying on my stomach, Reggie sitting beside me. He massages my shoulders, pressing deeply into the arches of my back. His hands move slowly as I groan with every touch. He turns me over, my eyes still closed, and slips my bra strap over my shoulders, massaging my breasts. My nipples are hard, calling for him to put them into his mouth and cover them with the warm moisture of his tongue. I moan as he sucks and caresses my breasts. The sensation between my legs gets hotter and stronger. Then I wake from my dream. Reggie is sitting beside me.

'You look beautiful when you sleep,' he smiles.

'How long was I asleep for?' I have been asleep for almost one hour. I feel exposed, as though he could see my dream and read my thoughts. I make my way to the bathroom. How embarrassing! It was only a dream, but it felt so real. Did I moan in my sleep? Locking the bathroom door behind me, I slide my hand into my knickers. The folds between my legs are wet.

For the next two hours, Reggie regales me with stories from his past. 'My grandad was a famous Jamaican gangsta, and I'm gonna be just like him. Money, power, and respect, that's what I demand.' His aura is potent and lingering; violence almost pours from his voice as he speaks. His angry roars light up the room like lightning strikes— violent but disturbingly beautiful somehow. 'The longest I've been in prison was three years, and I ain't going back there,' he says. When he was twenty, he burgled an artist's house in Hampstead and only got caught because he smeared his freshly excreted faeces onto the living room wall in an attempt to 'leave my mark,' like a cat marking his territory. This act of artistic machismo eventually costs him his liberty and three years of his life in the company of Her Majesty's prison alongside some of the country's most notorious criminals. He has dreams of building a huge drug cartel, supplying drugs to London's rich and famous, but right now, he only sells crack to desperate addicts. He spends hours re-watching Scarface and Pablo Escobar films. 'My granddad caught one of his workers stealing money from him and blew his brains out.' He laughs. I listen intently, imagining the man's brain splattering like a watermelon exploding into the air, pieces of his intelligence glistening as the sun's rays burn through his dissolving thoughts, and I wonder why he trusts me with all his confidence.

I look at my watch. 'It's getting late. I better get going.'

'Let me take you home,' he offers.

Grabbing his keys, he puts on a black leather jacket and takes my hand. A few of his friends are still hanging around outside, but Paul is gone. Reggie drives a red BMW with a black leather interior. A pair of scented boxing gloves with the flag of Jamaica printed on them hang from the rear-view mirror.

'Red is my favourite colour.' I say as he opens the door for me.

'And you're my favourite girl,' he replies, leaning in and planting a wet kiss on my lips.

He drives so fast that I feel overwhelmed with a mix of fear and excitement. The revving of the engine and the smell of the leather stirs a feeling within me that silently whispers, 'Be careful what you wish for.' I motioned for him to pull over. 'Drop me off here. I don't want to chance Mary seeing you.'

He opens my door and helps me onto the pavement. 'Damn, you smell so good,' he says, stroking my cheeks. I smile as he grabs my waist, draws me close to him, and kisses me again. "And you taste good, too.' As he kisses me, I feel something hard between his legs. Drawing myself away, I look down. 'See what you do to me,' he says, touching himself. He takes my hand and leads it between his legs. 'How does this feel?' he asks.

'I don't know, hard.' I blush. He laughs and squeezes me so tightly, I struggle to breathe. We arranged to meet again the following day.

'You're mine,' he says before driving away.

13

The Blink of an Eye

I CAN BARELY SLEEP; every toss is filled with thoughts of him. His smell lingers at the base of my nose, and I can still feel the warmth of his touch and the feel of his soft, velvety lips against mine. I am a virgin, but I know I won't be for much longer. I am ready to become a woman, and he is the man that will turn me into one.

It's still dark when I awake, and Mary has already left for work. The morning bird song that used to greet me in our old house has long been replaced by pigeons cooing on our neighbour's balcony. I lay in bed, staring up at the stained chipboard wallpaper thinking about my day ahead. I wonder what my first time will be like. Will it hurt? What if I bleed? Will I feel the sensation I felt in my dream? I fall asleep again but am awakened by a knock at the door. 'Who is it?' I shout from the top of the stairs. It's Paul. He doesn't look me in the eye, preferring, instead, to look at the floor.

'Reggie wants to meet you at twelve,' he says, shooting me a look of disgust.

'Paul, we have been friends for a long time, and I hope we always will be. I really like Reggie, so please be happy for me,' I say.

'Like him? You don't even fucking know him!' he shouts, slamming his hand against the door. I don't think I have ever seen him this angry.

'Well, you introduced him to me, and he seems really nice,' I say.

'I'll meet you downstairs in a bit.' he says, and I slam the door behind him. I look at my watch; I have one hour to get ready—oh, where is Jamie when I need him? He is so good at putting outfits together.

The weatherman says it will be a hot, sticky day, so I decide to wear a red organza dress that pulls in at the waist to accentuate my curves. It has twelve buttons that run down the front; I decide to leave the top four undone. I pair my outfit with a gold key chain pendant and gold hooped earrings and tie my hair into a messy bun that sits carelessly on the crown of my head. Finally, a pair of wedge heels make my legs look even longer— outfit complete! I meet Paul at 11.45 AM, and he walks me over to the precinct. He looks at me like a hungry beast that hasn't eaten in months. 'Forget about Reggie; you should be mine,' he jokes. I know he is serious, but he should have acted sooner if he wanted me. I like him, but I need some excitement in my life. If I'm going to be with anyone, it's going to be the boss.

Reggie is waiting for us by the laundry. Butterflies swarm my stomach as we approach him. He looks at me and can't contain the huge smile that engulfs his face, exposing his jewelled teeth. 'Hey, beautiful,' he says, pulling me towards him and kissing me on the lips. Paul tries not to look, but Reggie catches him staring at us. He quickly tries to divert his gaze, but it's too late. 'You missed your chance, Paul, she's mine,' he says, grabbing my hand. 'What do you wanna do today?' he asks.

'Whatever you like.' I don't really mind. I'm just happy to be with him.

We drive to the new, recently built shopping centre in central London. It's laid out over five floors and has over four hundred and fifty shops, including a designer village filled with all the top designers, from Louis Vuitton to Gucci and Prada. I try to hide my excitement as we stop outside the concierge entrance. A valet opens the car door.

'Thank you,' I say, beaming.

'You're very welcome,' the valet replies, staring at my chest as if in a trance. This seems to agitate Reggie, and I wonder if he feels pride, jealousy, or fear. Pride that I'm now his. Jealousy, as he can't bear the thought of any man wanting me or fear that I may desire someone else. He takes my hand and leads me into the building.

I stare up at the ceiling as we make our way up the escalator. A huge crystal chandelier glistens, soaking up the rays of the sun that beam down through a large glass atrium. This is my first time in a shopping centre. Jamie has told me about them, but I've never been to one be-fore. The only place I've ever shopped for clothes is at the market. I gaze into the shop windows, mesmerised by the displays. One window is so lifelike, I almost think the mannequins are real. Reggie leads me into a shoe shop. 'Choose whatever you want,' he says. Before I can re-spond, a sales assistant approaches us.

'Can I help you?'

'She needs help choosing a pair of shoes.' Reggie points his chin towards me. My mind races. All the shoes on dis-play are so beautiful, it will take me hours to decide. The rich smell and the feel of the leather remind me of the seats in Reggie's car. My eyes dart from shelf to shelf, searching the array of heels resting on a pair I like until they are drawn to another and another. Then I spot them. They are black and red with a platinum engraved sole.

'I'll try these,' I say.

'Great choice,' the assistant says.

Suddenly, I feel like Dorothy in the Wizard of Oz, magically transformed. I am now ten feet tall, walking on air, looking down from a pedestal. Emboldened, I walk over to Reggie sitting in a chair playing with his phone. 'What do you think?' I ask.

He looks down at my feet and smiles. 'They look amazing on you, babe,' he says, standing to kiss me before I parade around in front of him.

'We'll take them,' I beam, handing the shoes back to the assistant.

'That will be £350.00.' Did I just hear right? Did she say £350.00? Surely, he won't pay that much for a pair of shoes. But without hesitation, he pulls a wad of £50 notes out of his pocket and hands the money to the cashier. I can't contain my shock and engulf him in my arms, planting a long kiss on his lips. £350 for a pair of shoes! They are now the most expensive thing I own. If this isn't love, I don't know what is.

Next, we go to a lingerie shop. The assistant measures me in the changing room before helping me pick out some items. I love almost everything in the store. Unlike the underwear I tried to conceal in the school changing rooms, the silk against my skin makes me feel sexy and confident. No more itchy lace or poly-silk for me! Once I choose several sets, the assistant leads us upstairs and into a private room above the store. The walls are covered with padded pink fabric and diamond-studded buttons. A huge, gilded mirror covers one side of the wall, and a glass pink chandelier hangs from the centre of the ceiling. An ice bucket with a bottle of champagne and two glasses is laid out on a table beside a large cream leather sofa.

'Enjoy,' the assistant smiles cheekily as she closes the door firmly behind her.

'What is this place?' I ask.

'The VIP room,' Reggie winks, opening the bottle of champagne.

There's a privacy screen in the corner where the assistant hung all the items I picked out. It's covered in embroidered silk with images of Japanese geishas sewn into it. Reggie pours me a glass of champagne, and we sit on the sofa. I want to pinch myself. I feel like a movie star, sitting in the VIP room and drinking champagne in a pair of shoes that cost more than anything I've ever possessed, with the man who will take me away from a life of poverty. 'I could get used to this,' I say, planting a soft kiss on his lips.

'Good, coz this is your life now. You're mine, yeah.'

Briefly, I wonder if this is a question or statement, but readily reply, 'Yes, I'm yours,' before disappearing behind the screen and stripping out of my clothes.

First, I try on a three-piece set made of red silk with a black French lace trimming. The bra has slits where the nipples sit; the silk and lace of the knickers cling to the curves of my hips. The assistant confirms that 34DD is my official bra size, my waist is twenty-four inches, and my hips thirty-six. I slip a pair of black lace stockings up my legs, slide on my new shoes, take my hair down from its ponytail, and look in the mirror. Running my hands over my breasts, I feel sexy and confident, ready to give myself to my new man. Reggie's jaw drops as I walk out from behind the screen and give him a little fashion show before spreading my legs and sitting on his lap.

'You are by far the sexiest girl I have ever met,' he says, kissing my lips and then my neck before making his way down towards my breasts, kissing them softly and gently. I moan as he pulls my bra straps down with his teeth and begins to kiss and caress my breasts, gently squeezing and licking my nipples.

'I want you,' I say, staring into his eyes. I am over-whelmed by the tingling sensation working its way from my breast and down to the area between my legs.

'I want you, too,' he says and unties his tracksuit bottoms.

'No, not here. I want my first time to be special, not in a shop.'

He lets out a frustrated sigh and stands up. 'Okay, I'll book us a hotel.' I've never stayed in a hotel before, and the idea fills me both with excitement and nervous anticipation.

After hitting a few more shops, we go for something to eat. 'You should come live with me,' he suggests casually through a mouthful of pasta. His suggestion shocks me. This is what I want, but I hadn't expected it to happen this quickly. 'You're sixteen, Ash. I've heard how strict your gran is. It's the only way we can properly be together. You can't be my girl if I don't know where you are or what you're doing.' I feel overwhelmed. I have always dreamt of this: a knight in shining armour to whisk me away, rescuing me from my poverty-stricken life. Maybe God is real. Mary is leaving for Jamaica soon, and it's my birthday in two months. Now I definitely won't be returning with her. I don't hesitate to accept his offer and decide I will tell Mary tonight.

14

Be Careful What You Wish For

MARY IS HOME EARLIER than usual. The smell of stewed peas and rice hits my nose as soon as I open the front door. I enter the kitchen; Marcia is sitting at the table doing her homework. Miss Goody Two Shoes, I think, as she shoots me a judgemental look from under her double-glazed glasses. I want to send it right back to her, but I'm afraid she will finally decide to tell Mary that I've been bunking off school. The funny thing is, I actually like her a lot more now as, even though she's caught Paul in the flat on more than one occasion, she has never grassed me up.

I promised Reggie I would tell Mary tonight, and although I wish Marcia weren't in the room, I take a deep breath and begin to tell her what I suspect she already knows. 'I'm not coming to Jamaica with you. I'm sixteen and can get a flat and a job and build my own life here.'

Her shoulders drop in defeat. 'Ashley, you is mi wash belly. I know I may have gone about raising you the wrong way, but I have only ever wanted the best for you.' I lie and tell her I know someone who can help me get a place to live and that I have found a job as a receptionist at the local doctor's surgery. 'Why can't you just study your books like Marcia? She wants to be a nurse and make something of her life.' I want to scream and tell her that I don't want to be a nurse or a bloody secretary, and that she's been so flipping busy earning pennies, I haven't been to school in months, and she hasn't even noticed. But I don't. Instead, I say thank you. Thank you for looking after me, for going hungry, for working every hour your God sends to keep a roof over our heads. I desperately want to ask about Eve; I think if she saw me now, she would be proud, but I don't want to hurt her feelings, so I decide not to.

Mary will receive her twenty-year bonus from the Heinz factory in three months and will then leave with Marcia and join Johnny in Jamaica. My heart feels low and heavy as I pack my bags. Mary is the only mother I have ever known, and now I am about to leave her and start a new life. I wonder why she hasn't asked me where my new flat is or if she can come and see it, then before I leave, she pushes a wad of ten-pound notes into my hand. *'Dear God, I beg you, take care of this child. You know, oh Lord, that I did my best, and you know my heart. Guide and protect her and save her from the sins of her mother.'* I open my eyes and look into hers, and there it is. She knows I'm not moving into my own flat; her self-fulfilling prophecy has finally come to pass. I really am no good, just like my mother.

Reggie collects me whilst Mary is at work. 'You ain't got much, have you?' he jokes as he packs my bags into the boot of his car. 'I tried booking us a hotel for the night. I want to make your first time special, but they are all fully booked.'

'It's okay, we don't need to go to a hotel,' I say. I'm disappointed; I wanted my first time to be extra special and have been looking forward to my first stay at a posh hotel.

'Don't worry, I promise I'll make it special for you,' he says.

Once I unpack, we drive to Chinatown for something to eat. I look at the menu, but before I can decide what I want, Reggie calls the waiter over. 'We'll have a number 2, 7, 16, 21, and 25 with two Cokes,' he says before handing the menus back to the waiter. He didn't even ask me what I wanted, I think, and I wonder if I have made the right decision. Yes, yes, I have. This is what I've always wanted: someone to love and take care of me. He's a man who's used to being in control, and I reassure myself he has a better idea of what to order anyway. I sit in silence, knowing I am about to give myself to him, watching as he eats and noticing that the palm of his hand is big enough to hold one of mine. He belches as he chews a spoonful of noodles and gulps a mouthful of Coke while his rope chain swings around his neck, hitting the plate and soaking up the brown juices from his noodles in oyster sauce. Once we finish eating, he pulls out a wad of £20 notes and prepares to pay the bill. I watch as he quickly shuffles the money between his fingers, wondering how much is in the bundle.

Once home, he rolls a joint and pours us both a drink. I sip it slowly, hoping it will relax me. A nervous energy engulfs me, knowing what is about to happen. My mind is full of romantic ideas, and when he had told me we'd be going to a hotel, I'd fantasised about what it would be like; I thought my first time would be luxurious and romantic like the movies—not in his bedroom. His room is cold and dark. Everything is black: his grimy, smudged mirror-covered wardrobe, the chest of drawers. The bed is covered with black cotton sheets, and a black rug hides a large section of the cold wooden flooring. The headboard is the only piece of furniture that isn't black; it's covered in hard-padded, red leather. I feel a lot more relaxed once I finish my drink and take a few pulls on his spliff.

'Come, let's go to bed,' he says, helping me up from the sofa.

I slowly climb the stairs, and he follows closely behind me. I sit motionless on the edge of the bed, scared to undress. I am about to undo the button on my shirt when he kneels down between my legs. He unbuttons my shirt, slips it over my shoulders, and begins ravishing my neck. Lowering my bra straps, he holds my breasts firmly in his hands, pushing me backwards onto the bed as he buries his head between them, eagerly sucking and squeezing my tender nipples. I tense slightly as he places his ring-laden fingers between my legs, pulling my knickers down over my thighs. 'Relax, I promise I'll be gentle,' he whispers. He can't contain his eagerness as he pushes my knees up towards my stomach. Removing my knickers, he stares longingly at my naked body before burying his head between my legs. I groan in pleasure as his tongue dances between them. 'You taste so good,' he says as my body relaxes. The feel of his wet tongue makes me moan and shake as he quenches his thirst. Loosening his belt, he hurriedly pulls his trousers off. 'Are you ready for me?' he asks, staring into my eyes.

'Yes, I'm ready,' I take a deep breath as I prepare for him to enter me.

'Relax, babe; it won't hurt.'

He tries entering me, but the hole between my legs isn't letting him in so easily. He fumbles and pushes until he eventually forces himself inside me, violently breaking through my preserved wedding veil. Pain shoots up my spine and out through my mouth, causing me to let out a loud moan. The walls of my vagina grip tightly onto him as he thrusts himself deep inside me, faster and faster. I close my eyes tightly, wishing it would end. He moans with angry pleasure as he moves eagerly inside me. I'm too scared to tell him he's hurting me. He might not want me if I ask him to stop and may tell me to go back home. I hide the invisible tears that swell beneath my lids and close my eyes, praying it will all be over soon.

'Does it feel good? Does it feel good?' he asks repeatedly between thrusts.

'Yes, it feels good,' I lie, hoping he will finish sooner if I pretend I'm enjoying it.

'Ah, ah, I love you, Ashley,' he gasps, shuddering as he releases himself inside me before turning his back to me and falling asleep.

My gift of virginity is now taken—sold—in what felt like hours, but my watch shows it was just under ten minutes. I smile. I am happy; he loves me, so it was worth every second. As he sleeps, I walk painfully to the bathroom and wipe the blood from between my legs.

15

The Grass is Never Greener

LIFE WITH REGGIE IS utter chaos, and my dream of living a life filled with restaurant dinners and shopping sprees is thrown out the window quicker than the day he took my virginity. His friends come around every day except Sundays, including the two girls I saw when I first met him. Sunday, a day I always disliked, quickly becomes my favourite day of the week. He calls it a rest day and won't allow anyone to visit except the weed man, who he meets at the door but doesn't let in. Instead of living with my boyfriend, I feel like I am shacked up with him and a bunch of strangers who won't even give me eye contact, much less talk to me. The same music I once enjoyed with Paul now blares from the stereo so loudly I want to throw it out the window and smash it into a million pieces. The smell of weed and brandy is our air freshener, and paracetamol is my best friend.

'I've got sex on demand,' I hear him joke to his friend one day. Since the day he took my virginity, he has never told me he loves me. When I tell him I love him, he just laughs. 'Love isn't real, babe; it's a temporary emotion that lasts as long as an orgasm.' Which, in his case, is five minutes—ten if he's feeling energised. I've never had an orgasm with him. Does this mean I don't love him? I really want and need to; how else will I get the things I want?

'So, why are you with me?' I ask.

'You were a virgin, and you're pretty. Most girls around here are as loose as a fucking elastic band.' he laughs. Inside, so many tears fill my heart, I feel as though it might burst. I try to hold them back, but tears spill from within me and run down my cheeks. 'What the fuck are you crying for? I fucking took you from your shit hole life, and now you live with me for fucking free. Stop the crocodile tears.' I swallow my tears, go to the bathroom, and cry them down the plughole, begging them never to return.

Reggie thinks he's been smoking and drinking a lot more than usual. 'I only brought this bag three days ago, and it's finished already. It usually lasts at least five days.' He thinks I don't drink or smoke and so doesn't suspect me. But after months of being trapped here, I've started. Paul used to teach me how to roll, so I can do that perfectly, and I mix my brandy with Coke so it isn't so strong. I need it to numb the pain, and drinking helps me to forget. Mary and Marcia have gone to Jamaica, and I'm stuck with him now. I either smoke and drink in secret or run away, and I'm too much of a coward to do the latter.

Reggie loves having sex with me, even if it only lasts a short time, so I decide this is the best time to ask for what I want. I feel like a caged bird that is only allowed out to fly once a week in search of food. I want—no, I need—new clothes, and I'm sick of the house always being filled with his idiot friends and bitches, as he calls them. I plan to confront him. For the first time during sex, I decide to do what I saw a girl do in a movie we watched last week and put his dick in my mouth. I feel his body resist, but he quickly relaxes as my tongue slides up and down the space between his legs. He doesn't come as quickly as when we have sex, and I feel nauseous, but I want to go shopping, so I keep going. I almost bit it when he rammed it deep into my throat.

'You stupid fucking bitch! What the fuck are you doing?' I want to laugh but apologise and stroke it gently before putting it inside me.

I know that once he's done, he will probably go to sleep, so I decide to ask him straight away. 'Can we go shopping tomorrow, hun? I need some new bits. Also, do your friends have to come round all the time? I love spending time with you on my own.'

He looks at me as though I've just farted in his face. 'You're a fucking whore, just like the rest of them, aren't you?' He says we're all the same and only want is his money. I wonder what else he has to offer. 'I ain't taking you fucking nowhere. This is my house, and I ain't changing nothing; you knew what you were signing up for. You want to live the fast life? Well, this is what comes with it.' Fast life? My life is as fast as a snail on the motorway; I had more fun rocking on a swing with Jamie and Paul. I hardly leave the house and am now just a bloody wash-erwoman and shoe cleaner. 'I'm hungry. Go and dish me out some food,' he says. I want to spit on his plate but don't dare. I feel angry with Paul; why didn't he warn me sooner? Paul was right; Reggie uses girls to transport drugs for him and recruits the guys to sell them. But then I remember that I'd rather live in hell than live in Jamaica with Mary and face her judgmental "I told you so's".

'Why are you so fascinated with guns?' I ask Reggie one day. He likes to read gun magazines and keeps a collection of them in his bedroom drawer.

'It's good business, babe.' He then leaves the room and returns with a gun in his hand. I freeze, unable to move; I have never seen a gun before. 'Don't worry, it's not loaded,' he says. Seeing the look of fear on my face, he hands it to me. Its cold, heavy surface conjures an image of a man lying in a sea of blood, the hole in his forehead still smouldering.

'Why do you need it?' I ask, handing it back to him.

'Don't ask stupid questions. You know how I make my money; I need protection on these streets, and if anyone disrespects me, this is what they'll get.' Looking me dead in the eye, he grips the gun against my chest, pushing me backwards onto the bed. A feeling of fear and regret rush over me. He is threatening me. Part of me wants to leave him, but I am terrified of what he might do to me.

Paul still comes to the house sometimes. He looks different somehow, more attractive and manly and still smells of sweet coconuts. Now, he even has a new BMW. He always said he would buy it one day, and now look at him. It seems as though he's doing better than Reggie.

'I can't stay in this game forever. I plan to make my own money and get away from here,' he used to say. He has dreams of building a property empire. I wish I could run away with him, but I know that ship has sailed. Reggie would kill us both if anything were to ever happen between us. He knows how close we were and always sends me upstairs when Paul's around. Sometimes, I dream about him, wondering what my life would be like if I had listened to him and turned back before reaching Reggie's door. Now I can barely look at him, afraid he might see inside my soul and know it's crying out in pain. Instead, I give him a sideways glance as I leave the room, and our eyes meet. I immediately feel concern from his kind spirit, certain he feels the hurt and shame I try so hard to hide. I lock myself in the bathroom, afraid that Reggie will see my tears again, and I wash them away, along with my pain and regret.

Occasionally, Reggie takes me out with him when he's doing a deal. I have long since realised that he likes the idea of having a beautiful young woman beside him much more than he likes me. He taught me to drive and sometimes makes me drive him around, forcing me to carry packages I know are full of drugs. We are on our way back from East London when we catch the attention of the police.

'Hold this.' he says.

'What? No,' I say, terrified.

'Hold it; they won't search you,' he snarls as he pushes the gun into my hand. I quickly place it inside my jacket pocket as the car draws closer. The police flash their lights, and I pull over. They question us both: where are we going? Where are we coming from? Thankfully, they let us go without being searched. We drive home in silence. Inside, I am furious. How could he do this to me? I rage silently.

'What the hell did you think you were doing?' I scream once we are inside the house. I take the gun from my jacket pocket. 'I could have been arrested! You put my life, my liberty, at risk over yours.'

'They wouldn't have searched you; they never search girls,' he says.

'I hate you!' I scream and turn to walk away, but as I do, he grabs my hair.

'Who the fuck do you think you're talking to?' he says, slapping me. My face feels as hot as an iron, and my eyes sting as tears stream down my cheeks. I feel dizzy and became unsteady on my feet, my head spinning from the shock. 'Get upstairs!' he demands, dragging me by the hair up to the bedroom. This is the first day of many he has sex with me without my consent. He rips my clothes off, throws me on the bed, and fucks me like I am a rag doll. Hot, angry tears stream down my face, soaking into my hair, as I lay silent, my head banging violently against the padded headboard. When he's finished, he takes a shower and leaves the house.

I lay on the bed sobbing quietly for what seems like hours. My insides feel like someone has ripped them to shreds, my heart is heavy, and my body aches. I look in the mirror, unaware of who is staring back at me. My eyes are dark, my face blood red, the imprint of his hand still visible on my cheek. He doesn't return to the house for two days, and for a moment, I think about leaving, but where would I go? He isn't all bad; he looks after me and gives me money for food shopping. I don't even have to work, so I should be grateful. If I don't complain, I'm sure I can make him love me again.

When he finally returns, he isn't alone. He's with Cynthia, one of his mules. I've never liked her; she is always the last person to leave the house, hanging around like a bad smell. It's obvious she likes Reggie and will do anything to please him. If he wants a drink, she jumps to make it; if he needs a light, she's the first to give it to him. She sits on the floor by his feet like a loyal dog. I want to ask what she is doing here but daren't say anything for fear of upsetting him, so I shoot her a disapproving look without saying a word. I desperately want to hug Reggie and apologise, but I can't risk facing his rejection in front of Cynthia.

While preparing dinner silently in the kitchen, I

watch Reggie and Cynthia sitting together, chatting and laughing as they drink and smoke. I hated the idea of smoking before I met Reggie, and I'd never tasted brandy, even when Paul used to drink it. Now, I can barely go a day without a drink and smoke. I've stopped trying to hide it now, and I don't care what Reggie thinks; without it, I wouldn't even be able to look at him. Most mornings, when he sends me down to make a cup of tea, I make myself a coffee with a dash of brandy and roll a spiff before brushing my teeth, and I instantly feel better. This, for me, is the best part of the day, especially as I know once I bring him his tea, he will want to have sex. At least now, I'm numb to his touch.

When I first met Reggie, I thought all my dreams had come true; I had snared the top man, the one with the most money, who is feared and respected, who loves me and will give me whatever I want. Now, just six months later, here I am, cooking and cleaning, forced to carry his guns and drugs. He treats me the same, if not worse, than all his workers. So, when I see Cynthia lean in to kiss him, I see red. As if possessed by an unruly spirit, I pick up the knife I have been using to chop the onions and charge into the living room.

'What the fuck do you think you're doing? Get the fuck away from my man!' I scream, pointing the knife at her.

'Ashley, are you fucking crazy?' Reggie shouts. 'Give me the damn knife!' He grabs the knife, and it cuts into his hand. The look on his face terrifies me. I've seen it before and know what's coming next. I edge backwards as he clenches his bloodied fists and lunges towards me. I turn to run upstairs, but just as I reach the top step, he grips the back of my neck. Something inside me cracks as I hit the floor, and his hands tighten like a noose around my neck. Squeezing my eyes shut, I try to cover my face as his St. Christopher sovereign smashes into my cheekbone, the imprint of the saint marking my left cheek as he hits me repeatedly, leaving me unconscious in the hallway at the top of the stairs.

When I eventually gain consciousness, I can't move, paralysed by the sounds I hear coming from our bedroom. My body aches, and my face throbs. For a minute, I forget where I am; I think I'm dreaming, but the taste of blood in my mouth reminds me of the beating I received earlier—reality reminding me that this isn't a dream; it's a living nightmare. Lying motionless on the floor, I try desperately to block out the moans coming from the bedroom, but the image of Reggie and Cynthia in our bed doesn't allow it. I attempt to raise my head, but the pounding is too great. My body surrenders; my spirit retreats...

I am awoken by Reggie's footsteps as he makes his way from the kitchen with two glasses in his hands. 'Get the fuck off the floor and clean yourself up!' he shouts as he slams the bedroom door behind him. The sounds of laughter from behind the bedroom walls feel as painful as my throbbing black eye. I almost don't recognise the reflection staring back at me in the mirror. My lip is bloodied and bruised, and my face is so badly swollen I can barely open my eyes. I run a bath and go down to the kitchen for some ice. A knock at the door startles me. Who the heck is it? I won't answer it; I don't want anyone seeing me like this. Then Reggie shouts from upstairs, 'Ashley, open the door and take the money from Paul.' Paul? He can't see me like this. I grab a pair of glasses off the table and slowly open the door, holding my hand up to cover my mouth. I see Paul's heart sink as he looks at my face.

'Ash, what the fuck happened to your face?' he asks, but he already knows the answer. He raises his hands, attempting to move the glasses away from my eyes. I wince as he reaches out and gently touches my face. Sadness fills his eyes when he sees what Reggie has done to me. Uncontrollable tears stream down my face. 'Baby, you've got to get out of here. He will kill you if you stay,' Paul whispers.

'He'll kill me if I leave,' I say quietly, pulling myself away from him. The warmth of his body is a feeling I miss and haven't felt in a long time.

'Ashley!' Reggie shouts.

'You better go,' I sob, pushing Paul away.

'Leave him, Ash. Come with me; we can move away from here.'

'Goodbye, Paul,' I say tearfully, closing the door behind him.

Life with Reggie becomes progressively worse; I constantly drink and smoke to mask the pain. Every now and again, he brings a girl back to the house.

'Why do you want me here?' I finally have the courage to ask one evening after drinking heavily. 'Why won't you let me go?' I slur. Despite always telling me I am the most beautiful girl he has ever met, he has killed my confidence, wringing it out of me, one squeeze at a time. I now walk with my head down, afraid to look anyone in the eye. He only allows me to leave the house with him, controlling my every move. I am his property to do with what he wants, and he will kill any man who dares attempt to approach me.

'Stop drinking,' he replies as he snatches the glass out of my hand.

'I hate you! I hate you! I hate you! I wish I was dead!' I scream in a drunken rage.

'Carry on like that, and you soon will be. Go to bed, you drunk.'

That evening, as usual, his friends come round. They smoke, drink, and play video games, and as always, I'm not allowed downstairs because of Reggie's jealousy. He knows Paul has feelings for me and has stopped letting him inside the house. As I sit at the top of the stairs, listening to them laugh and joke, I hear a voice that sounds like my younger sister, Donna. I haven't seen her since she went to live with Eve, and I wonder if she's seeing one of Reggie's friends. Silently, I make my way downstairs. I blink twice, thinking my eyes must be deceiving me, but they aren't. It is Donna, and she's sitting on Reggie's lap, kissing him.

'What are you doing, Donna?' I ask.

She smirks at me. 'What business is it of yours?'

'You're kissing my boyfriend.'

She let out a wicked laugh. 'He's everybody's boyfriend, Ashley. You're just his slave.' The room erupts with laughter.

'Go back upstairs!' Reggie grabs me by the throat and pushes me outside the room, dragging me upstairs into the bedroom.

'I'm sorry,' I plead as he undoes his trousers.

'Turn around,' he says, pushing me up against the mirrored wardrobe door. Grabbing my waist, he lifts my skirt, pulls my knickers to one side, and enters me. 'When I tell you to do something, you do it!' he shouts repeatedly, ramming himself between my legs, hard and fast, until he's done. I feel a raw burning sensation between my legs and a painful cramping in my stomach, and a pain shoots up from inside my uterus whenever I try to move. Congealed, sticky blood moves slowly down my legs. I look down to see a pool of red clots gathering on the floor between my feet.

I am awakened early the following morning by a loud banging on the front door. Reggie, who is still downstairs in the living room, comes rushing up into the bedroom. He goes to the wardrobe and pulls out a case filled with packages of white powder. Frantically, he attempts to hide them under the loose floorboards concealed by the bedroom mat. But before he can, the front door comes crashing in, and suddenly, police are everywhere. 'Put your hands up!' they scream, pointing guns at us. An officer notices my bloodied clothes and bruised face and leads me away, calling an ambulance. Reggie and his friends are arrested. The police found a hoard of cocaine and a gun at the house. Reggie is sentenced to ten years in prison.

16

Like Mother, Like Daughter

UNTIL NOW, I NEVER really believed in God, but Reggie being sent to prison can only be a gift from Him. My prayers have been answered, and I hope I never see him again. Hoping to find some of his money or jewellery, I return to the house one last time, but the police have ceased all his valuables, so the only things left for me to take are the clothes I came with. I leave the shoes and underwear behind; I don't want to bring his worthless memories with me. I wonder how I will pick up the pieces of my life that lay shattered in a thousand pieces. Part of me desperately wants to call Mary. In the months before she left, our bond had grown more than ever; her heart softened almost overnight. But fear and the little pride I have left forbid me. I couldn't bear to hear the words, 'You're just like your mother' again. My life is a mess. Mary has returned to Jamaica, and I have a mother I'm not sure I'd recognise if she walked past me in the street. The only real friend I have is Paul, that's if he wants anything to do with me.

Following the raid, I am taken to the hospital; my body weak, my spirit ready to surrender. 'Just take me now, God,' I pray silently as I lay in the ambulance. At the hospital, they take a sample of my urine and draw blood from my bruised arm before helping me out of my clothes. I imagine pieces of my skin tearing away from my body as the nurse cuts and peels away my blood-soaked clothes and helps me into a blue paper gown. I clench my fists, trying desperately to stop my teeth from clattering.

'Open your legs for me, love,' the nurse says. I wince, sensing the pain I have yet to feel. 'Don't worry, I won't hurt you. Just try to relax,' she reassures me.

There is a machine that looks like a gigantic computer next to the couch. She lifts my gown and presses her hands into my tender stomach. The walls of the room are painted brilliant white. A round ceiling light filled with dead flies illuminates the room. One, two, three, four. I try counting them, wishing I were one of them—dead, warm, and protected from this cruel world.

'What happened to you?' the nurse asks. My mouth remains closed, and I continue to count flies. 'This will feel cold, but it won't hurt,' she tries to reassure me again as she squeezes jelly onto my stomach and spreads it out with a funny-looking wand. 'Were you raped, dear? Who did this to you?' I've lost track of the fly count and have to start again. 'There it is,' she says, 'A nice strong heartbeat.' Heartbeat, what heartbeat? 'Well, the bad news is you've lost one, but the other one is fine.' Other one? What other one? I am seventeen, eight weeks pregnant, and want to die.

Before a social worker arranges for me to be placed in a refuge for battered women, Paul comes to visit me.

'Paul, I need some drugs; you got a smoke?' I'm feeling so low I wish I could bury myself.

'Ash, you're in hospital. Look at you; you need to get off that shit. You're too good for this. Come and live with me; I'll look after you.'

I looked at him cynically. 'I'm pregnant, Paul. What would you want with someone who's carrying another man's child?' His eyes widen as his shoulders drop in defeat. I see his hopes of us being together now Reggie is in prison vanish instantly, and he tells me what I already know but cannot bear to hear. He has always loved me but doesn't think he can love another man's child, that this is not just any child, it's Reggie's. He just can't do it. Sadness and sympathy pour from his eyes. 'I'll always be your friend, Ash, and I will always be here for you.' I hold him tightly and begin to cry, hoping my tears will soak his heart.

Paul visits as often as he can, giving me money and making sure I'm okay, trying to encourage me to get help with my addiction. 'Ashley, you're pregnant. Drinking and smoking ain't good for the baby.' I know he's right, but drink and drugs help mask my reality. They help me avoid facing up to the mess I've made of my life and ease the painful knowledge that I'm a fool. I feel so stupid. What was I thinking, being with Reggie? As if he would ever love someone like me. Why would he? I'm a worthless nobody.

Apart from going to the supermarket for food, alcohol, and cigarettes, I barely leave the refuge, preferring to hang out with the other girls, smoke weed, and drink whatever cheap alcohol we can afford. All the girls who live here are either pregnant or have babies. They quickly become my new family, and I feel at home around them. We all share a common thread; we are victims of abuse or addicted to alcohol, weed, crack or cocaine. As time passes, I see less of Paul; he hates seeing me high, always lecturing me about what damage I could cause to my unborn baby, but I'm getting my social security money now, so I don't really care if I see him or not.

Alice, one girl I am especially close to, takes cocaine. She was introduced to the 'white devil', as she calls it, by her uncle, who abused her. Now pregnant, her mother has abandoned her. This reminds me of Mary and Johnny putting Eve in a home for something that wasn't her fault. I tell her I hope the bastard rots in hell when she tells me he recently hung himself following his prison sentence.

One afternoon, as Alice and I sit in her room smoking, she pulls out a clear plastic bag full of white powder. I've seen it many times when I was with Reggie but have never tried it. I watch as Alice pulls a £10 note from her bag, rolls it up like a pencil, tips some of the powder out onto the tea-stained coffee table, and chops at it with her travel card. She then holds the rolled note up to her nostril and, like a vacuum, sucks the powder off the table up into her nose.

'What does it feel like?' I ask curiously.

'Better than sex, better than alcohol, better than any feeling in the world.' She looks at me, perplexed. 'You've never snorted before, Ash?'

'No, never.'

'Well, there's a first time for everything. Here.' She hands me the note, and I try my best to mimic what I have just witnessed. Holding the note up to my left nostril, I cover my right nostril with my index finger and sniff the powder up slowly and cautiously. Instantly, I feel a tingling sensation run through my body. I feel alive and happy, more alive than I've felt in a long time. Weed makes me feel drowsy and numb, but the white powder gives me back the confidence Reggie had beaten out of me, and I love it. Suddenly, I feel aroused, and for a moment, I consider calling Paul. 'How does it feel?' Alice asks as I hand the note back.

'It feels amazing!' I laugh. 'You're right; it is better than sex.' Alice laughs as she leans in to kiss me. 'What are you doing?' I back away slightly, but I miss that feeling of soft lips on mine, so I don't push her away. We spend the rest of the evening listening to Alice's favourite band, The Rolling Stones, snorting and drinking a box of Tesco's liebfraumilch until we pass out.

The next morning, I am rudely awakened by the Sun burning through my lids, momentarily wondering where I am before memories of the night before flood my brain. As I stand up, I see Alice lying with her head on the coffee table, the rolled-up note still in her hand.

What seems to be white foamy froth is covering the rim of her mouth. She has always been pale, but now her skin appears to be almost blue. I shake my head, hoping to see things clearly, but the room spins faster, and my head pounds. Alice is still; not a single breath leaves her body. I go to touch her but hesitate and lay my ear close to her blue lips. I shake her body, begging her to wake up, but I know she is gone, as the Bible says, no longer of this world. There is another bag of powder on the table. I slip it into my pocket and prise the note out of Alice's stiff hand before alerting the other girls in the house. I tell the police I found her after entering her room this morning. I feel guilty, like it's somehow my fault. Not only has she lost her life, but that of her unborn child.

Alice's death has left me stunned and shaken. A voice in the back of my mind tells me the same fate awaits if I don't change my ways and that I must clean myself up and think of my baby. The problem is, I now have another demon to face: I've had my first taste of the white devil, and I loved it.

A few days later, Alice's cousin comes sniffing around. Men aren't allowed at the refuge, but they always sneak in after-hours once the wardens are off duty. The coke Alice had belonged to him, and he wants it back. Her room has been cordoned off, but he picks the lock. I stand in the corridor as I hear him throw her bed and furniture around the room in search of his stash. He knows Alice and I were close, and I think he suspects me. But as far as he is aware, I don't do coke, and so he believes me when

I tell him I know nothing. There are almost ten grams of coke hidden in my room; I should have given it to him, but I can't risk being implicated in Alice's death in any way. Later that evening, memories of the sensations I felt the night before resurface. That feeling of euphoric happiness plays in my mind, and I want it again. But then I remember Alice's cold, lifeless body slumped on the floor. I dig a hole in my brain and bury the memory deep inside. I will myself to flush the remaining drugs down the toilet, but it's too late; my brain receptors have been awakened. Give me more, give me more, they whisper. They've tasted the white devil and want to taste it again and again and again. The temptation is too great; my demons outnumber my angels, and as soon as night falls, I lock myself in my room, remove the powder from the pocket of a jacket hidden at the bottom of my laundry basket, and finish what I had started the night before. Again, I feel that rush, that euphoric feeling of happiness, joy, and love. I drink wine, snort coke, and dance for hours. My world swirls blissfully as I hug my pillow.

'I love you, Paul,' I drawl, kissing the image of his head I drew in blue ink. As I dance, I feel a wetness between my legs. I look down to see my feet standing in a pool of water. Fear replaces my joy as pain shoots from between my legs, cutting into my stomach. I scream out in agony and slip on the puddle, falling to the floor. I try to shout, but no one comes. 'Help me,' I groan, barely able to speak. Pain grips my stomach as my uterus contracts. Terrified, I try to resist the overwhelming urge to push, but the feeling is too great, and I push and push and push. The girl in the room next to mine eventually hears my screams. Banging on the door, she calls out, but it's locked, and I can't move.

'I've called an ambulance and the wardens,' she shouts.

By the time the ambulance arrives, I have given birth to a baby girl, almost eight weeks premature and weighing just four pounds.

'You must have a guardian angel watching over you; you've lost a lot of blood and are both lucky to be alive,' the paramedic tells me as he cuts the umbilical cord. I say a silent prayer to Alice as I glimpse a look at the most beautiful being I have ever seen. They take us to the same hospital I was born in, and for the first time, I believe Mary's self-fulfilling prophecy: I am just like my mother.

My baby is placed in intensive care, where she stays for almost four weeks. The only thing I can think of while in hospital is where I can get my next fix. When one girl from the refuge comes to visit me, I give her some money and beg her to buy me a drink and some drugs. Initially, she refuses, but I promise to split it with her, so she agrees. The hospital staff notice something isn't right and monitor me, asking where I am going every time I leave the ward. They say my baby is showing what they think might be withdrawal symptoms.

'Just because I'm young, you are judging me!' I shout.

They disagree and tell me they have a legal obligation to report any concerns to social services. Nurse Eileen tries to ease my conscience by telling me she's taken a liking to me and that she doesn't want to report me

147

but has a duty of care. She reassures me I am in an unfortunate position but that I am a beautiful, smart young woman with potential who has just fallen into the wrong company. Her words touch me like Jesus touching a leper. No one had ever called me smart before; they only see my beauty, which doesn't go deeper than the surface of my skin. Eileen is genuinely kind and sits and talks with me for hours, listening as I tell her about my life and how I ended up pregnant and alone. I omit the parts about my taking drugs, although I suspect she knows that anyway, as she seems dubious whenever my friend comes to see me. I lie and tell her we're going for a walk in the hospital gardens. Sensing my anger, she hands me a book on forgiveness.

'I know bad things have happened to you, Ashley, but if you want to truly move on with your life, you will eventually have to forgive those who have hurt you.' I look at her and wonder if she's a bloody preacher or a nurse.

Eileen begs me to accept all the help social services offer if I want to keep my baby, or they may take her into care. That baby girl is the only thing I have left in this world: someone to love and someone to love me back without condition. I thank Eileen and decide at that very moment I will try my best to get clean. 'I can't go back to that refuge. The temptation was too great,' I tell her. She assures me they will help me find alternative accommodation and rehabilitation out of the area. When my friend Janet comes to visit the following day, I refuse to see her. Eileen makes up an excuse, and she leaves.

A lady from social services arrives, and Eileen stays with me during the entire interview, listening as I lay my soul bare.

'Ashley, can you tell me what happened to you?' she asks. I stare at her feet and wonder why she isn't wearing socks. Her second toe is almost twice as long as her big toe; it sticks out like a razor clam that's just popped out from the sand. Marcia has a long second toe, too. Mary used to say having a toe that long means a woman will rule over any man. I sit and wish I had a toe that long. The thick skin on the bottom of her feet is covered with black ridges that cut lines deep into its surface. I imagine slicing two inches of skin away only to reveal more layers of calluses. 'Ashley, I know it's hard. It seems like you've had all the confidence knocked out of you, but you're going to have to talk to me, even if you can't look me in the eye,' she says.

Reggie would never allow me to look at anyone. His eyes would follow mine like an eagle, focusing on whatever I was looking at, even if it was just a woman or a baby. When I unknowingly looked at a man, he would accuse me of flirting with a stranger I didn't even know and would never meet. I am honest with her and plead from the darkest corners of my heart. For my daughter's sake, I desperately want to clean myself up, move away, and make a fresh start. I want to finally prove Mary wrong.

17

Misery to Miracles

DURING MY PREGNANCY, I was so preoccupied with drugs and alcohol that I never stopped to think of the damage I may have been causing to my unborn baby or whether she possessed the same powers I had been cursed with. But now, sitting here, staring into her hazel brown eyes, I do, and I am consumed by a guilt so heavy I want to bury myself under a mound of dirt and stay hidden away forever. How could I have knowingly put my daughter through this? 'I promise you that from this moment on, I will be the best mother I can.' She coos and smiles as if to reassure me we will be okay. I have never known a love like this. She is what my midwife Cathy calls a perfect baby. She eats and sleeps all day and won't wake at night unless I wake her, which I have to do because she is premature, so I feed her as much as I can, trying my best to get her up to the optimum weight. Sometimes, I even have to change her nappy using cold water just to rouse her, or she will continue to sleep for hours. Watching her sleep is one of my favourite things. Her small chest rising and falling reminds me of the breathing machines they have in hospitals. When she smiles in her sleep, I wonder what she is dreaming about, her deep dimples lighting up my heart. She was born with her two bottom teeth almost visible.

'They're called natal teeth. This is rare but not uncommon, so you shouldn't worry,' Cathy tells me.

'I'm sorry for being a bad mummy when you were in my tummy, but I promise from now on, I will be the best mummy; I promise I will.' She smiles at this, and I think she can hear me even in her sleep.

She is three months old now and weighs thirteen pounds. Cathy says this is the ideal weight for a baby her age. She thinks I am doing a good job and should be proud of myself. But the guilt won't leave me. It hangs over my head like a cloud that never stops raining.

'What if she's damaged, and we just don't know it yet?' I ask.

Eileen and Cathy reassure me she's fine and say that even at three months, she is advanced for her age. She lifts her head up and has almost started crawling. Her bright eyes follow even the slightest movement.

'It's as if her senses are heightened,' Cathy says.

I'm sure she knows when we're talking about her. Her coos seem like words. She kicks her legs and waves her arms whenever we say her name. I named her Esther after

Mary's great-grandmother. 'It means wise one,' I whisper into her perfect little ears.

Mary surprises me when I call and tell her I've had a baby. 'You have been blessed with the gift of motherhood. Try to raise her the best you can.' She tells me to try not to make the sins of my parents fall on her. 'You have a chance to change the cycle, Ashley. I know you will be a wonderful mother.' I can't believe what I am hearing. She has never said I'm good at anything, and now she's telling me I will be good at one of the most demanding jobs in the world. 'If you need anything, anything at all, you call me,' she says before I end the call. Something has change in her, and I'm not sure what it is.

Being a parent, I now understand why Mary was so strict. I would never lay a finger on Esther, but I feel an overwhelming need to cocoon and protect her. Sometimes, I think if I could wrap her in cotton wool, I would lock her away from this cruel and dangerous world. How can I ensure she doesn't make the same mistakes I did? I can only do my best and trust she will do hers.

Margret, my social worker, has become like a mother to me and is determined to help me get clean, arranging my benefits, grants, and housing. Eileen is more like a friend now and brings me clothes, toys, and books for Esther. I've been in counselling since Esther was born, and my counsellor visits once a week. Our conversations are confidential, so for the first time, I open up and am honest about everything. She says I am one of the bravest, strongest young women she has ever met, and that my resistance to drugs and alcohol since Esther was born is inspirational. I'm not sure she would say that if she knew what I did last weekend. I was watching TV, and a group of women were standing outside a club, smoking and drinking wine. I missed that feeling and wanted to feel the same way. I was missing Paul and had been thinking a lot about Reggie recently. What if he's let out of prison and tries to find us? How will I protect Esther from him? Do I have the right to stop him from trying to contact her? I needed a drink. It was 6:00 PM and getting dark, so I wrapped Esther in a blanket and walked to the off-license. All I could afford was a bottle of Lambrini. Just one glass, I promised myself. I awoke at ten the next morning, the empty bottle in my hand, my head pounding like a jackhammer. I ran into the bedroom, and there was Esther, lying awake in her cot, smiling. Then she said one word that changed my life forever, 'Mumma.'

When Esther is twenty-four months, we move into a two-bedroom flat on the eleventh floor of a tower block in Woolwich. Margret helps me apply for money to buy things for our new home, and Eileen helps me find second-hand furniture.

'Have you thought about getting a job?' Eileen asks one day during a visit. I've thought about it a lot, but I'm nineteen, have no qualifications, have never worked a day in my life, and fear leaving Esther alone with strangers.

'I'm not good at anything. Who will employ someone

who has never had a job?'

'Don't be so hard on yourself, Ashley. You're a lot smarter than you give yourself credit for.'

The Job Centre offers all sorts of training and will even pay for sixteen hours of nursery fees. I look at Esther walking around and know it will be good for her to play with other children. If I want to provide a better life for her, I'm going to have to do more than rely on state handouts. But I refuse to leave her alone until she can talk properly, so on her third birthday, I decide it's time to enrol her into nursery. I'm sure her vocabulary is twice as wide as mine was when I was her age. Since the day she was born, I read her books, and although money is tight, I buy her a new book every month. I treat every day like we're in school, reading in the mornings and numbers in the afternoon. Every three months, I buy different seeds from the garden centre that we plant and watch them grow on our balcony. Margret thinks this is a great idea as it will teach her how to nurture. I am determined she will be the brightest child in her class and will never be bullied the way I was. Eileen suggests she take an IQ test.

'She is very smart for her age and may even be able to start school early.'

I am proud of this possibility but want her to enjoy her childhood in a way I never did with children her own age, so I decide against it. After her first day at nursery, her teacher asks me what my secret is and jokes about whether I'd like a job at the nursery.

'She is a little genius, and I can't believe she's been

potty trained since she was two years old,' she laughs.'
She even volunteered to read to the class. 'You have a very
special child there,' she tells me.

Being without Esther for the first time in three years
leaves me feeling lost. So, I decide to wash all the windows
and rearrange the furniture, and by midday, I can't keep
still, so I rearrange my wardrobe, colour-coordinating
everything from my jeans to my underwear. As I empty
the contents of an old handbag, a piece of paper falls at
my feet. I unravel it to reveal the letter P scribbled in
black ink. My heart stops momentarily; my gut feels like
someone has punched me in the stomach and left me
gasping for air: Paul, the only man who ever truly loved
me. I have left my past behind and made a fresh start in
my life, but maybe Paul could be a part of my future. I sit
and stare at the paper until my eyes dry out, and I splash
my face with water before checking the paper again
to make sure his name is still there. Mary always says
everything happens for a reason, so why could this not
be the fate I deserve? Holding the paper over a candle, I
ponder on whether to burn the eleven numbers starting
at me or dial them. I do neither, and instead put it back
in my bag and try to forget it. I go into Ester's room
and arrange her books in alphabetical order. I am about
to refold her T-shirts, but I can't. Images of Paul now
occupy the front and centre stage of every thought. I take
the number out of the bag. He loves me; he loves me not;
he loves me; he loves me not. He loves me, I tell myself
as I dial.

'Hello?' For a few seconds, I say nothing. It is him; it

is Paul. 'Hello?'

I inhale deeply before answering. 'Hello, Paul; it's me.' There is silence on the other end. 'Paul, are you there?'

'Ashley, I can't believe it's you. I think about you every day. How are you?'

'I'm fine.'

'What about your baby?'

I tell him about Esther. 'Can we meet up? I'd love to see you and, to be honest, I could do with a friend,' I say.

The tension in his voice is so taut I can almost feel it. He hesitates before continuing. 'Reggie is out of prison.'

I try to speak, but my voice falls silent. My body stiffens in shock at this revelation. I've just got my life back and felt safe knowing Reggie was in prison. Now, with a few words, I feel like I am living in one. Even though I'm on the eleventh floor and you'd have to be Spider-Man to get inside my flat, I urgently check all the doors and windows, making sure they are all locked shut. I know the nursery will allow no one other than myself to collect Esther, but I want to get her and bring her home immediately. 'How? When?' I finally ask.

'Where do you live now? I went to your old refuge, and they told me you'd moved out.'

My mind is racing. Why does he want to know? How can I trust him? What if he tells Reggie he has spoken to me? 'Does Reggie know about the baby?' I finally ask.

'Yes, he heard. Look, let's meet up. I promise I won't tell anyone I've spoken to you.'

I don't give him an answer right away, but I have so

many questions I need answers to, so I call him back three days later and arrange to meet.

I don't have much, but the little I have, I take pride in. Visiting second-hand shops has become my favourite pastime. I've developed a skill of turning the rubbish of strangers into treasures of mine, ensuring my flat is always spotless. I use a portion of my weekly food budget to buy Paul a small bottle of brandy and a chicken that I plan to cook for us. The last time Paul had seen me, I was in a dark place, and I want to show him I've changed, that I have cleaned myself up and am a good mother to Esther. I decide to meet him at my local station. A large part of me knows I can trust him, but I have Ester to protect and can't risk giving him my address. As lonely as I may be, I can't afford to mess things up and risk losing my daughter.

Paul's eyes widen, and his smile, as bright as ever, reveals almost every tooth in his mouth.

'Ashley, you look better than ever,' he says. I smile and continue to walk. 'What's wrong? Why won't you look at me?' he asks. I close my eyes as he takes my chin in his hand. 'He's still getting to you, isn't he?' he says. 'Don't worry, you're free of him now'.

As we walk back to the flat, he fills me in on all the Conleigh gossip. Reggie only served part of his sentence. He grassed on his dealer, someone the police had been after for years. He is now seen as a snitch and has been moved out of London under a police protection programme. Fear that lingered within me since Paul told

157

me about Reggie disappear from my stomach, and my body is suddenly light with relief. I can stop looking over my shoulder and finally let fresh air into my home.

Esther is so excited we have a guest over and is intent on playing police detective. 'How do you know my mummy? Where do you live? Why do you have a funny-coloured tooth in your mouth? What do the letters on your T-shirt mean?' she doesn't stop until bedtime when she volunteers to read Paul a story.

'You've really cleaned yourself up. I'm so proud of you, Ash. You have a lovely home and are clearly a great mother; that's one bright kid you've got there.' He places both hands on either side of my shoulder, sending a surge of electricity through my neck that threatens to fry me until he takes them away. I stare at his lips while he speaks and wonder if they feel as soft as they look, his fingernails still as neat as ever. I smell his skin and try to guess how many coconuts it takes to make his lotion. I am about to pour him another glass of brandy when he wraps his arm around my waist, burying his head into my neck, covering it with what feels like a million tiny kisses, and I finally feel safe.

'I'm sorry for everything, Paul. I've treated you badly, and you've never given up on me. Thank you.'

'I'd better be going, or I'll miss my last train.'

'You can always stay over. I'll get some sheets, and you can sleep on the sofa.' I suggest, and he agrees.

The comforting feel of his fingers stroking my hair almost makes me fall asleep in his lap.

'You're so beautiful,' he whispers, kissing me gently

on the forehead. 'I love you, Ashley,' he whispers again. I don't resist as he kisses me, my body melting to his touch. Reggie was the last man to have kissed me, but it never felt like this. Paul's kisses are filled with love; I feel his energy transfer into my body with every touch. This is what real love feels like, I tell myself, my tears falling softly as Paul kisses them away. 'Everything's going to be all right,' he assures me. 'No one will ever hurt you again.' He repeats these words over and over again until I believe them, and my tears stop falling. He kisses me gently, tenderly caressing my body, before we make love. My body feels alive with energy. This is love, I tell myself, and I feel it more and more with every stroke. 'I love you, Ashley,' he says, and for the first time I responded.

'I love you, too.'

Esther's calls wake us early the following morning. I get her ready for nursery while Paul goes to buy some eggs for breakfast.

'So, do you like Paul?' I ask Esther as I comb her hair.

'I like him a lot, Mummy. Will he stay here all the time?' she asks. I hesitate at this question, but after last night, I am certain of the answer. It may have taken years, but we are finally together.

'Yes,' I say, 'He will stay with us all the time, except when he has to go to work.' I laugh.

Looking at my wardrobe, I realise we'll need to get another. If Paul's tracksuit collection is anything like it used to be, we might even need another two. Hopefully, the one I saw in the second-hand shop is still available.

It's brown, but I will sand it down and paint it white to match mine. I wonder what side of the bed he sleeps on. I hope it's the right, as I can only sleep on the left side. Anyway, once we both get jobs, we can start saving for a house. I'd love to have more children, and this place is definitely not big enough to expand our family. I smile so much my cheeks hurt.

'I'm glad you're happy, Mommy,' Esther says.

'You always make me happy,' I say.

'I know, but I think Paul makes you happy, too.' She's right; I'm glowing as bright as a light bulb and feel a radiating happiness I've never felt before. I am the luckiest girl in the world. How many people get a second chance with someone they should have loved but threw it away?

I make breakfast and play Ella Mai's Boo'd Up on repeat, lost in my thoughts, imagining my new life with Paul, being his wife and him being Esther's father. My daydream is broken when he kisses me tenderly on the nape of my neck.

'I've got to go, Ash.'

'What time will you be back? I'll cook dinner. What would you like to eat? You should bring some clothes with you; you can move in,' I gabble before finally taking a breath.

'Slow down, baby,' he says, reaching for my wrists.

'I'm sorry. I'm just so excited. I can't believe after everything we've been through, we're finally together.'

He looks at me hesitantly, and I immediately sense

something is wrong. His eyes tell me this isn't going to be the happy ending I've been dreaming of. 'Ashley, you know I love you …'

'Please, please, please don't say it,' I whisper. I can feel a big *but* coming. A feeling of dread fills my stomach, so I sit down to quell the dizziness whirling through my mind.

'You know I love you more than anything, but we can't be together like that.'

'What do you mean, *like that*?' I feel my blood boil and want to smash every plate on the counter.

'We haven't seen each other for years, Ash, and things have moved on. You've got a daughter, and I've got one on the way. You remember Angela? Well, she's pregnant with my baby.'

'Angela, the whore who sleeps with anyone?' I look up at him in disbelief. 'You slept with her? And what's worse, you got her pregnant. Is it even yours?' I say bitterly and instantly regret it. 'Why didn't you tell me this before you made love to me and told me you loved me?'

'I do love you, but I can't help the situation. She's pregnant with my baby, and I have to be there for her.'

Tears threaten to flow from my eyes like a dam on the verge of bursting. Why me? Why am I always being used and let down by the people I love? I refuse to let him see me cry again. 'Well, you better leave then,' I say, handing him his jacket and walking him towards the front door. He has the audacity to try and hug me before he leaves, but I shove him away, pushing him into the doorframe.

'I still want us to be friends, to make sure you and Esther are okay.'

'Are you serious? We were doing fine until you came along. What was last night all about? I cried with you, told you I loved you. You made love to me for the first time, and now tell me you don't want me. Is this how your sick mind works? Finally get what you want and then throw it away.'

'I promise, I never meant to hurt you,' he says.

'Are you trying to make me pay for being with Reggie and not you all those years? Well, you've succeeded; the tables have turned. Now that I love you, you get to walk out on me. Now I know how you felt all those years,' I yell, slamming the door behind him. Numb, I fall to the floor, cradling myself tightly as I bawl quietly inside myself. Esther's call broke my tears. 'Pull yourself together, Ashley; you have a daughter to care for, and she's all that matters.' I tell myself. I hold Esther and sob silently as she wraps her soothing arms around my neck. 'It's just me and you now, kid, just me and you.'

18

Faith of a Mustard Seed

After Paul leaves, I feel like an elephant mother protecting her young, and I am now more determined than ever to make a better life for Esther. Mary's adage, *failing to plan, is planning to fail*, rings as loudly in my head as church bells while I sit at the kitchen table scribbling out the next chapter of my life onto a previously untouched notepad. Esther will attend nursery full-time, and I will get a job. But what kind of job? It will have to be one that pays enough to cover the extra nursery fees and all my bills.

I spend countless afternoons at the local Job Centre, trailing through job posts. The only positions that don't require experience are cleaning jobs. I don't mind cleaning at home, but it isn't a job I want to do. Anyway, I will never be able to make ends meet on such a low wage. Something inside me is telling me I am destined to be more than a cleaner. I want my daughter to be proud of me.

I make an appointment to see a careers advisor, who shoots me a disapproving look as I walk into her office with Esther in her pushchair. She sits at her desk, looking down on me like God on a throne, surrounded by mounds of paper, a cup of coffee, and a half-eaten doughnut barely concealed in a white greasy bag. Her blotchy skin flakes as she scratches the bridge of her nose, pushing her glasses further up her face to get a proper look at me.

'Do you have a CV?' she asks.

'A CV? No, I don't.' I know what a CV is; I remember my old form tutor, Mrs Kennedy, telling us we would need one once we left school, but I have never actually seen one, and the way Miss Blotchy is making me feel, I am too embarrassed to say. She must be able to read my mind.

'Here's an example of what a *good* CV looks like,' she says. She pulls a piece of paper from underneath the rubble and hands it to me. 'It lists all your qualifications and achievements. Go away and write your own. Once completed, I will check it with you and iron out any mistakes. You can use our computers over there,' she says, pointing to the bank of computers at the back of the room. 'We'll use your CV to approach employers, and if they're interested, they will call you in for an interview.' She pauses. 'Don't worry,' she says, as if the look of anxiety on my face has given rise to hers. 'We'll teach you interview techniques and help you with money to buy clothes for work. My job is to help prepare you as much as I can. We also offer a wide variety of training courses, so if you need to brush up on your key skills, we have plenty of resources to help you.'

Now I think her skin isn't that bad and thank her as I stand to leave. It seems Mary is right; God really does come in all guises.

After putting Esther to bed later that evening, I read through the CV requirements and the realization that I have no qualifications finally dawns on me. This is another part of my life I kept buried yet inevitably rears its ugly head once I bring it to the surface. I decide to bend the truth; after all, they didn't ask for proof of my qualifications, only that I write them down. I write, scribble, cross out, and tear until my CV is complete, my notepad almost empty, and finally, after two days, I had achieved an A in Drama, a B in Maths, a C in English and history, and a D in Science—clearly my weakest subject. The job centre lady seems impressed by my efforts, especially my B in Maths.

'Who will care for your child while you work?' she asks. 'Most jobs are nine to five. To keep a child in nursery for that many hours isn't cheap. Do you have anyone who can look after your daughter while you're at work, even for three hours a day?' I think about this for a second; I have no one. But I do have Mary, and although she's in Jamaica, she will do anything for me. When we last spoke, she said she couldn't wait to visit her great-granddaughter.

The job centre helps prepare me for interviews and the world of work. I visit almost every day, leaving Esther in the on-site crèche. I am really enjoying learning; all those extra classes and books I read at home are finally being put to good use. It's also nice to have a break from caring for Esther, if only for a few hours. Being around adult company and people who are also trying to turn their lives around gives me a much-needed confidence boost. I attend several interviews before eventually getting a job as a receptionist at a recruitment agency, where I am paid just over minimum wage. I drop Esther off at nursery at 8:00 AM and start work at 9:00 AM, finishing not a second after 5:00 PM, allowing me enough time to collect her at 6:00 PM.

The job of answering and directing calls is easy and requires little skill. Despite coming from a tough inner-city estate, my English has always been good, and I quickly learn from the other women in the office. I enjoy my job, but it's impossible to make ends meet. Esther's nursery fees are high, and I am falling behind on my rent. With all the will in the world, working is proving impossible. I seem to be better off out of work. I have to quit; after all, what good is a job if the postman has no letterbox to post my P45 into? I feel like a failure, but a roof over our head is the only stability I can offer Esther, and I can't risk losing our home.

A few months later, Mary calls to say she is coming to England.

'Come and stay with me. You can sleep in Esther's room, and it will be a great opportunity for you to get to know her.'

Mary has glaucoma in one of her eyes. 'I have to get it seen to. If I go blind, I won't be able to drive, and without my independence, I can't live in this country.' As a pensioner and British citizen, she is still entitled to free healthcare here. In Jamaica, the same operation would cost over £1,000. 'It's not just about the money. I miss England. If I could, I would move back in an instant.'

Johnny is happy on his farm raising chickens, goats, and cows and says he would rather die before he steps foot back in England. I feel sorry for Mary; she has given up what she loves for a man who seems to love his farm animals more than he loves her. I hope he's worth it, but I don't think any man is worth that much.

Esther goes to church with Mary, and she loves it. 'You should have seen her singing away at the songs like she's heard them before,' Mary said. Esther asks if we can go every week, but I ignore her question and tell her to go and take off her good dress. Having Mary around feels like a load has been lifted off my shoulders. She carries Esther around with her like a little handbag, taking her to every market in London, parks, and even museums.

'When did you start going to museums?' I joke.

'We all change, Ashley. Time will do that to you,' she says.

I quietly observe the way she is with Esther. It's as though an alien has invaded her body; she acts like a completely different person. If Esther spills milk or refuses to finish her dinner, she strokes her head gently and tells her it's okay, that she is perfect and knows when she's had enough, or, 'It's okay; accidents happen.'—I almost choke on my tea when she says this. Accidents never happened when I was a child. Since Mary arrived, Esther sleeps with her every night, and I awake most mornings to find her delicate arms wrapped around Mary's neck.

Mary's operation goes well, and she is preparing to return to Jamaica. She has a large barrel delivered, which she fills with everything from toothpaste to toilet roll.

'Don't they have these things in Jamaica?' I ask sarcastically.

'Not like this,' she says as she pushes an enormous pack of one thousand Tetley tea bags into the barrel.

'I want to go to Jamaica with Grandma, Mummy,' Esther says as we secure the lids of a ten-pack of fairy liquid with masking tape.

I want to ignore her, but Mary is sitting right in front of me, and judging by the probing look on her face, she will not stop until she gets an answer. Mary looks at me, waiting, her eyes willing me to say yes. 'I think it's a great idea,' she finally says.

'Please, Mummy, please. I can go to Auntie Marcia's nursery school, play on the beach, and learn to swim.' She gives Mary a cheeky smile, and I wonder if they've been hatching this idea during their journeys to church.

'If she only came for six months, it would give you a chance to sort yourself out and get a job.' I avoid looking at Esther's puppy dog eyes and tell them I'll think about it. 'We'll need to arrange her passport, so don't think too long.' Mary says.

I lay awake for half the night, my mind unable to quiet itself as I draw up a list of the pros and cons of sending Esther away. The pros outweighed the cons by half a page. I could work, save, study, and visit Esther as often as possible.

Mary has been here for ten weeks, and Esther hasn't crawled into my bed once since she arrived. I miss her already, and she hasn't even gone anywhere yet. I know the experience would be great for her: playing on the farm, visiting beaches, and experiencing a different culture, but that's not my worry. What if something happens to her? I would never forgive myself. I think Mary can read my mind because, the next evening, she answers every question that has been whirling around in my head. 'You know I would rather die than let anything happen to Esther, don't you?' You would die because I would kill you, I think. 'I would never lay so much as a finger on her, Ashley; I promise you. Marcia, Johnny, and I will take good care of her.'

She doesn't have to convince me of this. Over the last few months, I have watched her with Esther and know she would never hurt her. I decide to put my feelings aside and do what I think is best for my daughter. 'Okay, only for six months, then I'm coming to get her.'

The next day, we take Esther's passport photos, complete the application, and book an emergency appointment at the passport office. It arrives almost two weeks later, and I wonder if I have made the right decision. I already feel like a piece of me has been cut away, and we haven't even left the house yet. Esther awakes at the crack of dawn, dresses herself in the clothes I laid out the night before and is waiting patiently on the sofa with her coat and backpack on before I even make coffee.

'I don't want to miss the plane, Mummy,' she says as I tell her to take off her coat and come and eat breakfast. She complains she can hardly breathe as I smother her face with kisses during the drive to the airport while she holds my sweating palm, rubbing it with her tiny fingers. At the departure gate, she takes a folded piece of paper from her pocket and hands it to me. 'Don't open it until you get home,' she instructs.

My heart feels weary, and I want to change my mind. 'I'm sorry—change of plans. You can't take her; you cannot take the only thing that has kept me sane all these years,' I want to say, but the excitement on Esther's face won't let me.

'This is my first ever time on an aeroplane,' she says to the lady at the desk. The tears I have been holding back since Esther's passport arrived are done hiding. They run out from behind my lids and stream down my face like a burst water pipe. Mary hands me a tissue, followed by the entire packet. I press hard into my eye sockets, willing the tears to stop. It is only when I look at Esther that they quell. Her hazel eyes are now filled with concern. She is now afraid to leave me. I take a deep breath, swallow the remaining tears, and kneel to meet her.

'You are going to fly high in the sky and have the most amazing adventure ever.' I hand her a red notepad. 'Mary and Marcia will help you write in here every day. Tell me what you are doing, seeing, learning, and eating. Write it all down, and they will post it to me, okay? And I will call you all the time.'

'Okay, Mummy. Missing you already,' she says, wrapping her arms tightly around my neck. I inhale her baby-soft skin one last time before it's time for them to go.

'Bye, sweetheart, I love you,' I say before they walk through the departure gate.

I wait until they are almost out of sight, and then she turns around and blows me a kiss that I catch and put into my pocket. I open the paper; the words '*Love you, Mummy*,' are written in red ink. I cry until I smudge the paper, and the tiny hearts merge into one. Even when I left and went to live with Reggie, Mary never gave up on me. It's time I stop giving up on myself.

19

Where There's a Will

WITH ESTHER GONE, I can think of nothing but why I sent her away and how to get her back as quickly as possible. Like Mary, I have become a planner. If she has a goal, she writes a plan, listing every step needed to get to where she needs to be. What I want is to provide for my daughter and earn enough money to give her the best start in life. But the reality is I've only ever had one job answering phones, and that didn't last long. So, it's back to the career office for me.

As I approach the high street, I notice a shop front, its window full of posters advertising jobs. *Temps needed, £15 per hour, start today,* one ad reads. The latter part is what catches my eye: *no experience necessary.* The sign above the door reads *Deliverance Recruitment.* God really is everywhere, I think as I ring the intercom. A woman answers and buzzes me in. The door leads into a small room with four tatty-looking desks in each corner, all of them occupied by women. At the larger desk in the right-hand corner of the room sits an older-looking lady with an ashtray almost overflowing with brown cigarette butts in front of her. 'How can I help you, dear?' she asks, blowing smoke between her wrinkled lips.

'I saw the signs in the window and wondered if you have any jobs available?' I ask, handing her my CV. I imagine the smell of cigarette smoke settling into my hair and wonder how long it took before the once-white walls became as yellow as her teeth. Her eyes scan the page.

'Are you available to start immediately?'

'This very minute,' I reply.

She then passes me over to Julie, who leads me down threadbare steps and into the basement to complete my registration. 'We'll be in touch if anything comes up; just make sure you're available and ready to go.'

I thank them all, probably one too many times, and leave.

Later that evening, I receive a call from Julie. 'We've found a temporary position we think will be perfect for you.' It's only for two weeks but pays £15.00 an hour, which is a lot of money for me. The company is based in Central London. 'Quite high-end, so you must look very presentable,' she says. I'm ecstatic they've found me something so quickly and play Destiny's Child - *I'm a Survivor* while dancing in the mirror as sweat beads burst from my forehead. Although it's only a temporary job, the more experience I gain, the more I'll have to add to my CV, which I made look longer by increasing the font size. I decide to wear my black suit with a white shirt, paired with black heels.

The closest I've ever been to Central London was on a visit with the church to St Paul's Cathedral. I have no idea where I'm going and don't want to be late, so I leave home extra early the next morning. The company, Kramer Brothers, is based around the corner from Berkeley Square in Mayfair. I arrive forty minutes early and sit in a café opposite the building. The longer I sit watching people in their smart clothes and expensive suits, the more nervous I become. I decide to turn back. This is a different world, a world someone like me doesn't belong in. I have only ever heard of Mayfair on the Monopoly board, and now I am here, it doesn't feel right. I pay for my coffee and am about to head back to the station when Julie rings.

'I'm just checking to make sure you've arrived okay,' she says.

'Yes,' I reply, knowing it's too late to turn back now.

The building is twenty-four floors high, and the Kramer Brothers occupy the entire twenty-third floor. A security guard signs me in and directs me to the lifts on the opposite side of the turnstile. The building is cladded with large glass panels; huge green plants and shiny black leather sofas fill the entrance gallery. The sound of shoes clanking on the white marble floor sounds like one big tap dance. There are four lifts, each made entirely of glass, that take what seems like seconds to reach the top floor. I inhale nervously as I approach the reception desk and ask to speak to Paulina as Julie instructed. The receptionist, Melanie, tells me to take a seat on the sofas by the coffee table upon which sits a white orchid. The large TV on the wall is showing subtitles of Sky News channel. A tall, slim lady approaches me. Her warm smile helps me to relax a little.

'Hi, I'm Paulina,' she offers her hand.

I extend mine and shake hers firmly, hoping my palms are not as sweaty as my armpits. This morning, whilst in the coffee shop, I read that a firm handshake is a sign of a strong character. Paulina leads me along the hallway to another open area. There are two desks in the middle of a space surrounded by four offices.

'You'll sit here, opposite me,' she says, explaining that together with her colleague Joan, who is currently on holiday, they look after the four men who occupy the offices. 'First, I'll start you off answering the phones, then I'll give you more work to do, depending on how you get on.' Paulina shows me how to use the phone system and answer calls.

The first couple of days are pretty quiet as the owners are away at a property event in the South of France. This is perfect as it gives me the opportunity to gain confidence without being too stressed. Kramer Brothers is a real estate company involved in everything from shopping centres to multimillion-pound residential developments. There are large black-and-white aerial photos on the walls of completed and ongoing developments. An architectural model of their latest project, a development in Canary

Wharf comprising apartments, offices, and retail units totalling one hundred acres, is displayed in the entrance hall outside the lifts.

I take to the role well, and Paulina's comment that she is impressed by my telephone manner gives me a much-needed confidence boost. My third day is a lot more stressful; the brothers are back in the office, and the phones ring so much, my ears continue to ring hours after leaving the office. Paulina explains that Jacob, Mike, Luke, and Daniel are brothers who now run the company their father founded sixty years ago. 'They usually arrive in the office by 8:00 AM but leave early on Fridays to have Shabbat dinner with their parents.'

The brothers are standing around the desks talking to Paulina when I arrive in the office the next day. Following my conversation with Paulina and feeling eager to impress, I attempt to get in early by 8:30 AM. Daniel, the youngest of the brothers, looks up and smiles as I walk in. If they ever wanted to deny they were brothers, it would be impossible. The identical nose that dominates their faces looks as though it had been made from the same surgeon's mould. Medium waves of dense black hair cover Daniel's head, his face bronzed by the southern sun. He is shorter than his brothers but by far the most handsome. As I approach, I notice something strange about the skin on his face. It isn't smooth like his brothers; by contrast, it's raised and bumpy, like the surface of grated cheese.

'Hi, I'm Daniel, and this is Mike, Jacob, and Luke,' he says, smiling, immediately putting me at ease.

I shake each of their hands, willing my clammy palms to keep their cool.

'We hear you've been a real help to Paulina whilst Joan's been away,' Jacob says. I smile politely and head towards my desk.

During lunch, Paulina fills me in on the brothers. They are all married except for Daniel, the youngest. 'He's a bit of a playboy and the apple of his father's eye,' she says.

I can't help but ask, 'What happened to his face?'

'Helicopter crash. He was flying alone when he attempted to carry out some sort of aerobatic manoeuvre and crashed.' The accident left him with many scars, most of which are kept hidden beneath his clothes, but the scars on his face are visible for all to see. The glass from the helicopter windscreen shattered and cut into his flesh as he crash-landed in a deserted field. Miraculously, he managed to crawl to a farmhouse and whisper Jacobs's number to the farmer before passing out. 'He's lucky to be alive,' Paulina finished. When I first shook Daniel's hand, I felt a strange chemistry pass through me, and now, listening to his story, I feel it inside me like a highly charged lightning bolt. How brave, I think, as I listen to Paulina.

At the end of my two weeks at the firm, Paulina thanks me and promises she'll be in touch should they ever need help again. It was nice while it lasted, I think, as I trail the jobs section of my paper. Good things only seem to last a minute in my life.

I visit the job centre every day for weeks and call Julie so much she starts avoiding my calls. Part of me is ready to give up, but the thought of Esther won't let me. I am lying in bed, willing myself to get up and at least brush my teeth, when I receive a call from Julie. 'Paulina would like you to come in and see her. She has a job proposition for you.' I can't believe what I am hearing. A job proposition—for me! I go to see Paulina the following day.

'The business has significantly increased its portfolio recently, and the workload has increased.'

She needs an assistant to answer phones and fulfil admin tasks, and she offers me the job of administration assistant, working directly under herself and Joan. I try to contain my excitement but act like a child who has just been given her first packet of gummy bears, and I accept her offer before she even tells me of my £27,000 yearly salary. It is more money than I dared dream of; me, a girl from Conleigh, am finally on my way to building a better life for my daughter. I go home and call Mary, screaming my news to her down the phone. I can now begin saving and have Esther back sooner than I ever thought possible.

'I'm proud of you, Mummy,' Esther tells me.

So far, she has fed the goats, collected eggs from the chickens, and this weekend, she plans to build a big sandcastle on the beach. The happiness in her voice reaffirms I made the right decision.

The Job Centre gives me a work grant of £150 to help buy clothes and anything else I need for my new job. I've paid close attention to what other women wear during my commutes to work and have already decided what my work style will be. I like the classic, timeless look and decide to go to Oxford Street to see what my grant can buy, staying far away from any markets. I spend the morning going in and out of shops, calculating items as I fill my basket, trying on clothes I know I can't afford, comparing the fit and feel of the fabrics against my skin, the cut of the bias of the dresses. There is an undeniable difference between the quality of the clothes I try on in the cheaper stores compared to those on Bond Street. I have lunch outside a café at the back of Oxford Street, weighing up exactly what I will buy after lunch. As I sit eating, I hear someone calling my name from across the street.

'Ashley, Ash!' The voice sounds familiar. I can hardly believe my eyes when I look up to see Jamie running across the road. 'Girl, what are you doing up here?' he asks, ordering a cappuccino. It's been years since I last saw him, but he still acts like the Queen of England, sipping his coffee with his diamond-incrusted pinkie finger pointing up to the heavens. I look at his perfectly manicured nails and hide mine under the table, making a mental note to buy some nail varnish before going home. 'Girl, I heard you were in a bad way, and as for Reggie, don't even get me started on his black ass.'

179

'I'm just glad it's all over now,' I say. I spent the next half hour telling him about Esther and my new job.

'Bitch, you got a three-year-old, and you still got the body of a goddess. I'm gonna hook you up.' I smile and tell him of my plan to get Esther back. 'Ash, you're a beautiful soul, and now you're free of that hood rat; I hope you see that. Honey, you're going places; don't let past mistakes hold you back.'

I reassure him that the past is firmly behind me, that I have cleaned up, and I'm ready and excited about this next new chapter of my life. Jamie is on one of his usual *buy-but-don't-pay* shopping sprees and insists on getting me a whole new wardrobe for work. A part of me wants to resist his offer. I've left my old life behind and have no intentions of going back. I can hear Mary's voice in my head, *honesty is the best policy*, but I really need a new wardrobe, and why have Top Shop when I can have Chanel? I agree to give him £150 if he gets the clothes I want, and we arrange to meet back at the café in four hours. In the meantime, I go shoe shopping and buy the highest pair of heels I can walk comfortably in without running the risk of breaking my neck.

I sit agitatedly in the cafe, waiting for Jamie as anxiety grows slowly within me. It's been almost four and a half hours, and he still hasn't returned. The shops will close soon, and it will be too late for me to buy anything. I'm an idiot; I should have given him the money after he returned with the clothes. The waitress peers into my empty cup and asks if I'd like another coffee. I have, after all, been nursing this one for the last two hours. I don't want one, but I am about to say yes out of sheer embarrassment when Jamie walks in carrying two large bulging bags.

'Girl, let's get out of here,' he says. We jump on a train and head home. I can't believe my eyes when I see all the clothes he's stolen for me. I'll be able to wear a different outfit every day for a month! He's even got me jewellery, tights, and two handbags.

'Jamie, my bosses are going to wonder how I can afford such expensive clothes.' I laugh with excitement and spend the next hour giving him a fashion show.

'Girl, if I wasn't gay, I'd ask you out,' he laughs.

He has stolen me over £3,000 worth of clothes. I feel guilty only giving him £150, but it's all I have. He says he feels guilty about taking any money from me.

'See it as a thank you for all the times you defended me when people teased and bullied me.'

'You're gonna have the men in your office weak, Ash,' he teases as I model a red pencil dress. 'It shows off your curves perfectly.'

I smile confidently, but inside, my nerves run as wild as an ant's nest. 'Lord, help me do a good job. Please let this opportunity last longer than the rest,' I pray.

20

Her Majesty's Pleasure

THE WEEK BEFORE I start work, the postman greets me as I arrive home from a food shop, handing me a handwritten envelope covered in love heart stickers. Who on earth could it be from, I think, as I eagerly rip at its edges. No one except Paul knows where I live, and it clearly isn't an official letter with stickers all over it. Then I see an address stamped on the back of the letter: HMP Brinsdown. What does HMP stand for? I sit on the sofa and unfold the letter. It is two small pages long, but I turn to the last page before I read it. It's from Paul.

Dear Ashley,

I hope this letter finds you and Esther well. I'm okay but have been better.

As you've probably gathered by now, I'm in jail. They have sentenced me to six years for some stupid drug shit. You know I'm a good guy, really, but sometimes poverty and greed get the better of us, and we do things we later regret.

You were right about Angela; her baby wasn't mine. I guess she just saw me as an easy target—knew I was the kind of guy who would stick around and take care of her. But when the baby was born two months early and was mixed race, well, you know the rest.

I'm so sorry, Ash; I let you down. I want you to know I still love you, and whatever happens, no one will ever take your place in my heart.

I would love to see you but understand if you never want to see me again, especially after the way things ended between us. I've enclosed a visiting order so you can come and see me if you want to or at least write to me.

I'm stuck in my cell for almost twenty-three hours a day, so things can get pretty depressing in here. I share my cell with this guy, Andrew. He's been convicted of murder, but he's actually a cool guy. I'd love you to send me some pictures of you. It would give me something to smile about.

I miss you, Ashley, and I am gutted about the way things turned out between us. When I finally had everything I wanted, I threw it all away.

I understand if you're upset and never want to see me again, but just remember that I'll always care for you.

Love Paul

'The fucking cheek! Now you're stuck in jail, you want to see me. You fooled me, broke my heart, then left me, and now you want me to come and visit you in prison?' I scream aloud while tears melt into my sheets as I read and reread the letter. Anger pounds my heart, but pity softens it as I read his words about poverty and greed getting the better of us; they had a hold of me, too, and as much as I try to forget my past, I've done things I'm not proud of. The love I felt for him the day he left resurfaces like a ball that won't sink. It's not his fault Angela fooled him into thinking she was pregnant with his baby. He did what any decent man should: stick by their child. I stare at the words written by the only man who ever loved me and know I can't let him rot in jail or let bitter emotions consume me. When I needed him, he was there, and now he needs me, so I will do the same. If I can forgive Reggie and let go of all the hurt and pain he caused me, I can forgive Paul. I remember something Eileen said to me once during one of our many chats in hospital. 'The heart has no room for bitterness. Whatever is in the heart will rapidly spread around the body, for it is the heart that gives the lifeblood to every organ that surrounds it. If the blood pumping from the heart is bitter, it is poisonous, and if it is poisonous, it will kill everything surrounding it.'

The prison is over 200 miles away. I use some of the money Mary gave me and take the train from King's Cross to Brinsdown and then a taxi from the station to the prison. I am informed that visits last two hours and told to bring money so I can buy things for Paul from the prison shop. The prison is another eight miles from the station in the middle of nowhere, surrounded by green fields. I wipe the steamy window of the taxi as I stare out at the grey, misty landscape. The prison, its high walls reinforced with heavy rusting barbed wire, comprises a series of buildings. There are no windows on the perimeter walls, just a set of large brown wooden double doors, enforced with iron strips and old heavy locks. As the taxi pulls up outside the prison gates, I notice a queue already forming. It's a chilly morning, and a frost has settled on the vast fields that surround the building. The air is clean and crisp, and I shiver as I stand in line. White clouds leave my warm mouth as I exhale. Some visitors are wrapped up in long coats, large scarves, and puffer jackets. Many are drinking what I guess is tea or coffee. They have obviously been here before and are well prepared. Looking at the high walls makes me think about Reggie and how desperate he must have been to escape prison. I think of the day he made me hold the gun and wonder what would have happened if they had caught me. I could be sitting on the inside of these walls, hoping for a visit from Paul.

Footsteps and clanging keys sound from behind the doors as an officer approaches. He is a thin, tall man wearing a black jacket, dark grey trousers, and chunky black boots. He calls out a series of names. I'm not sure if he is calling the names of the prisoners or the visitors until he calls 'James'. That's Paul's surname, so I move out of the line. As I step forward, shivering in a few thin layers, the guard eyes the length of my body with a slight expression of perplexity. The sun was shining when I left London and seemed warm enough for me to wear a blazer over my tight black and red cotton dress that falls just below my knees, matched with a pair of black ankle boots. He escorts us through the gates, behind which lies a series of brown brick buildings. One has windows as small as the bricks themselves; lights glow dimly through the glass. I stare up at the tiny windows, wondering what lies behind the walls. Paul later tells me that the inmates in this block are so dangerous that the lights have to be kept on twenty-four hours a day. There are a few caged basketball areas, all topped with barbed wire. The entire place reminded me of a zoo.

We approach another door. This time, a female officer with yet another set of keys opens it and ushers us into a room which houses a metal detector and an airport-style conveyor belt. The guard calls each visitor individually. I watch as she frisks each visitor thoroughly from head to toe. A series of instructions follow: 'Open your mouth, spread your legs, hold your arms out, spit out any gum.' Some are sent back to the first room for having too much money with them or carrying liquids. 'The rules are clearly written on the posters,' the guard says, pointing to the wall. 'You should have left this in the locker,' she keeps repeating. We are told to take our shoes off and place them on the conveyor belt, together with our bags and overcoats, which are then checked and scanned. I find the experience degrading and invasive. We've done nothing wrong, so why are they treating us like criminals?

'I'm just doing my job, love. You'd be surprised at some of the things people try to smuggle in here,' a guard says, clearly sensing my frustration. I offer a fake smile and collect my belongings from the other end of the belt.

Yet another queue. I am ready to turn back when we are made to line up again. This time, they usher us in groups of ten into a small space with thick electric glass doors. The guard opens it slowly before ushering us inside. The door then closes fully behind us before the exit door opens into a seating area. I scan the area. Not even Houdini could have escaped this place, I'm sure. Finally, a guard starts calling names again. This time, the door he opens leads to the visitors' hall, where the inmates are waiting. When he calls Paul's name, my stomach fills with nervous anticipation. I approach apprehensively. 'Number 23,' he says, pointing to a table at the far left-hand corner of the room.

It is a large, warm room filled with sets of small low tables and chairs. Each table has an inmate sitting behind it, waiting for his visitor to arrive. They all wear a red sash over their chests, making them easily identifiable amongst any male visitors. Guards sit in a raised pulpit in each corner of the room, while others stand near the inmates, close enough to see what they are doing but far away enough to give them a false sense of privacy. There is a shop at the back of the room that sells food and drinks and also a large gated play area for children. Some inmates stare at me as I make my way towards the back of the room. Some even stop their conversations midway as I walk past, their heads turning to follow me. I sprayed so much perfume before leaving my handbag in the prison locker I almost choked on it and am now followed by the invisible scent of jasmine flowers.

Paul jumps to his feet as our eyes meet, opening his arms as I advance towards him. Prison seems to have aged him. No longer smooth, his once-shiny skin is now dry, almost ashy grey. His beard is so overgrown it almost hides his lips that now appear cracked and withered. Obviously, there are no manicures offered here as his once-perfect fingernails are now longer than mine and filled with what looks like rims of black dirt. I fall into his grasp and cry as he cradles me to his chest.

'Don't cry, baby; I'm fine,' he reassures me.

'Have you been working out?' I ask jokingly. His chest is large and firm, and I feel safe in his arms.

'I've been trying to keep fit. There's not much else to do in here,' he laughs, showing off his biceps. We sit down, and he draws my chair close to his. I am about to throw my arms around him again when a guard appears.

'Less touchy-feely, please,' he says.

Paul thanks me for coming to see him and explains how he ended up in what he calls *Her Majesty's Hotel for Men*. 'I could be out in three to five years with good behaviour. I know it's a long time, and I don't expect you to keep coming to see me, but try not to forget about me, Ash. At least write to me.'

'I can do that,' I promise. I loathe being searched and hate the entire experience of visiting, but it is worth it to see the smile on Paul's face, so I promise to write to him every week and visit as often as I can.

On the train home, I rummage through my pockets for loose change. My teeth haven't stopped chattering since I left the prison, and I can no longer feel my feet. I hope I have enough change for an overly-priced £2.00 cup of coffee from the train's drink station. I pull the recent letter Esther sent out of my pocket.

'Mummy, I love you so much. See you soon when you come to get me.'

I read it over and over and decide I'm never going to visit Paul in prison again.

21

Pretty Girl Privilege

As PER JAMIE'S STRICT instructions, I prepare my outfits for the week ahead. 'Girl, you need to channel your inner Karl Lagerfeld on Monday with that cute ass.' So, a black pencil skirt, white ruffled shirt, and black heels it is. I cook enough chicken to last me until Wednesday and buy some fruit and a few snacks, too. Wasting money in expensive sandwich bars isn't a luxury I can afford. The office has a kitchen area where people sit and eat; there's also a subsidised restaurant on the ground floor of the building. The Job Centre has paid for my first months travel, so that is one less thing to worry about until I get paid at the end of the month.

Darkness and the rattle of a garbage truck greet me as I awake early, ready for my first day. My official working hours are from 9:00 AM to 5:00 PM, but I aim to be in the office by 8.30 AM every morning. This job is a God-given opportunity, and I am determined to work hard and make the most of it. I accessorise my outfit with silver cufflinks and a white pearl necklace, douse myself in perfume, and slip on a pair of leather gloves, draping a pink shawl over my shoulders. 'A pair of shades is a must,' Jamie says, and I agree; I hate eye contact with strangers.

Before I leave, I say a prayer, 'Lord, thank you for this opportunity. Give me strength and guidance to do a good job, today and always.' My faith has never been strong, even after all those years of going to church with Mary, but the past few months seem to have instilled a faith in me I never knew I had until I needed it.

My journey to work is less than forty minutes, door to door. The glares I receive from some passengers make me feel uncomfortable. Can they see beyond my facade of nice clothes and jewellery and tell I'm an imposter from the local estate? There is a single vacant seat, which a man kindly offers to me. I smile nervously, unsure whether to accept it or offer it up to someone else. He insists, so I sit and bury my head so deeply into the newspaper my neck hurts. The eyes of people staring make me uneasy. Before Reggie, the gaze of strangers never bothered me, but after him, I avoid eye contact, even with animals. I try to distract myself from the stares, holding my head low, counting the cracks in the pavement, and lowering my gaze as I approach security to collect my new pass. One guard, Dembe, takes the picture for my pass.

'I hope you don't mind me saying so, but you are the most stunningly beautiful woman to have ever entered this building,' he says, clicking the camera.

'Excuse me?' I say, surprised by his comment. Dembe is from Uganda and has the darkest, smoothest skin I have ever seen on a man. I immediately want to touch it to see if it feels as smooth as it looks. His tall, lean frame makes me think he spends every spare minute in the gym. His teeth gleam like sun-kissed ski slopes and shine every time he smiles, which is often. He never fails to greet visitors with his huge, friendly smile.

'I hope you don't think I'm being out of place or anything. I'm just saying, I take a lot of pass photos, and of all the employees in the building, you are by far the most beautiful. In fact, I think you're the most striking woman I've ever met.' I feel my face heating up and hope that only I can feel its heat. 'And I love your style. You look sharp, like you mean business.'

A faint 'thank you' is all I can muster as he places the pass in my hand.

'What are you doing for lunch? I would be happy to show you around the area if you like?'

'Maybe next time,' I say.

'Okay, no problem. Have a great day.'

I am greeted by Melanie, the receptionist, who almost doesn't recognise me. 'You look amazing, Ashley, all ready for your first day?' Melanie always makes me feel welcome. We went to lunch a few times when I was temping and have since become friends. I sit at my desk and begin arranging the stationery Melanie has given me. The brothers are just ending a board meeting and look surprised to see me already at my desk.

My first day goes so fast it's almost a blur. The phones ring constantly, and I photocopy enough documents to fill a small forest. But, overall, I settle in well and quickly became part of the team. Melanie gives me the name 'Miss Unsociable' as instead of heading to the bar with the team on Fridays, I opt to go straight home. After a couple of months, I finally succumb to the pressure and decide to join them once a month on payday, but I set my limit to £20.00—almost half of my weekly shopping budget. The drinks at Banners are so expensive that this barely gets me a couple of drinks.

Since Esther left, I've started drinking again—not heavily, but I do treat myself to a bottle of wine on a Friday night that usually lasts the entire weekend. It's a nice way for me to relax and unwind after a long week at work. I look forward to my long soaks in the bath, listening to music with a nice glass of red. On Saturdays, I usually have a movie night with my neighbours Chloe or Jen. I met Chloe when I first moved in, and we have been friends ever since. I call Esther every Sunday and am always surprised by how much she seems to grow and mature each week. 'Auntie Marcia says I am smarter even than the six-year-olds,' she tells me. She spells a new word to me every week and is helping Grandad Johnny plant flowers. I tell Mary about my new job.

'I know I've never told you this before, but I am proud of you, Ashley. Despite everything, you have turned your life around.' On hearing her words of approval, I feel as though a veil has lifted. I can finally see that I am somebody; I do have some worth. I put the phone down and cry myself to sleep that night and awake feeling like a new woman with pride and purpose.

After three months, Daniel calls me into his office, asking how I'm getting on and if I am happy. 'So, tell me about yourself,' he says.

'What do you want to know?' I reply, knowing I can't tell him about my past.

'Well, the reason I'm asking is that I need an assistant. Can you type?'

'No.'

'Can you take minutes?'

'No.'

'Shorthand?

I shake my head.

'Well, what can you do apart from answering the phones, which you're obviously very good at.'

I think for a few seconds, my mind racing at this unexpected line of questioning. 'I'm good at organising. If you need someone to organise your diary, meetings, or holidays, then I'm your girl,' I finally say.

He smiles. 'That's perfect! Just what I need: someone to help me get organised. Would you like to be my PA?' I want to say yes but don't know what a PA is, which I think he quickly figures out by the look on my face. 'You'll be my personal assistant, take my phone calls, organise my diary, my travels... basically, you'll organise my life, making sure I'm where I need to be when I need to be there.'

'What about the job I'm doing now?' I ask.

'We'll get Melanie to help. Take some of the pressure off you. Oh, and you'll get a pay rise.' I smile so wide my teeth can probably be seen from heaven. 'An increase of £2,000,' but keep the increase between us, okay?' All I can think of is Esther. I want to run into Daniel's arms and smother him with thankful kisses, but instead, I say thank you, accept his offer, and leave his office before he changes his mind.

Joan and Paulina are eager to know what we have been talking about for so long, and I begin to explain. Daniel tells them I will still help them out but also be his PA and answer directly to him. He also makes it clear that his requests will always take priority. 'Melanie sits at reception watching TV most of the time. I see no reason why she can't help out a bit more.' He says. Joan is happy for me, but Paulina is anything but.

'Pretty girl privilege,' she mutters under her breath as I walk past.

I tell Melanie about my promotion during our lunch break. 'You deserve it,' she says. Melanie is a part-time carer for her sick mother and would one day like to go to university to get a degree. But for now, she is studying an access course in business management. 'People think I just sit here staring at the screen, but I use this time to study. I can't wait to get out of here,' she tells me.

The first task Daniel sets for me is a laborious one. He has hundreds of business cards that need to be put into his online contacts system. This takes me the best part of a week to complete, and my wrists ache at the end of it, but at least my typing speed has increased. Mostly, though, I vet his calls, make his overseas travel arrangements, book flights and hotels, and manage his diary. One day, he gives me the task of gift shopping.

'I need a gift for my newborn niece, one for my mother—it's her birthday—and one for my girlfriend as a way of an apology.' Mr playboy has a girlfriend. I wonder what he's apologising for. He gives me his credit card and tells me to call him if I have any problems.

'What's my limit?' I joke as he hands me his card. I have no idea what to buy. I've never met these people. I decide to call Jamie—my go-to fashion queen—who advises me to go to Harrods. 'Harrods?'

'You've got his credit card, ain't you? And from what you told me, he's worth at least a few mil.' I've never thought about this before. It suddenly dawns on me that I am the personal assistant to one of the biggest property developers in the country and am about to jump in a taxi with his credit card and go shopping in Harrods! The enormity of the task ahead and its potential effect on my future finally hit me like a football in the stomach.

I begin in the children's section. The staff are great, helping me choose a silver money box. I call Daniel to ask him for his niece's name and date of birth, which I have engraved on the side of the box. First purchase complete. Next, I head to the women's section, becoming lost in the rich scents, alluring music, and optic lighting. I can read the minds of the snooty assistants a mile off. 'What is she doing in here? She can't even afford to buy a button for a shirt.' I approach the only assistant who looks remotely friendly. Once I explain I am buying gifts on behalf of my boss, she can't be more helpful and transforms into saleswoman of the year, showing me gifts ranging from £200 to £5,000. The assistant tries to convince me to buy a platinum pendant for Daniel's girlfriend, but I decide on the silver heart; after all, I'm not sure what he's sorry for, and platinum is more of a grovel than an apology. I spend the most on gifts for his mother: a silk scarf covered in horses and a pair of South Sea pearl earrings. I have all the items gift-wrapped and make my way back to the office in time for lunch.

'Very impressive,' Daniel says, 'And you have impeccable taste, but I already knew that,' he winks.

My next challenging task is to book dinner for him at a restaurant.

'An old school friend of mine is coming to London. I haven't seen him in years. We need somewhere to go on Saturday evening, so can you book something for me?'

'Do you have anywhere in mind?' I ask.

'No, you choose.' Really, Daniel? I have no clue about restaurants, and he must know that. Why is he making this so difficult? He could at least tell me what kind of food he likes. His 'I eat everything' comment isn't helping me, and I don't think the Chinatown restaurant Reggie took me to will be to his taste. I am about to ask Paulina for some suggestions when I remember the restaurant guide Melanie keeps at reception. It lists all the best restaurants in London, the average price of a meal, star rating, and everything else one needs to know about a place. After a few hours, I eventually decided on a French restaurant, Le Pashe, in Covent Garden. The maitre'd laughs when I say I want a table for Saturday evening.

'We have been fully booked for months, Madam; I can't even add you to the waiting list.' His tone changes to that of an apologetic child when I explain I am calling from the office of Mr Kramer, who has a VIP client in town, and he graciously accommodates my request for an 8:00 PM booking.

'How did you manage to get a table there at such short notice?' Daniel asks, impressed.

'I have my ways.' I smile.

'I bet you do,' he says. I feel his eyes watching me as I walk out of his office.

I plan to spend Saturday evening with Chloe, watching movies and eating pizza. Chloe is from Brighton and left home at sixteen with dreams of becoming an actress, but she became pregnant shortly after arriving in London. She is a single mother to her daughter Megan. Chloe is lucky. Megan stays with her father every other weekend, giving Chloe some time to herself. It is about 6.30 PM when my phone rings. Daniel's name flashes up on the screen, and I go into automatic panic mode. Is something wrong with the booking? I am momentarily stunned into silence when he asks me if I'd like to join him and his friend for dinner. 'Sorry, I can't. I have a friend over,' I say.

'That's even better, bring her too.' I hang up and scream at Chloe in excitement. 'We've been invited to join my boss for dinner at Le Pashe in Covent Garden.'

'Why is he inviting you to dinner?' Chloe asks suspiciously.

'I don't know. Perhaps they're bored and want some female company.'

'I've got nothing to wear,' Chloe sighs.

'You can borrow something of mine,' I say, pointing to the wardrobe. I decide to wear a long black-and-white A-line skirt, which gives the illusion that my waist is smaller than it actually is, and a fitted red polo-neck top that sits just below my belly button. Chloe chooses my black jumpsuit with a silver belt. Thank God I washed my hair, which I leave loose, letting big bouncy curls fall to one side, almost covering my right breast. I never wear make-up to work, but tonight, I wear eyeliner, mascara, and my favourite red lipstick after taking my obligatory bath and dousing myself in perfume.

I read in a magazine that it's always good for a woman to keep a man waiting, so we arrived on time—twenty minutes late. Daniel and his friend Nick are waiting at the bar when we arrive. Daniel won't take his eyes off me as we approach. I am unbothered by his gaze, too preoccupied by the magnificence of my surroundings to care. Moving closer, I watch his eyes trace the length of my body as if unzipping a sleeping bag; we blush as our eyes meet. He orders a bottle of champagne, and the waiter shows us to our table. The atmosphere in the restaurant buzzes like a busy New York bar in Sex and the City, and the rhythm of the jazz music makes my bones sway to the beat. Our table is a round high booth with a sofa covered in soft green velvet. A small antique chandelier hangs above the table from the gilded glass ceiling. I pray only I can hear the churns coming from my stomach as the waiter hands me a menu. Typical, it's in bloody French! Great, my boss invites me out to dinner, and I don't even have the sense to look at the menu beforehand. I am relieved when Daniel calls the waiter over, who talks us through the menu. I listen intently and decide to order the sea bass with pommes dauphinois and mange tout for my main meal and ceviche to start. I watch in awe as the sommelier expertly opens the champagne. The flame of the candles makes the 24-carat gold-plated cutlery sparkle and shine. I sip slowly, but our glasses are never empty. The sommelier miraculously appears from nowhere before every last drop. Daniel orders wine to accompany our meal. I eye him as he reads through the list, which seems longer than the free magazine I read on the way to work. Who knew there was such a large variety of wine in the world?

Laughter slowly creeps in and engulfs our alcohol-infused evening. I lose count of the amount of wine we drink but am careful to nurse mine slowly. I wish I were sitting next to Chloe so I could tell her to slow down. I'm less merry than she is, so I notice her octaves rise with every glass.

'So, what is it you do, Nick,' I ask. He leans in and explains that he is an engineer. He recently developed a new technology that allows for a more effective extraction of metals from the earth, particularly in difficult terrains like deep ocean beds. Attempting to come back with a more impressive answer to a question no one wants to know the answer to, Daniel shares details of his latest multi-million-pound deal.

'I've visited nine countries in the past month, selling my software,' Nick intervenes.

'Have you ever been to Australia, Chloe?' Nick asks. She smiles as they share a private joke.

Every so often, I catch Daniel staring at me. Oddly, this doesn't make me feel nervous or uncomfortable. I like it and wonder if his apology didn't work. Maybe I should have gone for the platinum pendant after all. Perhaps then he'd be sitting here with his girlfriend rather than his assistant.

The meal is the best I have ever tasted. The sea bass is so soft it melts like butter in my mouth, and the wine Daniel has chosen makes it taste even better. After dinner, Chloe and I visit the bathroom. It's like going back in time. The walls are covered in woven silk wallpaper with thousands of colourful butterflies; the ceiling is decorated with pink, white, and blue fake roses that hang in mid-air, and water flows from the gold swan-shaped taps into pink marble sinks.

'Wow, Ash, Daniel is totally into you,' Chloe gushes.

'No, he's not; he's my boss, *and* he has a girlfriend. He sent me shopping to buy her a gift the other day. Anyway, he's rich and can have any woman he wants. What would he want with me? I'm just a normal girl, a single mum. I have nothing to offer him.'

'I'm telling you, he likes you. He can barely take his eyes off you.'

I shrug off her remarks, but while I'm in the cubicle, I think about what she said. Does he really like me?

I order tarte tatin with vanilla ice cream for dessert. This time, I notice Daniel lick his lips every time I take a mouthful. It is almost 11.30 PM when we leave the restaurant. Daniel's driver is waiting outside in a silver Rolls Royce, and he insists on giving us a lift home.

'We're fine. We can get the tube; it will be much quicker,' I say hastily. The last thing I want is for him to see where I live. But the stubborn mule won't take no for an answer.

"I insist. It's late; it's the least I can do. You've both been such wonderful company.' He opens the car door and watches as we climb in. I reluctantly give the driver my postcode, knowing it doesn't matter if I whisper or shout at the top of my voice. Daniel is about to see where I live, and the closer we get to my flat, the more anxious I become. As if reading my thoughts, Daniel reassuringly holds my hand in his.

As we approach the estate, the air outside suddenly appears misty grey. There are always several large metal bins outside the entrance to the building; I'm used to them.

This is, after all, their stationary position, but tonight, they seem extra large, extra dirty, and extra smelly. I wish we could bypass the entrance and be teleported straight to my front door. The car pulls up in front of the bins, and Daniel jumps out. I feel so embarrassed that I invite them up for a drink. That way, at least they'll see inside my home and realise it isn't all bad. We make our way to the lift and up to the eleventh floor. Until now, I have never noticed the screeching sounds the lift makes as it ascends or how dim the lights are, and I am transported back to my first day in Conleigh. I sigh silently with relief when we finally reach the eleventh floor and the doors open. The warm smell of vanilla hits my nose as I open the front door and lead them into the living room.

'This is nice,' Daniel says, staring out at the BT Tower that is clearly visible from my living room balcony. 'What an amazing view.' Chloe goes to her apartment and returns with a bottle of red wine. I offer them a drink, and Daniel follows me into the kitchen. 'You've made a nice home for yourself, Ashley. You'll make someone a good wife one day,' he jokes.

As I turn away from the fridge, he pulls me into him, kissing my cheek. I spin my head to the side, trying to avoid his lips. 'What are you doing?' I ask.

'I've been dying to kiss you since the day I first laid eyes on you,' he says.

'But you're my boss; we can't do this.'

'It can be our secret. No one needs to know.'

'I don't think it's a good idea,' I say and continue to prepare the drinks. He says nothing. I suspect he is someone who's used to getting his own way. He stays in the kitchen while I take the drinks out to Chloe and Nick, who are sitting on the sofa, having an intense debate about football. I return to the kitchen and sit and talk to Daniel.

'So, tell me about yourself. I know little about you. Who are all the people in those pictures? And who's the baby?' He points to the hallway. I suddenly remember my private life is a secret; no one at work, not even Melanie, knows about my personal life. I'm not hiding it; I'm not ashamed of my daughter, but it's just something I have never shared. The alcohol has loosened my tongue, so I readily tell him I am a single mum to Esther and that I've sent her away temporarily whilst I save in order to take better care of her. He listens silently as I tell him about my past, leaving out the parts I feel too embarrassed to share. When he finally speaks, he says he feels a newfound admiration for me. He can see how much I love and miss Ester and understands the sacrifice I've made in trying to give her a better future.

'You won't be single for long; you'll be snapped up in no time,' he assures me. I smile at this but don't say a word.

Daniel isn't in the office when I arrive on Monday morning. I wonder if I've messed up his itinerary, as there are no meetings scheduled in his diary. He finally arrives at midday and asks me to buy him some lunch. He never tells me what he wants, always leaving it up to me to decide what he eats. I only know the things he doesn't like, so avoid them, but there are only so many sandwich combinations to choose from! As I lay his lunch out on his desk, he tells me he's just bought a new car. He scrolls his phone, eager to show me pictures of his new toy, an Aston Martin DB9.

'Looks like a James Bond car.' I shrug.

He laughs. 'You're right; it is a James Bond car, as you describe it. I can take you for a spin in it later if you like, or I could give you a ride home? I need to break it in as much as possible,' he says, sounding like an over-excited child.

I shake my head. 'Okay, you can take me for a spin later.'

At 5:15 PM, Daniel asks me to meet him in the basement car park under the building. I have never been down here before and marvel at the array of expensive cars. Daniel is waiting for me in his car by the lift entrance. It is a racing green convertible with a cream leather interior, and the engine roars like a ferocious lion every time he presses his foot on the gas. It is so polished I can practically see myself on its shiny green surface. He turns to me as I settle into the seat. 'Where would you like to go?'

'Home, ideally.'

'It's such a beautiful day; let's go for a drive.'

After about a mile, we stop to take the roof down. He is careful not to take it down too near the office; the last thing he wants is to set tongues wagging. I watch as he presses the button, and the roof folds in on itself, with different parts of the car lifting and closing again as the roof goes back. People stare, some even take photos. For the first time in a long while, I feel special. Here I am, on a sunny Monday evening, sitting in this beautiful car. He heads towards the motorway. We don't speak much; there is just too much noise from the wind. We drive for about thirty minutes before turning off the motorway into a quaint village and pulling into the car park of a pub. Again, people stare as we get out of the car.

'This car certainly gets a lot of attention,' I joke.

'It isn't the car they're staring at,' he smiles. We take a seat at a table in the pub gardens and sit listening to the rare sound of birds singing. 'You have the most alluring smile,' he says, staring at me. 'I've been thinking about what you told me at the weekend.' I wait for him to continue, my mind racing. I shouldn't have told him anything. Is he going to sack me? 'I'd like to help you get your daughter back.'

'Help me how?' I ask, relieved I'm not about to lose my job.

'We can come up with a plan, but I'll pay for you to get her and bring her home. I'll pay for a nursery or schooling, whatever help you need.'

I wonder why he wants to help me. I've barely known him five minutes. 'Why would you do that?' I finally ask.

'Because I want to and because I can,' he says, taking my hand.

'Ashley, I'm a very wealthy man. I like you, and I want to help you.' I want to speak, but the words won't leave my throat. I will do anything to get Esther back, but this sounds too good to be true. I want to scream a million yesses, but I am terrified this is a joke. How can this happen? How can I be so lucky? 'I admire you, Ashley. You clearly love your daughter, and sending her away was a brave thing to do.' The waitress brings our food to the table, and we sit and eat in near silence, me deep in thought. Mary always told me that what someone gives freely with one hand, they take away with the other—the Jamaican way of saying, 'There's no such thing as a free lunch.' In the back of my mind, I already know this is an exchange I am willing to make. I learnt early on from Eve and Mary that money, sex, and love go hand in hand, and of all the men they've ever had, I think I'm about to catch the best.

After dinner, he drives me home, but I make him stop a block away from my building. It's still light, and I don't want my neighbours to see me get out of his car. I thank him and promise to think about his offer. He presses my back up against the car door and strokes my cheeks as he leans in to kiss me. This time, I don't resist; I kiss him back. His kisses feel soft and full of affection. I eventually pull away when I feel myself becoming aroused.

'You smell so good,' he says, kissing my neck gently.

'I'll see you tomorrow, and thanks for the ride,' I say as I turn to walk away.

He grabs my hand. 'Ashley, promise me you'll think about my offer. You've had a tough start in life, and I just want you to experience the happiness you deserve.' I promise him I'll think about it.

I barely sleep that night. I can't get Daniel's offer out of my mind. The little sleep I do have is filled with dreams of having Esther back and being with Daniel, the three of us living happily together as a family. I tell Chloe about Daniel's offer.

'Are you mad? I don't even know what there is to think about. If you don't want him, I'll have him,' she jokes.

'I want Esther back, but what if I end up getting hurt?'

'Ashley, girls like us rarely get a happy ending, and this seems like yours. Don't throw it away,' she says.

I know she's right, and I know I will definitely accept his offer.

22

Fools Paradise

Daniel doesn't pressure me for an answer, and work continues as normal. He even encourages me to enrol in a training course the company will pay for. 'You're smart and have potential, but you'll need to be qualified to really progress,' he tells me.

It's the end of the month, and after a stressful week, I am really looking forward to Friday night drinks with the girls. Sitting in the prime location of reception, Melanie sees and hears a lot, so after a few glasses of wine, she is keen to spill the beans on all of her weekly observations. 'Apparently, Angelica from Finance is having an affair with Jacob.' Jacob has been married for almost ten years and has two children with his wife, Janice. I've met Janice a few times when she's come into the office to see Jacob. 'And what's happening with you and Daniel?' Melanie quizzes, looking at me with a knowing smile.

'Er, what do you mean, what's happening?'

'Oh, come on, Ash; we all see the way he looks at you! And giving you a promotion after two minutes of being here, he's definitely got a thing for you.' I quickly dismiss her comments before changing the subject. The last thing I want is to become the centre of office gossip. If, or rather, when I start seeing Daniel, I have every intention of keeping it private and away from work.

I'm still in bed when Daniel calls the following morning. He's going to look at a plot of land for sale near Oxford and asks if I'd like to accompany him. I agree to meet him outside my local station at eleven. It takes about two hours to reach the site. He outlines their plans to build a mixture of commercial offices and retail units. We then go for a walk around the nearby town. I love the old golden stone buildings and am fascinated by the architecture. Over lunch at an old country inn, Daniel tells me about his family. He isn't fiercely religious but observes most Jewish customs. If he isn't away on business, he visits his parent's house every Friday for dinner. 'I'm not allowed to marry outside my faith, and my parents are always pressuring me to find a nice Jewish girl to settle down with.' I immediately wonder where this leaves me. Then, as if reading my mind, he lays his cards on the table. 'I'm going to be honest with you, Ashley. You know I like you—a lot—and I would love to be with you. But if we see each other, it's going to have to be in secret. No one can ever know about us. And if you don't want that, I understand. I will still help you get your daughter back.' Like a pin, his words burst the imaginary bubble that has been floating around in my mind. I had envisioned our new life, dreamed that Daniel and I would get married and start a family, but like a windscreen wiper, he quickly erased this fantasy from my mind.

Fairytales don't happen to girls like me. Mary is right; if something seems too good to be true, it usually is. Nevertheless, I'm going to make the best out of this situation, get Esther back, get some qualifications, and get a head start in life. It may not be ideal, but it's the best offer I've had in a long time. As far as I'm concerned, Daniel is my way out, and I'm taking it, happy ending or not. I have a good job, so I can save and build a new life with a wealthy boyfriend. Okay, so no one will ever know about him, but that's a small price to pay. My main focus is Esther, and as long as I can give her the best start in life, that's all that matters.

We sit and talk for hours. Daniel winces when I tell him how Reggie used to rape me and about the baby I lost. He says he admires my resilience even more now and that after all I've been through, I have found a way out and am now sitting here with him. He appreciates the sacrifice I made by sending Esther away to try and build a better life for us both. Most of the girls he knows only worry about how much money Daddy is putting in their bank accounts or what handbag to buy. 'They wouldn't survive a second if they had to go through what you have,' he says.

I plan to collect Esther at the end of the summer holidays in time for the start of the new school term. It will be her fourth birthday, and I can't wait to surprise her. Daniel advises me on how to look for schools. I begin researching them immediately; I want Esther in the best school possible. Driving home, he stops to buy me a bunch of beautiful red roses and a bottle of champagne. After listening to my story, he seems eager to spoil me. He confesses, saying he feels guilty but has already started developing feelings for me, and although he thinks I will be better off without him, he can't let me go, despite knowing I can never really have him, and he can never love me the way I deserve. I say nothing; I long to be loved and am grateful for his love, no matter how sporadic or inconsistent it may be. We sit and drink champagne, watching the sun go down over London from my balcony. Daniel loves listening to my stories and can't stop laughing when I tell him about Jamie.

It's getting late, so I decided to run a bath. My bathing ritual is something I look forward to at the end of each day. I run a bath, light scented candles, and pour drops of jasmine oil into the water. Then, I undress and slip on a silk bathrobe. Daniel's jaw falls open when I walk into the room and ask if he'd like to join me in the bath. Taking his hand, I lead him to the bedroom, where I help him undress. Slowly, I undo the buttons of his pink shirt and slide my hands along the length of his arms, causing his shirt to fall to the floor. Kneeling down, I unbuckle his belt and unzip his jeans. His hairy legs feel muscular and strong under my soft palms. Pushing him onto my bed, I part my bathrobe to reveal my naked body. He breathes silently as he slowly examines my curves.

'You're as perfect as I imagined,' he says. 'Your skin feels like freshly spun silk,' he jokes as I press my breasts softly against his chest.

He holds me close to him as he kisses me tenderly, his lips as smooth as velvet against mine. Placing my breasts in his mouth, he playfully licks them, watching as they grow firmer and larger with every touch. He is totally in tune with my body and observes every response I make to his touch. Listening to the way I moan when he squeezes my breasts and sucks on my nipples. I reach down and pull his pants off. I can feel the stiffness of him against my thighs and want him desperately. He teases me with his tongue, kissing and biting my neck and stomach, covering my thighs with what feels like a million soft kisses. I want him more and more with every touch. He squeezes and caresses my breasts, toying with me as he playfully moves up, down, and around my body.

'I want you inside me,' I moan.

'How much do you want me?'

'I want you so badly, please, Daniel,' I beg.

Gently, he eases himself inside me. I moan as he glides in and out of me, our bodies moving together in unison as ecstasy rapidly engulfs our spirits. It's the strongest, most powerful orgasm I've ever experienced, and in this moment, I feel a deep love for him.

'Wow, what was that?' Daniel breathes heavily as I lay against his chest. 'That was out of this world! Are you some kind of witch doctor?' he jokes. I laugh as he kisses me, holding me tight. 'You feel like heaven to me, and I'm never letting you go,' he says. My insides light up like a candle in a darkened room. Maybe we will be together after all.

We fall for each other quickly and deeply, and the more time we spend together, the deeper we fall, openly discussing our feelings but deciding to live in the moment and enjoy what we have rather than worry about what the future may or may not hold. Neither of us can imagine life without each other and spend as much time as we can together before Esther returns, working hard to hide our affection for each other in public. Daniel's brother, Luke, does notice, though. He knows his younger brother well and has never seen him so happy. He knows Daniel is no longer seeing his ex and confronts him when he catches him staring at me with what he calls *starry eyes*.

'He thinks you might sue me for sexual harassment,' Daniel says. 'I told him I would put my neck on the line that you would never betray me.' He stares at me as if inviting a response.

'I love you and would never do that,' I say eventually.

'You're my best-kept secret,' he says. Except, now I'm not.

Now, Daniel barely makes eye contact with me in the office but never seems to worry about trusting me, saying he trusts me as much as he trusts his own family. We often text each other while at work. I'll see him in the boardroom with his brothers or a group of lawyers and send him flirty text messages. It is our little secret that makes the relationship even more exciting. One evening, we plan to go for dinner after work, but Daniel's meeting runs over. I'm waiting for him in a bar nearby when he calls and tells me to come back to the office. It's getting late, and everyone has left for the day. I find him in the boardroom on the phone. He beckons me towards him, grabs my waist, and pulls me to sit on his lap. Naughtily, I begin to unbutton his shirt and kiss his neck as he continues his conversation, trying his best not to make any suspicious noises. I kiss his lips in between words.

'Yep, five million, yep, yep.'

The more I kiss him, the more distracted he becomes. His manhood obediently rises to attention as I stand before him and unbutton my shirt, exposing my black lace underwear and undressing until I am almost naked in front of him. Kneeling between his legs, I slide my hands along his thighs to the prize between his legs. He is finding it increasingly difficult to concentrate and talk at the same time. I smile cheekily as I watch him struggle, trying not to make any revealing noises. I run my tongue up and down his erection before wrapping my lips tightly around it and putting it in my mouth.

'Jim, I'll call you back,' he says, hastily hanging up the phone.

He lifts me off the floor and bends me over onto the long glass boardroom table. Pulling my knickers to one side, he grabs my waist, entering me from behind. 'I'll never be able to concentrate in here again,' he laughs as we get dressed.

Daniel offers to take me to the airport to collect Esther, but I decline, so he arranges a car for me instead.

'She has been extremely well behaved,' the air hostess says as she hands me Esther's suitcase. Mary had offered to travel with her, but for an extra £100, I paid for her to be accompanied during the flight. It's been a year, and she seems to have grown at least ten inches, but she is still every bit my little baby. Her hair almost reaches the middle of her back, and her sun-drenched caramel skin makes her hazel eyes seem even lighter than they used to be. I hold her tightly and inhale her scent. The baby smell she had when she left is now replaced by the smell of rosemary.

'Grandma grows lots of rosemary bushes, so we make rosemary oil.' She tells me how they soak the stems in oil and leave them under the sink for two weeks, after which time, the oil is infused with its scent. 'It's good for mosquitoes,' she tells me. 'Grandma says my blood is sweet, and that's why they love to bite me, but once I put the oil on, they leave me alone.' I stare at my little madam. Her feet seem to have grown two sizes bigger. 'Grandad made me a special net that hangs over my bed when I sleep,' she says.

She talks non-stop during the entire journey, telling me about her new friends and informing me she has four mangos, a breadfruit, and a piece of yam in her suitcase that Grandma hid in newspaper. Once home, she hands me her diary. It's full of drawings of animals and flowers and photos taken by Marcia with little captions written underneath each one. 'Every day after class, Aunty Marcia gives me extra lessons,' she says. Her handwriting is almost better than mine, and I feel so grateful to my sister. She notices the note she left me.

'To mummy, I love yuo ver much and wil thing of yuo ever day.'

I photocopy it and keep it in a frame next to my bed. I also keep a copy in my purse as a reminder of why I am doing what I do—to make a better life for her. Once she's settled and ready for bed, I call Daniel.

'I would love to take you both for lunch. I'd love to meet her.' I'd love for him to meet her too, but I don't think it's a good idea.

'The last thing I want is to confuse her,' I say. He agrees, but I can hear the disappointment in his voice. 'It wouldn't be fair to her. She will love you and get used to you being around, and, who knows, you could disappear at any moment.' He seems desperate to play happy families but respects my decision.

I have enrolled her in one of the best private schools in the area. A school bus brings her to and from school, and when she isn't doing some form of after-school activity, I pay Chloe to look after her if I have to work late or when I am away with Daniel for the weekend. I'm happy Esther loves her sleepovers with Chloe's daughter, Megan. This allows me to spend time with the people I love without feeling too guilty. After nearly being caught one too many times by Jacob, Daniel decides it's best that we spend some weekends away. He thinks I'm an old dinosaur fresh out of extinction when I tell him I don't have a passport.

'Take the day off and get yourself down to the passport office,' he tells me.

My favourite trip with him was to the South of France. When Esther was away, we would often spend lazy Saturday afternoons watching old black and white movies, and my favourite was To Catch A Thief with Grace Kelly and Cary Grant. We watched it over and over until I noticed Daniel had fallen asleep during the fifth sitting, so I decided we wouldn't watch it again. I met him at the airport on Friday evening after work, and he wouldn't tell me where we were going.

'How will I know what to pack if you don't tell me where we're going?' I argued.

'Come empty-handed if you like. I'll take you shopping once we arrive.'

'At God knows what time of night?' I replied.

'Okay, think summer wardrobe,' he teased.

We made our way to the first-class check-in.

'Your flight leaves in two hours,' the assistant said.

'We're going to Nice. Are the people nice there?' I joked. But the joke was on me.

'It's Nice,' he corrected me.

'So why is it spelt Nice?'

'I don't know; ask the French,' he laughed, kissing me on the lips.

My bum had barely warmed the seat when the hostess offered us a glass of champagne. 'White or rose?' she asked.

'I could get used to this,' I joked.

As we descended, the ground beneath us looked like a huge fairground, lit up by hundreds of rides. As soon as we disembarked the plane, we were greeted by a chauffeur and escorted by car to a helicopter. My heart raced. Flying in a plane is one thing, but a helicopter with one driver and four seats—no way. Daniel, sensing my fear, immediately reassured me. 'We'll be fine. We'll literally be in the air for no more than fifteen minutes. I promise I won't let go of your hand,' he said, taking mine into his. I reluctantly agreed, but the feeling of his hand in mine eased every fear.

I recognised the building immediately: the Carlton Hotel.

'You see, I do pay attention,' he said.

I felt like a princess in a fairytale. We stayed in an enormous suite overlooking the French Riviera. The marbled bathroom was filled with luxury soaps and cosmetics that I stuffed into my case every morning so housekeeping would leave more. Daniel shook his head and laughed when I did this.

'What? We can't get these at home,' I joked.

The best part of the trip was the picnic. Daniel hired a blue convertible similar to the one in the film, and the hotel made us a picnic. We drove for hours, eventually stopping off at a secluded spot, where we sat under a tree and had lunch looking down at the yachts below sailing the Mediterranean Sea. Being there with him, I was certain he loved me, although I've yet to hear him say those three words.

When we are away, we feel free from the worry of prying eyes. We hold hands and kiss openly in public, like a pair of lovesick teenagers with a secret only we know. Daniel always insists on taking me shopping, but I only ever buy gifts for Esther and Megan, buying them a teddy bear from every country we visit. I am living what feels like a dream I don't want to wake up from. The more time Daniel and I spend together, the deeper the intensity of our lovemaking becomes, drawing me tighter to him. When we are together, I feel like the happiest woman alive, but when we're apart, I feel a hole inside as deep as a crater.

'I think about you every night.' He confesses one evening. I want to ask him if he loves me but am too afraid of what he might say. Chloe thinks I'm getting too emotionally involved.

'Keep going like this, Ash, and you're going to get hurt.' She says.

'You were the one who encouraged me to do this in the first place,' I say.

She reminds me of why I started seeing him in the first place: to get Esther back and make a better life for us both.

'I mean, don't get me wrong, he seems really nice and clearly has some good intentions, but he's definitely putting his own needs before your own.'

I argue that he's putting Esther through school and helping me financially, and she reminds me that he's a multimillionaire, and the money he gives me doesn't make the slightest dent in his wallet. I know she's right, the pain I feel when we're apart makes my chest ache, and I cry myself to sleep most nights, praying we will eventually be together despite his religious beliefs. I've even started wearing makeup to conceal the dark rings forming under my eyes. I no longer just want his help; I want his love. I've opened my heart, left it unguarded, and allowed Daniel's love to seep into my veins, and I'm not sure it will ever wash away.

23

Shattered Illusions

IT'S BEEN ALMOST THREE years now since Esther returned. She is thriving at school and has won almost every spelling bee competition. Sending her away was one of the best decisions I could have made. We speak to Mary and Marcia every week, and I cannot stop thanking them for the part they have played in helping her grow into the smart girl she has become. Listening to her speak, I cannot help but admire her confidence, something I still don't have enough of.

'When I'm older, I'm going to be a doctor or maybe an astronaut,' she says.

'You can be anything you want,' I tell her. When I was young, I didn't think I could be or do anything, not even a nurse or a secretary like Mary tried to encourage. I think I would have loved to have been a singer or a dancer, but I thought people on TV lived a million miles away on another planet and that it was impossible for me to do anything like that. So, I try to encourage Esther as much as I can. 'Your future is as bright as all the stars in the sky,' I say to her every night before bed.

'Mummy, what did you want to be when you were little?'

Nothing. I was always told I was just like my mother, so maybe I just wanted to be like her; maybe I still do. I don't think my life has turned out too badly, though. I have a good job, a wealthy man who takes care of me and Esther, and a nice little flat. Mary doesn't know about Daniel, but I finally have her approval. She is proud I have a good job and am a good mother. I think even Eve would be proud of me. Sometimes I wish I could find her, that she could meet Esther, that I could tell her all about Daniel and how well he takes care of us. Show her I don't need to take pokes for money but for love.

Recently, Daniel has been asking to see me during the week instead of at weekends. He says he's super busy and needs the weekends to catch up on the backlog of work. The first few times, I refuse, but when he tells me he may not be able to see me for at least a month, maybe two, I readily agree. I hate leaving Esther with Chloe during the week, but the truth is, I'm scared he might leave me if I refuse.

'It's not like you need to be home to tuck her in,' he says.

I remind him that even though Chloe lives next door, I will have to carry her home to put her to bed, and she will probably wake up. Meeting in the week quickly

223

changes the nature of our relationship. We no longer go for dinner or spend any real quality time together. We mainly meet in the new company flat, have sex, and then he calls me a cab and sends me home quicker than I can put my knickers on.

'Daniel, what's going on with us?' I ask him one evening before my taxi arrives.

'Ashley, you knew the nature of our relationship from the start,' he says, reminding me that our *arrangement,* as he now suddenly calls it, will never be more than it is. But this is less than what it was, I want to say, but I feel I am holding a cup full of water, and one more word will tip it over, never to be full again. 'I'm the one helping you out, remember? And in return, well, you know,' he says. His words pierce my heart like a pin to a balloon and my eyes well with water. I know it may sound stupid, but I really thought I could make him love me. How can we be so intimate, spend so much time together, and not fall for each other? 'Ashley, please don't cry. Just remember what I'm doing for your daughter, okay.' The hate I once felt for Reggie, that pain I thought I would never feel again, quickly resurfaces, and I fucking hate him now and want to claw at his face like a wildcat. I want to ask him why he treated me so good and now so bad. I feel as though he lured me in and has now become tired of me but doesn't quite know how to end it. I remember Chloe telling me about her ex.

'He didn't want to be with me anymore, but he was a coward who hated confrontation,' she said. So, he did everything he could to get her to break up with him instead. He started ignoring her calls, turning up late or not at all, starting arguments out of a two-word sentence. 'He even came home one night smelling so strongly of perfume, I swear he stopped off at the sample counter and sprayed it on himself,' she joked. And the minute she said she'd had enough, he said okay and packed his bags quicker than a thief in an empty shop. She never saw him again.

This is what I'm sensing from Daniel. Something has changed, and he's too afraid to say, as if he's trying to let me down without banging my head on the floor. Well, I'm not making it that easy for him. I try to talk to him about it, but my taxi arrives, and he practically shoves me out the door. No goodbye, no kiss, no see you tomorrow— nothing. I want to tell the taxi to turn around, to go back and confront him. 'How fucking dare you treat me like some prostitute,' I want to say. But then my mind falls silent, the cloud lifts, and all is suddenly as clear as ice-cold water. Ashley, you are a fucking prostitute. Yes, Daniel may be nice, and yes, you may stay in nice hotels or plush apartments and eat at fancy restaurants, but the relationship is a trade. He gives me money, and I give him sex. Mary was right all along. I really am no better than Eve. I thought I was better than her for being with a rich man rather than someone like Ernie. But now I see I'm no different to her. I am going to find her, tell her I know all her dirty little secrets, and demand she tell me why she left me. And I'm going to confront Daniel, too.

I love him and don't want to lose him, but my heart is aching, and I want it to stop.

'I'm tired, Mummy,' Esther says the next day. Today, for the first time, she didn't jump out of bed and wake me up; I had to wake her. I didn't sleep much, either. I can't forget the way Daniel pushed me out the door, almost causing me to trip on the threshold. It reminded me of when Ernie used to tell Eve to leave as soon as she wasn't being poked anymore. The last few times during sex, he's even called me a bitch. I wanted to say something but was too scared. I can't go on like this anymore. I'm now putting him and his needs before Esther's. The next time we meet, I will definitely confront him about this. I just pray he understands. I need my job, Esther needs to be in school, and I desperately don't want to lose any more of his love.

For the first time since starting with the company, I decide to call in sick. Telling Paulina that Esther has chicken pox and that I will hopefully be in next week. Guilt consumes me when they send her a teddy and a get-well card signed by everyone in the office, including Daniel. I just need this time to think and decide what I am going to do. Yesterday, Daniel sent me a test message:

I'm sorry I've been a bit off lately, but I have been having a few issues with the family. Thinking of you xxx'.

What on earth does that mean? One minute, he's as cold as a lump of ice, and the next, he's as hot as an ember. A part of me is dreading seeing him again, but I need to know where I stand once and for all.

I've asked Mary for Eve's contact details. It hurts that after all these years, she has never once reached out and tried to contact me. What kind of mother can just cut herself off from her children as if they never existed? Fear swirls around in my gut. What if she doesn't want to be contacted? What if she rejects me? I am terrified of the answer, but if I don't try to contact her, I think I may regret it for the rest of my life. If she doesn't want to see me, it will hurt, but I will eventually get over it. I can't risk living with the 'what if' question roaming my mind like the lost child I sometimes feel I still am.

The following Monday, Daniel calls me into his office. I immediately know something is wrong when I see Jacob sitting with him.

'Take a seat.' Jacob says, offering me a chair. My ears throb in anticipation, and my heart pounds so loudly I fear they can hear it. I look at Daniel, who quickly averts his gaze as if he's afraid his eyes may trigger the tears hiding behind mine. 'There's no easy way to say this, but we have to let you go. We are restructuring, and unfortunately, your position has been made redundant.' Jacob's voice is as cold as a frozen lake. I don't look at either of them, preferring to stare out of the window at the London skyline I know I will never see from this vantage again. Jacob continues, 'We will pay you for the rest of the month and include £5,000 as part of your redundancy package. There's no need for you to work out your notice; you can leave as soon as this meeting is over.'

He then produces a confidentiality agreement I am made to sign before leaving the building. My chest tightens; my breath stifled by his words. I am too humiliated to say goodbye to my colleagues. I want to run, to jump out of the window, and fall with the wind eleven flights down onto the concrete below.

I see Dembe as I leave the building and remember how kind he was to me, how I actually considered getting to know him better before meeting Daniel, and now that chance of a relationship with him is gone.

Daniel follows me into the street as I hail a taxi. 'Ashley, wait. Let me take you home,' he says, jumping into the taxi behind me. 'Ashley, I'm so sorry it has come to this. I had no say in this whatsoever. My brothers know about us and have threatened to force me out of the business if I don't stop seeing you, and my parents are pressuring me to get married. I had no choice but to agree. I'm sorry it had to end this way. You deserve better. I could never really love you the way you deserved to be loved.'

My tears, hot and humiliated, stream down my face. I want to hurt him. I want him to feel my pain. My heart aches with a pain so strong I begin to scream. I hate myself! My life is like a merry-go-round; I make the same mistakes again and again and again. Daniel tries to comfort me, but his touch stings like nettle. He reassures me he will continue to pay for Esther's schooling. She has five more years in school, but he writes me a cheque to cover six. I take the cheque and turn to him before getting out of the taxi. 'I hope you live forever feeling as I do now,' I say before slamming the taxi door in his face.

He calls me every day for weeks before finally giving up. Each time leaving a barrage of voice messages. He says I'm right, that he will never be truly happy without me, that I was the only true happiness he has known in many years, and now I'm gone. His future life will be a misery, being forced to marry someone he doesn't love. He hated the way Reggie treated me and had prided himself in always caring and protecting me, but now he has hurt me and let me down, just like all the others have. He is no better than them.

* * *

I spend the next few months in a daze, holding my life together by a thread. If it weren't for Esther, I would stay in bed and will myself into an eternal sleep. Good things only happen to good people, and I'm not one of them, I hear a voice say. I pray hard, and each time, I am told to let go of the hate and forgive Daniel. Slowly, I realise that being upset with him only makes me unhappy and bitter, and I don't want Esther surrounded by such toxic energy; it isn't good for either of us. I ask God to take my pain away, to soften my heart that has become hardened by pain and resentment, trying desperately to remember all the good times we shared and our decision years ago to enjoy the moment. It's time to accept that the moment has passed. While it lasted, it was good, but now it's time to let go, forgive, and move on.

Melanie, who still works for Daniel, told me he got married six months after I left to the daughter of a business associate, a match arranged by his brother, Jacob. 'Together, our families will form a powerful alliance,' she overheard him telling Daniel. Although I knew it would happen, my heart wept when I heard this.

'Hi Julie, it's Ashley.' After all these years, I find myself back in the smoke-stained offices of Deliverance Recruitment. The old lady, looking even more wrinkled, still occupies the corner desk, her ashtray now filled with paper clips instead of cigarette butts, as it is now illegal to smoke in the workplace. Looking back, I can't believe it ever was.

'I've got the perfect position for you. It pays slightly less than your previous job, but there is a pretty good chance for promotion relatively quickly, so I think it's worth the drop,' Julie says. The position is for a property administrator at a local estate agent. 'If your reference from Kramer Brothers was any more glowing, I'd think you were shagging one of them,' Julie jokes. I don't laugh at this. 'If you're interested, I'll put your CV forward,' she says.

If I'm interested. Right now, I think I'd accept a job at a chicken factory, anything to get back into work and keep my mind occupied. The last few months have been a rollercoaster. I enjoy taking Esther to school and being there to greet her at the school gates at the end of every day, but those hours in between are as silent as an empty graveyard. I didn't realise how much I was missing out on by working full-time. My bright star is now head girl and top of almost every subject except religious education.

'I just don't believe God will make me burn in hell if I take a sweet from the tuck shop. Not that I would ever do that,' she adds quickly. There are just too many parts of the Bible that are too contradictory, she argues, and I agree.

'Take what you want and leave the rest,' I tell her. Mary tried to beat religion into me as a child, and it never worked. My mind was never fully present at church. It wandered the streets, sometimes even travelling to different countries. I'm not sure I believe in the God I was taught about, but I certainly believe in something much greater than myself.

Elite Property Services is based in Tower Bridge, a lot closer to home than my previous job. They are a small team of five but manage a portfolio of over three hundred offices. The entire office is almost the size of the boardroom at Kramer Brothers. Their toilets are so small you almost have to sit on the seat before pulling your trousers down. The kitchen-come-dining-area houses a glass table with six chairs, only five of which are in use—the fifth one, I'm informed, was broken by the apprentice, Tom. He has an obsession with trying the hottest chilli sauce he can find, and one day, rather than swallow his usual teaspoon, he upped it to a tablespoon. It was so hot he fell off the chair, leaving it without a leg, and spent the rest of the afternoon in the men's toilet. They are all married except Tom, who says his parents have been married for almost thirty years and are the most miserable couple he has ever met. So, he thinks he will give it a miss, even though he behaves like he's just been potty trained. I carry out administration tasks for the lettings team: posting ads online, applying for customer references, changing utilities, answering phones, and whatever other admin tasks are required. My 9:30 AM start means I can drop Esther off in the mornings but can't pick her up, so we're back to relying on the school bus.

'If you don't mind me asking, how can you afford to send your daughter to a school as prestigious as St Marguerites?' the office manager asked me two weeks into the role.

'My mother pays for her,' I lie. 'Mind your own bloody business. How I pay for my child's education is not your concern' is what I really wanted to say.

I've started looking at secondary schools for Esther, and it's not looking great. She is doing so well at school, and the last thing I want is for her grades to slip by sending her to the local state school. Frustratingly, we are literally one hundred meters too far from the best state school in the area. St Marguerites has been preparing the students for their eleven-plus entrance exams, and Esther has already decided she wants to go to St Etienne girls' school. Madeline, the other brightest girl in her class, is going there, and she has set her sights on joining her.

Apparently, Madeline's parents own their own island off the Maldives and so could afford to send her to a school on Mars if there was one. Her form teacher, Mrs Fitzpatrick, says she has as good a chance as any of getting in.

'Mum, I'm going to ace every exam,' Esther tells me confidently one evening after finishing her homework. Usually, she completes her homework at the after-school clubs, which gives me great relief as sometimes I look at her math workbook and think even Einstein would struggle with some questions. By the time she was six, Esther knew her entire times tables. To this day, I only know my 2s, 5s, and 10s.

At weekends, I always try to take her somewhere new, even if it's a city park or an old church. She loves the science museum, which we have visited at least twenty times. She spends her Sunday afternoons writing about what we did on weekends and even includes detailed sketches of things she sees. It's as if she has a camera in her mind, adding colours and textures.

'Mum, when can we go away on holiday together?' she asks me after half term holiday. Almost every child in her class goes away during the holidays to Spain or France, or even to Egypt, to swim with the fish, she tells me.

'Soon, honey, soon,' I promise. Together with my redundancy pay and the extra money Daniel gave me, I have saved quite a bit, but I am too scared to spend any of it. The thought of being broke terrifies me so much that I check my account balance twice a week just to check it's still there. I know it sounds a bit obsessive, but who can blame me? One minute, I'm sunbathing at the edge of a salt-water pool in Italy, and the next, I'm swallowing salty tears in my high-rise council flat. Living a lavish lifestyle with Daniel one minute and being back in my flat alone and jobless the next has taught me that nothing lasts forever and to take nothing for granted.

Esther is so determined to win a place at St Etienne's she studies constantly, even asking to forgo our Saturday outings for a month before her exams. I don't know where she gets her work ethic from, and if I'm honest, I find it a bit unhealthy. I hated school, and when I was her age, all I wanted to do was play in the park. 'Esther, I think you're working too hard. It's okay if you don't get in,' I say after prying her away from her books so she can eat something. She looks at me as though I've told her every book in every library in the entire world has just been destroyed by fire-breathing aliens.

'Mum, I don't think you understand how important this is. If I don't get in, I will have to go to a state school, and Mrs Fitzpatrick says I'll have no real future if I do.' I want to march down to that school and give Mrs High-Horse Fitzpatrick a piece of my mind. The night before her exams, Esther reminds me that she is going to be a doctor and save people's lives when she is older, and it seems nothing will stop her.

As usual, she is up before me the next day, excited to visit her potential new school. We get the train to St Paul's and walk ten minutes to school. The building is so tall I can barely see the sky, and it reminds me of an old gothic cathedral. Its grey stone walls, dark and imposing, are covered in what look like carvings of gargoyles holding swords, and a gold lion sits proudly atop heavy black cast iron gates. The crest is blue and white.

'Carpe diem, that means seize the day,' Esther dutifully informs me as I stare up at the building.

It was Daniel who suggested she take Latin as an extra-curricular activity. I argued that learning an extinct language was a waste of time; I was obviously wrong on that front. Even Daniel's Aston Martin would pale in significance to the cars parked here. I've never seen so many Rolls-Royces and Bentleys in my entire life, let alone in one car park, and half of them have a Geeves in the driver's seat. Wiping the invisible dust off my jacket, I adjust my sleeves and straighten my collar. I know I shouldn't think it, but part of me wishes she doesn't get in. I can't imagine how she will ever fit in here, and judging by the look of the uniform, a month's salary might just about buy her the sleeve of a blazer. Esther squeezes my hand, breaking me from my thoughts.

'Mummy, if I'm not nervous, you shouldn't be,' she says as if reading my mind.

One thing St Marguerites has given her is confidence. She walks into a room like she owns the entire building, and it makes me so happy. It also reminds me of all the times I walked into a room and wished I could become invisible.

'The results will be sent out in approximately two

weeks,' Mrs Pillar tells the parents.

Despite the smell of money oozing from everyone in the room, I am not made to feel uncomfortable and even exchange pleasantries with a few of the parents. For the next two weeks, Esther is like a child with ants in her pants and doesn't keep still, jumping whenever she thinks she hears the postman. It's almost three weeks later when the letter arrives. Esther is still at her after-school club, and I arrive home from work to see the blue and white crest staring up at me from an envelope on the hallway floor. My heart races the way it does when I run for the train in the morning. Should I open it or wait for Esther to get home? If she opens it and she's won a place, great. But what if she hasn't? What if she failed? I decide it's best to open it before she gets home. Holding the envelope to my chest, I pray. 'Dear God, please make it a yes.'

Dear Ms Clarke,

It was an absolute pleasure meeting Esther. As you know, our scholarships are in high demand, and places for them are extremely competitive. Unfortunately…

I stop reading at 'unfortunately'; I already know the rest. Lighting the back ring of the cooker hob, I stare into its blue flame. I am about to burn the letter when the buzzer rings. Esther has arrived home from school.

'It's arrived, hasn't it!' She is so intuitive, I sometimes think she could read the pages of a closed book. 'Where is it? Where is it?' she asks, following me into the kitchen before spotting the letter on top of the stove. I try to grab it, but her little hands are a lot swifter than mine.

Unfortunately, we cannot grant a full scholarship at this time. However, we will waive half the fee for the first year and, subject to her results at the end of the first year, offer a full scholarship for the duration of her time at the school. This offer is conditional and subject to yearly reviews.'

'I've got in, Mummy! I've got in!'

I am too busy trying to calculate the cost of half a year's school fees, uniforms, school meals, travel, and whatever else she'll need. 'Well done, baby. I'm so proud of you,' I say.

'Don't worry, Mummy. I promise I will work hard and get a full scholarship next year.'

'Let's go get some ice cream to celebrate,' I say. I would really like to call that bloody school and ask why they will only pay half the fees; I can't imagine any of those other kids needing any assistance. But I don't. I take Esther out for ice cream and spend the rest of the evening with a notepad and calculator.

The following week, on my way home from work, I receive a call from an unknown number. My heart stops momentarily when I hear Daniel's voice on the other end of the phone. 'Ashley, I really need to talk to you,' he pleads. I want to tell him to go to hell that I never want to see him again, but then I think about Esther's school fees, so I decide to see him.

We meet at Claridge's, where he is staying. He's already

waiting for me in the reading room when I arrive. I wear a red pencil dress with a long black coat, lace tights, and the royal blue suede shoes he bought for my birthday. 'You look stunning, as always,' he says, standing to greet me. I slip my coat over my shoulders and hand it to the waiter in exchange for a token. His eyes undress me as they glance wantingly over my body, lingering over my breasts before we sit down. 'Tea, coffee?' he asks. Tea or coffee won't settle my nerves, I think, as I order a glass of champagne. We sit in silence for a moment before he begins. 'I'm so sorry, Ashley. I never meant to hurt you.'

I sit and listen to him talk about his wife and how unhappy he is, even though she is pregnant with their first child. I feel a mixture of pity and sorrow towards him. His spirit is low, and I have never seen him so deflated. Imagine being so wealthy and yet so unhappy. He reaches out to touch my hand that is resting on the table, but I pull it away. I don't want him to think I'm giving in that easily.

'The way I dealt with things was wrong. I tried running away and hoped things would work themselves out, and that was wrong of me.' I want to roll my eyes; I thought we were over this. Is this what he called me here for, to join his stupid pity party? 'I just want you to know that I'll always love you, and I'll always be here for you if you need anything, anything at all.'

Bingo, now's my chance.

For a while, I say nothing. The sadness in his eyes kind of makes me want to love him again. 'I'm still hurt by the way you treated me, but my heart is healing, and I hope you find true happiness one day. I really do,' I say.

"I already found it with you, Ashley. But the truth is, my father's right. Life isn't about true love; it's about making the best of what you have. True love is that of the family. Sometimes, a man must sacrifice his own happiness for the greater good of the family, and that's what I had to do.' The man I once loved is now sitting in front of me, looking as if he's had his spirit rung out of him. Or maybe this is who he was all along, weak and hopeless.

'So, what are we doing here? I ask.

'I understand if you don't want to see me again, but I could really do with a friend right now,' he says. His words tug at my heart, and I stand to hug him. 'No, not here. I'm staying in room 56. Meet me there in fifteen minutes.'

'Okay,' I say before ordering another glass of champagne. I haven't eaten, and my head whirls as I try to make sense of what is happening. So, we are going backwards, but only this time, he's married, so we'll be having an affair, which means I will hardly ever see him and will be left crying into my pillow while he rests contently on his, playing fake happy families. He's got some fucking nerve. He's miserable and unhappy, so now he wants to walk back into my life and turn it upside down again. I don't think so. I'm not taking another penny from him. I will have to use almost every penny I have to get Esther through her first year of school, but I will do it alone on my own terms. I'm done being used by men. I order a

Dorset shell crab salad, jacket potato with caviar, chives and sour cream, a lemon tart, and three more glasses of champagne. 'Charge it to room 56,' I tell the waiter before heading home.

24

A Mother's Love

'Mummy, will I ever meet Eve?'

Esther has just turned twelve, and the family tree project she's started at school is raising more questions than I have answers for. The truth is, Mary gave me Eve's number months ago, but I'm too scared to call it. Just staring at the piece of paper raises feelings I have worked hard to repress, but they are still there, quickly rising in my blood, hot with anger. That stupid fucking bitch. She made me what I am: a worthless slut, who sleeps with men for money. A woman who was only willing to love if I got something in return. Looking in the mirror, all I see is a cheap whore staring back at me. I am determined Esther won't be the same. Her worth will not be defined by what someone is willing to pay for her. Every time I stare at her number, I disappoint myself. I thought I was free of her, that she could never affect me in the way she used to, and now, here I am, sweat running down my back, sitting on my hands to stop them from shaking. When will I finally be free from the grasp of a woman I've only ever seen a handful of times and don't even know? I am about to answer Esther's question, but she answers it before the words leave my mouth.

'Auntie Marcia and Nanny Mary told me about her when I was in Jamaica.' She runs to her room and returns with the diary I gave her the day she left for Jamaica. 'Look, I have a picture of her here.' For years, she's kept that diary in a paper bag inside her dresser. I've lost count of the number of times I have wanted to take it out and read it, but it's filled with her private thoughts, wants, and desires. So, as hard as it was, I always resisted the temptation. But now I feel swamped with the desire to read it word for word. Unexpected tears stream down my face, flowing uncontrollably like a mother's breasts in need of sucking. Soaking my t-shirt, they run through the creases of my neck, pooling in its crevices. Eve looks older but still as beautiful as the last time I saw her. But there is something hiding behind her eyes: shame, guilt, fear—I don't know, but I know it isn't happiness, love, or contentment. I stare at her eyes, and I feel it. Pain stabs my stomach, and fear grips my heart, squeezing it so tight I have to lie down. 'I'm sorry, Mum. I'll put it away,' Esther says, dabbing my eyes with the cuff of her jumper. I try to speak, but the words, lost in grief and despair, remain stuck in my throat. Why doesn't she want me? What did I do wrong? Why do I still crave her love more than anything, even after twenty-eight years?

'I'll be fine. I just need to have a rest,' I say. 'Go and do your homework.' She leaves the room, forgetting to take the picture and her diary with her.

I don't know how long I fall asleep, but my dream is filled with images of Eve being poked. Ernie's voice as deep as a baritone, and Eve tells me she wishes I was dead and plots to leave me in a phone box. Then nothing. Blank. I wonder what her life is like now. Where is she? I want—I need—no—I demand answers to my questions. I eye Esther's diary. *Keep Out* is written on the front in red ink. I know her now impeccable script has only just written these words recently. I pick it up and stare at its cover. Still impeccable, not a single tear. I turn it over, and there it is, the reason I have to face my demons and call Eve. A drawing of Johnny, Mary, Eve, and Dad. A dad she has never known. Not once has she asked me about her father, yet she has been missing him all this time. I yield to temptation and open her diary, turning to a page near the back.

I think about my dad a lot now and wonder where he is and what he does. Why doesn't he come to see me? Nanny Mary says that some people are bad, so we should just forget about them. She says I'm a lucky girl to have a mummy who loves me so much. She said my mummy never lived a day with her mummy, and she doesn't know who her dad is either, so I must be thankful I have a mum and should just forget about my dad. I love my mummy and don't want to upset her, so I will never ask about my dad. I will just think about him in my head.

I want to tell her he's dead, buried, and living in hell. That he is an evil, abusive bastard who doesn't deserve to know her, but I can't. Suddenly, I see the wall I have built around us crumble, knowing that if I don't take it down, she will eventually pull it down. Why did Mary never tell me about this? But as I ask myself the question, the answer appears: to protect and save me from worry. I close the diary and put it into my drawer. Maybe reading the wisdom of my daughter's thoughts will help me with mine.

'Mummy, are you okay?' Esther knocks on the door.

'Come in, sweetheart,' I say. She climbs onto the bed and hugs me tightly. She is almost as tall as I am, is now captain of the lacrosse team, and is head girl.

'She truly is one of our school's greatest assets,' her headteacher told me as they awarded her a full scholarship.

I have been promoted at work to property manager and am studying part-time for my degree in Real Estate. I've started saving again, and if all goes to plan, I will buy a small house by the time Esther is fifteen.

I decide to call Eve on a Friday. This way, I'll have the entire weekend to cry her rejection out of my system. My scars, no longer visible, are still there, buried in an open coffin, huddled together with all the other pains of my life.

'Hello,' my heart races from first to fifth gear, and I wish I could put the brakes on. 'A-Ashley.' I can hear her heart beating through the phone. How on earth does she know it's me when she has never heard my voice? 'Do you remember the day I came to take you back? Mary told you to go inside the house, and you replied, "Yes, Mummy." Since that day, I have carried your voice with me everywhere I go. A day doesn't go by when I don't imagine what it would be like if you said those words to me.' I am stunned into silence. She thinks about me every day. But then I remember climbing through the window to rescue Donna and Marcia and wonder if she thinks about them, too. 'I would really love to see you, but I understand if you don't want to.' I stop her here. I imagine smashing my phone into a million pieces, wishing it was her head.

'If you wanted to see me, why didn't you ever contact me?' I ask.

'Please, Ashley, can we meet? I have so much to say and think it's best said face to face.'

A part of me wants to tell her to go to hell, but I know I can't. At this point, I don't even need answers; I just need closure so I can finally put my lingering, unhealthy emotions to sleep, nail the coffin closed, and burn it once and for all. We arrange to meet the following week at a coffee shop in my local park. I count the days until we meet. My dreams are now a series of vengeful frenzies detailing my plan of attack.

I know what you did; you took money for pokes. I know Ernie is my dad; you're lucky I never told Mary. You've ruined my life. For years, I thought I could gain love by giving myself away. I still remember when you told me to save my virginity for the highest bidder, and do you know what the highest bidder did to me? The same thing Ernie did to you. I'm going

to tell Mary, Johnny, and whoever will listen what a bitch
you are. I'm going to ruin your life the way you ruined mine.

I sense her presence before I see her, my past feelings of abandonment immediately rise to the surface. I can almost hear my cries pleading with her not to leave me behind. I turn around and, standing in front of me, is the most beautiful woman I think I have ever seen. Her skin looks as soft as silk, and her hair smells of the sweetest lilies. She smiles, and my heart immediately softens, blood flowing freely through its arteries like an unblocked drain.

'Ashley,' she opens her arms, and before I can resist, I am trapped inside them; they hug my shoulders and squeeze me tight. A howl as loud as a wolf's cry escapes from my stomach, reverberating around the room as tears rush from the pit of my stomach and out of my eyes, soaking my face that is pressed tightly into her neck. She is wearing Chanel, Jamie's favourite perfume. 'It's okay; let it out,' she says, rubbing my back, and for the first time, I feel a bond that I have only ever felt with Esther. 'I'm so very, very sorry,' she says. I don't know if I won't or can't let go. My body feels like a magnet that has to be prized apart, or I will stay like this forever. The dampness of her wool coat pressed against my face feels like a pillow of clouds, and I want this feeling to last forever. 'I will never let you go again,' she finally says, releasing me from her grasp.

The shop is almost silent; people stare at us as if they have just witnessed an exorcism. A waitress offers me a handful of tissues, and I wipe my face as Eve orders water and a coffee, and we sit and talk for hours.

'I have wanted to contact you for years but just couldn't face you rejecting me. My entire life has just been one rejection after the other.' She says she made bad choices for the wrong reasons. I already know this, and although I was geared up to tell her, I just can't.

'Why?' I ask, 'Why did you do the things you did?'

'Ashley, you are the first person apart from my therapist I have ever told.' She was abused. She doesn't say who by, and I don't ask. 'Sometimes, when bad things happen to someone, they become the very thing that made them that way. Only time and life can change our minds, forcing us to see things differently.' She is not proud of her past but is not ashamed of it either. She is now a counsellor who helps victims of rape and abuse. I feel ashamed. Ashamed that I have spent so much time blaming her for something that wasn't her fault. 'I went through one of the darkest periods of my life whilst I was pregnant with you. I thought that by forgetting you, I could forget who I was then.' It wasn't until recently that she accepted her past. 'I am not proud of what I did, but I am no longer ashamed. The fact I now get to help others who may find themselves in similar situations is a blessing to me,' she says.

I can't help but think she's right. If I hadn't lived the life I have, I wouldn't be the mother I am to Esther. The past, no matter how painful, makes us who we are, and there are lessons to be learned from every experience, no matter how painful they may be. Everything I have been through, good and bad, has helped shape me into the woman I am today, and as a result, I now have a daughter who could run the country one day if she so chooses. It's not about what we've been through but how we get through.

'Ashley, use your experience to strengthen you. Let it drive you forward into your true greatness,' she says.

I want to stay and speak with her forever, but it's getting late, and I have to collect Esther from Chloe. I have one more question I am afraid to ask, but as we say goodbye, it pops out of my mouth. 'Where is my dad?' I know the correct question should be, 'Who is my dad?' but I think I already know the answer to that one.

'Your dad's name was Ernie. He was my first true love.' Tears fall from her eyes now, and I feel sorry I asked the question. 'He died a month ago'. My eyes widen, and my mouth falls open, exposing every filling and molar in my mouth. She convinces me to visit Ernie's grave. 'I've forgiven him, and for your own sake, you must do the same,' she says. I know she's right. If I can forgive her, I can at least try to forgive him.

My feelings of anger and hatred have somehow been replaced by a feeling of gratitude. She could have had an abortion, put me in a home, or left me outside a church or in a phone box, but she didn't. She gave me the chance of life, and it's up to me how I choose to live it. The pain and blame ascend from within, and I leave feeling as light as air, ready to finally let go of the past and start living my future.

We arrange to meet a few weeks later, and this time, I promise to bring Esther with me. With the past now fully behind me, I am ready to really move forward until the past comes knocking at my door—literally.

25

Same 'Ole Love

IT'S BEEN YEARS SINCE I last saw Paul. I did write to him for a while, but my letters became less and less frequent and eventually stopped. Thoughts of Daniel drift into my mind whenever Esther wins a prize or speaks French, reminding me of how lucky I was to have his help. She continues to excel in school, and my career as a property manager is going well. I will never forget this is partly thanks to him. My heart jumps whenever I receive a phone call from an unidentified number, and today is no different.

'Hello, is this Ashley?'

'Yes,' I answered hesitantly.

'Ashley, it's Paul.'

Again, his voice, like a memory box, instantly transports me back to my life in *Conleigh:* my time at the refuge, Alice's dead body lying slumped on the table, my head bashing against the headboard as Reggie raped me, him stepping over me after having sex with another woman in our bed, the foetal blood of our baby moving slowly down my legs. Everything I've tried so hard to forget suddenly comes back to haunt me with the sound of his voice. A part of me feels I've betrayed him. He has always been good to me, and I had all but forgotten him once I started my relationship with Daniel. Why is he calling me? What does he want?

'How are you, Ashley?' His tone, calm and warming, makes me feel at ease. 'How is that beautiful daughter of yours?'

'She's great and doing very well at school.'

'You were always a good mum. I should have married you when I had the chance,' he jokes.

'How are you?'

'I've been better, to be honest, Ash. I've been out for a year now. I'd really like to see you, would be nice to catch up.' There is a nervous desperation in his voice I've never heard before. I am slightly hesitant about meeting him, but swayed by guilt, I agree.

My mouth falls open, and I stand silent, unable to move, shocked by this gaunt figure that stands before me. His clothes, hanging loosely from his fragile frame, appear to almost swallow him. Has prison been that hard on him? His blotchy skin bubbles like boiling gravy. But bizarrely, the most noticeable difference I observe is his fingernails. Oddly, I had always loved his fingernails, and so had he. Paul is the only man I have known, except Jamie, who insisted on having a manicure every week.

But now his fingernails have changed. They have gone from being small and perfectly manicured to almost twice the size they used to be. How can someone's nails change so much, I wonder? 'You've lost so much weight, Paul, and you look different somehow,' I say.

'Well, you haven't changed a bit,' he says, giving me a hug that must hurt him as much as it hurts me. We order some drinks at the bar and sit on the sofa by the fireplace. 'How are things going with you and Daniel?' is his first question.

Letting his words slide inside one ear and swiftly out the other, I tell him about my recent reunion with Eve. "And what have you been up to?' I probe.

He inhales and sighs so heavily that I fear his shoulders will sink into the sofa and never resurface. Since his release, he has moved to a small town on the outskirts of London, adamant never to return to his old life or ways again. 'I've been working in a food factory. I started as a packer but have worked my way up to assistant warehouse manager.'

'So, are you single, seeing anyone, have any children?' I ask, curious about his private life.

'No, Ash. I've been saving myself for you,' he jokes again.

I try to maintain an icy composure in the hope it will cool my reddening cheeks. Even after all these years, he still makes me feel as dizzy as a kid on a merry-go-round. 'So, Paul, why, after all this time, have you contacted me now?' The hesitant look he gives me as he takes a sip of his drink signals something is very wrong.

'I'm not sure, to be honest. I haven't been feeling very well lately. My doctor has referred me to the hospital for a scan. My appointment is in two days. Will you come with me, Ash?'

I want to say no, to tell him to leave and let me get on with my life, but the fear in his eyes begs me not to. 'Of course I will.'

I take the afternoon off work and drive Paul to the hospital. I'm not sure why, but I follow him into the cubicle and help him undress into his robe. He appears weaker and smaller than he was even two days earlier, as if his illness is causing him to shrink, eating at him from within. Paul has always worn baggy clothes that disguised his thin frame, but nothing could have prepared me for what I now see. He has lost so much weight I can see almost every bone protruding from his body, ready to burst out from under the thin layer of skin that covers them. I fear that if he so much as bends over, a bone might puncture his skin, tearing it apart. I gulp and swallow the tears that threaten to spill from my eyes. Something is seriously wrong, but I can't alarm him. His skin is wrinkly and dry, as if it hasn't been moisturised for months. Like his fingernails, his toenails have also enlarged to almost twice the size they used to be, spread across his nail bed as if they are searching for extra bold vessels to supply oxygen to their dying owner. His once strong muscular body is now as frail as an eighty-year-old pensioner. I pray I don't hurt him as I help him into his hospital gown. Pacing the length of the waiting area, I pick up leaflets and put them down again while Paul sits silently with praying hands, staring at the posters about cancer and emphysema. I think, by this point, we are both certain something is seriously wrong; I don't need test results to tell me that. There is almost nothing left of Paul's once-fit, healthy frame; he is little more than skin and bone. Once the scan is over, I help him get dressed.

'We'll send the results to your doctor,' the receptionist says as we prepare to leave.

On the way back to Paul's flat, we stop to buy some Jamaican food. I go back to his flat and stay with him for a while. He has a small studio flat. His room is furnished with a double bed with a brown leather headboard, matching side tables, and a chest of drawers. In the corner of the room stands a tall, dark-blue cabinet, on top of which sit two turntables, three bottles of champagne, and two bottles of Hennessy. I wonder what he is saving them for. If they were in my house, I would have drunk them already. Although, since leaving Reggie, I've never touched a drop of brandy. Champagne is definitely my drink of choice. The cabinet houses his amplifiers and mixing decks surrounded by hundreds of records. Paul always loved records and has built up a vast collection over the years, mostly of old hip-hop artists, like LL Cool J, Tupac, Jay Z, A Tribe Called Quest, and Gang Starr. Directly in front of the bed is a TV and his beloved PlayStation with a row of games. He has always been addicted to that thing.

As we eat, Paul asks if I want a drink. 'I know you love your champagne,' he says, taking a bottle off the top of the cabinet and placing it in the small fridge that sits in the corner of the room before rolling a joint.

'You still smoke?' I ask, which is a stupid question because the smell of weed hit me as soon as I entered the room, and there is a box on the bedside table full of rizla, cigarettes, and a weed grinder, so it's kind of obvious that he still smokes.

'You know me, never change,' he says, coughing.

'That cough doesn't sound good, Paul, and if I'm honest, you don't look great either,' I finally muster the courage to say.

'Yeah, but I'm getting it sorted now. Whatever it is, they will fix it,' he says in between coughing fits.

Since we met two days ago, I've been trying to shake an unnerving feeling lingering within me, and being here with him is only strengthening it. It's now screaming, begging me not to leave him alone. Growing up, I always ignored my instincts, but as an adult, I have learnt to listen and let them guide me. They are telling me not to leave Paul alone this evening, so I call Chloe and make arrangements for Esther to stay with her. I drink champagne and inhale the second-hand smoke from Paul's weed as we reminisce about the past. I love the smell but will never smoke again.

'Remember when you first moved to Conleigh, and Samantha stole your shoes?' Paul says, laughing wheezily. I laugh so hard I almost fall off the bed.

'Those were the days. Whatever happened to her?'

'She went to jail for smuggling drugs from Jamaica, but she's out now and has two kids. She still lives in Leigh; I think she works in Ikea.'

Paul falls asleep before I do. One minute, he's talking, and the next, he's in such a deep sleep even a roaring lion couldn't rouse him. I used to tease him, saying he could sleep through an earthquake or even standing up. His breathing is shallow, and his lungs appear to be fighting for oxygen. I stare at his face and wonder what is going on under his skin. What would life have been like if I had chosen him instead of Reggie? I'm certain he would have been an amazing father and loving husband. If I could turn back the clock, I would, and I would choose him. I fall asleep watching a movie, but I am woken abruptly by Paul hitting me repeatedly in the face. I jump up, ready to defend myself, but realise Paul is having a fit. His eyes are rolling in his head, he is shaking uncontrollably, and blood is running from his mouth. Not knowing what to do, I immediately call an ambulance. It arrives within fifteen minutes and takes us to the local hospital. A doctor confirms Paul did have a fit and explains that this is a sign that something's wrong with his brain, so they arrange for him to have a brain scan. My leg shakes constantly as I wait for Paul to return from his tests. He is eventually checked into a ward, and the nurse asks about his next of kin. He looks up at me as if searching for the answer to her question. Knowing he is an only child who never knew his dad and his mother now lives in Jamaica, I say what I have to.

'I'm his next of kin.'

'I'm afraid it's not good news. You have a brain tumour,' the doctor says. 'It has spread from your lungs.'

'My lungs?' Paul asked.

'Yes, you have lung cancer and a brain tumour.' The doctor continues to speak. Paul watches his lips as they move, but I can see he's gone temporarily deaf and can't hear a word. He finally blinks, waking from his temporary coma when the doctor says, 'I'm very sorry,' before walking away. Looking up at me, tears settle on the brim of his eyes. I hug him as tightly as I dare.

'Don't you worry, Paul. We'll fight this; this is not the end. There are so many things they can do these days. You could have chemotherapy and other treatments.'

Over the next few days, I visit him in the hospital while they carry out further tests. During my third visit, I have that feeling again. 'Paul, if you could do anything at all right now, what would it be?'

'I'd marry you,' he replies, taking my hand.

I would love nothing more than to marry him, to make him as happy as possible for as long as possible, but it's not just about me. Esther is my priority, but something tells me she will approve. I look into his dying eyes, and the words jump out of my mouth. 'Then let's do it. Let's get married,' I say. He stares at me, not knowing whether to take me seriously. 'I mean it, Paul. I love you—I always have—let's do it.'

As I look at him lying helplessly in the hospital bed, I realise he is the man of my dreams, the man I have always loved, the one who has always been there for me. Seeing him lying there, knowing I am about to lose him, I realise that what I have always wanted I already have in Paul. I had to almost lose him to realise that he is what I've always wanted, not the empty, money-fuelled lifestyles offered by Reggie or Daniel. My brain reasons that marrying him will make him fight for his life, and my heart knows it's right; it knows he doesn't have long left on this Earth, but while he is still here, we can make his final moments as happy as he could ever wish for. I know he always wanted to be with me, and I am determined to give him his last wish, to become his wife, take care of him, and fight this together. I will love and cherish him and make up for the past when I abandoned him, and I will do my best to make him as happy as I can while he still has life on this Earth.

I am stunned when the doctor asks Paul if he has ever had a fit before, and he says he has, that he's been feeling unwell for a while and has been ignoring his symptoms. A few of his friends visit him in hospital.

'So, you're the famous Ashley,' his friend Marlon says. 'This guy talks about you so much I feel like I know you.'

Paul glances at me and smiles. 'We're getting married,' he says.

'What do you mean, you're getting married?'

'We've decided to get married. We've wasted enough time. If Ashley hadn't stayed with me that night, I wouldn't be here right now; I'd be dead. So, we're seizing the moment and getting married.'

I have already started looking for a church when Paul is discharged from hospital five days later. They put him on medication, including strong steroids, to ensure he has no more fits. The doctors plan to operate and remove the tumour from his brain and then tackle the lung cancer. We decide Paul will move in with Esther and me. I know she will love Paul, but I worry that, like me, she will quickly become attached to him, and who knows how long he has left. I tell Paul to make himself comfortable before going to collect Esther from Chloe's. Before we return home, I take her for a walk and tell her I've been at the hospital with my friend Paul.

'I've known him for a very long time,' I say. 'He's very unwell and needs someone to look after him.'

'If he's your friend, why don't you look after him, Mum?' Esther asks.

My heart fills with pride at her response. 'That's what I plan to do, sweetheart. He's coming to live with us. But there's something else.' I paused as Esther gazes at me. 'We plan to get married.'

Her smile widens, showing even her back teeth. 'Will he be my dad?' she says.

My eyes fill with tears as I draw her close. 'Yes. Yes, he will be your dad.'

Paul and Esther hit it off instantly. 'Do you know you are the smartest girl I have ever met,' he says one evening after attempting to help her with her homework. They both share a love of art.

'I am trying to recreate the Mona Lisa but with a modern twist,' Esther says.

'How about a black Mona Lisa with cornrows and a nose ring?' Paul jokes.

Esther thinks this a great idea, and for the next two weeks, they sit around drawing and sketching until Esther has what, to me, looks even better than the original. 'I'm calling her Evold, an evolution from old to new.'

Her art teacher says it's very original and creative and gives her an A. From that moment on, Paul is officially her Art muse.

Over the following weeks, Paul has several appointments for further tests. I take time off work to accompany him whilst juggling wedding planning. Not knowing how much time he has left, we want to get married as soon as possible. We decide to get married in Mary's old church. The vicar gives us a date as early as four weeks' time, so we decide to take it!

'Are you crazy, Ash? You can't plan a wedding in four weeks.' Chloe worries we are moving too fast. 'I know Paul is sick, but are you sure you really want to marry him? By marrying him, you are taking on the responsibility of being his carer.'

'Exactly. I am going to be there to love and care for him and make him as happy as I can for as long as he has left on this Earth.'

'Did the doctors tell you how long he has left to live?'

'No, not yet. We have a hospital appointment this week.'

'Wow, Ash. What you're doing is amazing. Few people would knowingly take on such an immense responsibility. I really hope he gets better and you guys have a happy ending.'

Following Paul's appointment with the neurologist, they booked him in to have the tumour removed a week later.

'We're confident we can remove the tumour without causing any brain damage,' the neurologist says as she talks us through the images on the screen. I tell her we were getting married in three weeks. 'Three weeks is fine.' She smiles. 'You're in the best hands here.'

The tumour is removed successfully, but despite Paul's condition, he continues to smoke. I reluctantly wheel him outside into the garden square opposite the hospital, where he enjoys smoking his cigarettes under the rays of the afternoon sun. His coughing fits increase, and he is forced to carry a small bucket around with him that he spits into. The smell of the fluid that expels from his lungs is almost unbearable. It smells like a toxic sulphur spring and is dark greyish-brown; the smell lingers in the air every time he coughs. Every day, I plead with him not to smoke, but he says he can't stop, that he's too stressed and needs it.

They release him from hospital the day before our wedding and give him drugs to take home, including morphine. Not realising the effect this will have on him, that night, he takes a large dose that sends him into a heavily induced sleep. The following morning, the morphine lingers in his system, rendering him as comatose as smoked bees. Even when I try to do the right thing, something always gets in the way. Paul can barely stand, let alone walk down the aisle. I prepare to call the church and cancel the wedding. Lying on the bed, half-dressed, Paul tries shouting at me.

'Don't cancel it, Ashley. I'll be fine,' he slurs.

The minister agrees to give us more time. 'Have faith; don't cancel just yet. God has told me you will marry today.' His faith is certainly stronger than mine, as looking at Paul half asleep in his boxer shorts, I have no idea how.

The minister is right; Paul is determined. He drinks what seems like a gallon of water that appears to wash most of the drug from his system. Esther, Chloe, and Megan are bridesmaids, and Paul's friend Marlon is best man. I still can't believe this day is happening, even as Chloe does my makeup and helps zip me into my dress. Our budget is tight, but I find a beautiful long white gown covered in pearls. Chloe, Esther, and Megan wear matching grey dresses, and Paul wears a black suit he bought years ago.

'You look beautiful, Mum,' Esther says, handing me the bouquet of calla lilies she made with Chloe. I stare in the mirror and try my best not to cry. Never in a million years did I ever imagine I would ever get married, and I am so thankful. I wish this moment would last forever.

Marlon drives Paul to the church, and the girls and I go in Chloe's car. I selected the traditional *Here Comes the Bride* song for the organist to play whilst I walk down the aisle. A content smile beams across Paul's face as he turns to watch me walk down the sun-drenched aisle towards him. Paul and I wrote our own wedding vowels that we decided not to share until the day, and I struggle to hold back tears as Paul reads his.

'Ashley, since the day I first laid eyes on you, you had my heart. I wasn't a man then and didn't know how to love and protect you. But I am a man now and will be eternally grateful to you for giving me the honour of being my wife. I will love you for the rest of this life and the next.' I even see a tear in the vicar's eyes as Paul struggles for breath, and the usher gives us two chairs to sit on for the rest of the ceremony. Chloe takes pictures, and Esther and Megan throw confetti as we exit the church. As we leave, there is a funeral procession driving past the church. I stare at the mourners, tissues to their eyes, grief on their faces, and fear fills my stomach. After the ceremony, we go to the local Italian restaurant for lunch, and for the first time in weeks, Paul doesn't smoke.

Two weeks after the wedding, Paul has an appointment with the oncologist. We arrive twenty minutes early for the appointment, eager to hear what the consultant has to say. The oncologist has a cold and uninviting manner reminiscent of Scrooge at Christmas, nothing like the team of doctors who had removed Paul's brain tumour. We nervously take a seat opposite his desk.

'Right, so you know you have lung cancer?' he begins. Paul nods. 'Well, in the beginning, we were hopeful. We have successfully removed many tumours from the lungs in other patients, but I'm afraid to say we can't remove yours.' We sit, stunned into silence by his words. He continues, 'You see, the scan shows the cancer has grown into your chest wall, so it is impossible to remove it completely. We could remove some, but it wouldn't make any difference. I'm sorry, there is nothing I can do for you.' He relaxes into the back of his chair. My heart races as I search for the right questions to ask this cold, unfeeling man in his white coat.

'Can't you remove whatever you can and treat the rest with chemotherapy?'

He ignores my gaze and looks directly at Paul. 'No. Listen, you have about a year to live, max, do you understand?' Paul nods, seemingly dumbstruck. He stands as if to usher us out of his office.

Before leaving, I ask, 'Is there anything we can't do? Can we travel?'

'Yes, do whatever you want,' he replies before opening his office door. 'I'm sorry, if we had seen you even three months earlier, we might have been able to save you.'

'I knew it. I had a feeling. I knew it was too late, but I just wanted confirmation,' Paul mutters under his breath.

My voice abandons me, and for a while, I remain silent, eventually asking, 'Is there anything you've always wanted to do, Paul? Anywhere you've ever wanted to go, any places you'd like to visit?'

Paul thinks about this for a few minutes as he stares out the car window at the passing traffic, raindrops falling heavily against the glass. 'I've lived for thirty-five years on this planet. That's 420 months, 21,840 weeks and 152,880 days. Twice as many raindrops fall every time it rains,' he reflects. 'Actually, there is somewhere I'd like to go. I've driven past it a few times, but I've never stopped there. It seems so beautiful. I'd like to go there.'

'Great,' I say. 'We'll go tomorrow. Where is it? Shall we bring a picnic?'

'It's just outside London. We don't need to bring anything. But let's stop off at my flat on the way home.'

I drive to Paul's flat, and he returns to the car with a bottle covered in dust. I can't help laughing as he hands it to me. 'Where did you get this old bottle?' I ask, wiping away the dust to reveal the label, 'Krug private cuvee.'

'I used to sell to this rich guy for years. One day, he wanted some stuff, but he was short of cash, so he gave me this bottle instead. It's worth a few grand. I've been saving it for a special occasion, and what could be more special than finding out you've got under 365 days to live?' he says as tears stream down his face.

'Well, I promise, they're going to be the best 365 days of your life.'

26

Ephemeral Encounter

DESPITE PAUL'S INSISTENCE THAT we don't need a picnic, I pack a hamper with a blanket, water, the chilled champagne, strawberries, and two champagne flutes Chloe gave us as a wedding gift. Paul packs his pill box. Preparing his medication is a ritual he has quickly adapted to. Before breakfast, lunch, and dinner, he lays his pills out on the table in front of him, swallowing them before eating. In contrast to the day before, it's a warm, sunny morning, and the black leather car seats are hot to the touch. I open all the doors and windows, allowing the cool breeze to circulate inside the car before we set off on our journey.

'Where are we going?' Esther asks Paul excitedly.

'You'll see when we get there,' he replies mysteriously. He is too weak to drive. His feet are heavily swollen and will only fit into his slide-on slippers, so he directs me as I drive. 'Slow down, you are driving too fast!' he shouts.

'Drive faster, Mum!' Esther shouts back. She loves the feel of the wind blowing against her face.

After an hour, we turn off the motorway and continue driving along the country lanes, passing through a quaint little village until we reach a large lake. Esther gasps as she inhales its beauty, and for the first time during the journey, she is silent, in awe of our surroundings. Trees and flowers reflect off the clear lake water as pristine as a landscape painting. The sky, as blue as the Azores, spreads out like a blanket, covering the sky for eternity. The sound of the birds singing makes my heart flutter with delight. Paul smiles as he watches the expressions on Esther's face.

'I think this is what the Garden of Eden was like,' she says, staring at the scene before her.

'I imagine so,' Paul says.

'Well, if this is where you go when you die, I'd be happy to live here forever.'

We make our way up a hill to a small pub. Paul chooses the table nearest to the lake, under a sycamore tree, where a gentle breeze carries its fragrance that fills my nose. Esther watches the bees carry pollen from one lavender flower to another, and small planes fly overhead.

'There is a flying school nearby,' Paul explains.

A waitress takes our food order, and Paul begins his tablet ritual. He takes his tablets out of the pillbox I bought him and lays them out in a line on his napkin. He takes five after placing his food order and the other five once it arrives. I look at him and laugh to myself. Ever since his diagnosis, he has taken his medication this way. He orders fish and chips with mushy peas—after fried chicken, fish and chips is his favourite meal.

'That is my last meal of the day,' he declares after lunch.

'You have to eat again, Paul. You can't take your tablets on an empty stomach. I'm cooking when we get home. What do you want for dinner?'

'I don't want anything. This is my last meal,' he says. I'm not sure what he means by his last meal, but I decide I will make another of his favourites, spaghetti bolognese, for dinner.

After lunch, we take the hamper from the car and sit by the lake. Esther makes friends with a group of children and plays happily with them in between moments spent telling Paul how much she loves him and how happy she is that he is her new dad.

Paul hugs her tightly. 'You know, Esther, we are only sent here for a while, and when God is ready, he will come and take us back to heaven.'

'I know that.' she replies. 'Our bodies will die, but our spirits will live on forever and ever.'

I shake my head and smile. 'Where did I get you from? How did you get to be so clever?'

'I don't know.' She shrugs and turns to run off to play with her new friends.

I turn to Paul. 'So, what do you think happens when we die?'

'Like Esther said, we never die. Our body is just a shell we live in whilst here on this Earth. There are many dimensions in the universe. When we leave this body, we simply pass from one dimension to another. We pass over from this universe to the next, each time occupying a new body, but our soul remains the same. It's like a fresh start. We won't remember our past life, but our core being, our soul, will remain as it always has been.'

'Are you scared?' I ask as we lay on our backs, looking up at the heavens.

'There's nothing to fear, Ash. When it's your time, it's your time, and it's my time now.'

I start to cry. 'But it might not be your time yet. We can see another doctor and get a second opinion. They could be wrong.'

'No, they're not, Ash. I knew it all along. I know my body is dying; I can feel it. You made me the happiest man alive the day you married me. To be with you is all I ever wanted, and you know it. You gave a dying man his last wish. You loved and cared for me when it mattered. These last few months spent with you and Esther have been the happiest times of my life. You knew I was sick and were prepared to give everything up for me. THAT is love, a love I never thought I'd experience in this lifetime, but thanks to you, I have. If I die tomorrow, I will be the happiest of men.'

'Well, you've got us for at least another year,' I joke. Paul smiles.

The night before we got married, he asks me if I am sure I want to take on the responsibility of caring for a dying man. 'I am just grateful you are allowing me to,' I tell him. I can see the guilt in his eyes. 'Don't worry, Esther and I will be fine,' I tell him, but I am really unsure if we will be. But one thing I know for sure is that this time next year, he probably won't be here. My only regret is that it's taken for him to be near death for me to realise how much I love him. I am determined to love and care for him until the very end, regardless of how difficult things may become. I open the champagne and fill the Swarovski-covered flutes. Esther comes running over as she hears the cork pop.

'Can I have a sip?' she asks.

'No,' I say.

'Just a sip,' Paul says, staring at me, his eyes pleading for forgiveness as Esther takes a small sip.

'Cheers to life and the afterlife,' she says before handing the glass back to Paul and running back to the other children.

I shake my head. 'Sometimes I feel like there's a wise old person living inside that girl.'

Once we're back home, I prepare dinner despite Paul's insistence that he isn't hungry. Esther lays the table, but Paul just sits watching the TV and refuses to join us. 'Paul, if you don't eat, you can't take your pills,' I plead.

'I'm not hungry, Ash. You two eat; I'm fine,' he says and continues watching TV, leaving his evening dose of medication untouched.

The next morning, I wake up and make breakfast. Esther eats hers and leaves for school, but Paul still refuses to eat.

'Please eat your breakfast and take your tablets,' I beg.

'No,' he replies in between coughing fits. 'I don't want to take them anymore. I'm not going to continue to take the pills to keep me alive. I'm not scared, Ashley. I'm ready to move on. You have made all my earthly dreams come true, Ash, but it's time now. I'm ready.'

'Will you stop saying that!' I scream.

I think he's being selfish. What about me and Esther? Has he thought about whether we're ready to lose him so soon? 'Please eat and take your pills,' I beg him.

He then begins coughing uncontrollably, and the fluid that fills his lungs expels through his nose and out through his mouth. 'I feel hot,' he cries, trying to tear the clothes off his body as though they are burning him. I try to help him undress, but as I do, he falls to the ground and curls himself up into a ball. 'I'm hot!' he shouts again, defecating on the floor, his insides spewing out as if someone had cut him open. Grabbing a handful of towels from the cupboard, I attempt to clean him up, but brown bile and urine pour uncontrollably from his body as he lies on the floor, shivering. I cover the floor with more towels and try to lift him off the floor and onto the sofa. He grabs the edge of the square leather pouffe to lift himself off the floor. I try to help him up as he coughs violently, and more fluid seeps through his nose and mouth, running like a hose without a stopper.

Turning him over, I hold him in my arms, screaming his name, shaking him repeatedly. His eyes are open, but I know life has left his body. As instructed by the emergency operator, I give him CPR until the ambulance arrive. They try to retrieve him, but it's too late; he has left this dimension and moved on to the next. I hold him tightly as his soul slips away from his mortal body into the billowing light that illuminates his soul. Before the ambulance crew leave, they move his body from the living room floor and place him onto our bed, where I cover him in blankets and lay with him until the coroner arrives to take his body away.

27

Life After Death

I AM SITTING IN the living room when Esther arrives home from school. Intuitively, she knows Paul is gone. 'Has he gone, Mum?' she asks. I burst into tears. 'Don't cry, Mum. His body is dead, but his spirit lives on forever; it will never die.'

The grief of losing Paul weighs heavily on my heart, and it takes three months before I go back to work. It had taken me so long to find Paul and realise he was my soul mate, only to lose him in the same breath. The only thing that stops me from sinking is Esther.

'Mum, I have a plan,' she says one day after arriving home from school. 'I think you should go back to work. You'll feel much better. You can't stay down forever; that's the last thing Paul would have wanted.' She tells me that the universe brought the two of us together for a reason. That I did what I needed to do, and now it's time to move on. 'Some experiences are meant to be ephemeral. In life, almost everyone wishes they could turn back the clock, but if we had the power to do that, life would stand still and never move forward because there would always be someone, somewhere, with regrets,' she says. Her lecture continues. I must be grateful and happy for the times we spent together, and that we were lucky enough to be able to get married and make each other happy. 'You were there for him when he died. Most people don't get a second chance, and you did. You always say that life's too short, so why don't you start that business you always dreamed about?' My fifteen-year-old daughter is as wise as a philosopher.

'Oh, and I have an idea about setting up a foundation. I did some research, and it turns out that sixty per cent of men die before the age of sixty-five from avoidable diseases; it's called avoidable mortality,' she tells me. The foundation would help raise awareness and encourage men to seek help if they feel unwell rather than wait until it's too late or ignore their symptoms like Paul did. 'Even if we save one life, it will be worth it. I can help you. I can set up a website and do all the social media for it. What do you think?' she said, finally coming up for air.

I look at her. 'God really blessed me when he chose me to be your mother,' I say. Esther is right; life is too short, and it's time I went back to work.

With Esther's help, we set up the Healthy Men's Club three years later. We travel up and down the country, giving talks on avoidable mortality and raising awareness. Both men and women thank us for highlighting these issues. I know it is all worth it when, at the end of a healthy living conference in Birmingham, a seven-year-old girl approaches Esther and me.

'Hi, I'm Kelly. Thank you for saving my dad's life.' Esther and I look at each other. 'He wasn't feeling well and went to the doctor after listening to one of your talks. He had prostate cancer, but because the doctors caught it early, he is better now.'

My eyes well with water, and Esther embraces Kelly in her arms. 'Thank you, Kelly. Hearing this makes us know what we do is worthwhile,' Esther says.

Because of Esther, we turned our tragic experience into a positive one, and I can finally see what she has been trying to tell me all along. 'Mum, life is like a road map; no road is ever straight. Sometimes, we go left, sometimes, we go right, and sometimes we take a wrong turn and get lost. Then, we find our way and continue our journey until we reach our final destination. And once we get there, we stay for a while and then decide we want to go somewhere else, and so we keep moving, always going from right to left, up and down, discovering new places and meeting new people along the way. And that's the best life you can live, one of freedom and adventure. If we do something we don't like today, we go to bed, get up the next day and say, I will not do that again, today is a new day. That's what Nana Sue says, "Life's journey is eternal, and you can always start over in this life or the next."'

'Who is Nana Sue?' I ask.

'She is the lady that talks to me in my dreams. She's always with me.'

I stare at her in disbelief. My daughter has a spiritual guardian. That's where she gets her wisdom from. I always thought she was an old soul. I hold her close, knowing that as long as we had life, we will live to see another day, and everything would be just fine.

Acknowledgements

I want to express my deepest gratitude to the strongest, most incredible woman I've ever had the privilege of knowing—my grandmother. Your unwavering strength and boundless love have been a guiding light in my life.

To my parents, sisters, family, and friends, I owe immense thanks for standing by me during the darkest moments of my grief. Your support and compassion have been my anchor.

To each of you, I offer my heartfelt appreciation. You've touched my life in profound ways, and for that, I am endlessly grateful.

In loving memory of Charles Christopher Bailey
1969 – 2016

Michelle's journey into writing started following the loss of her husband to cancer in 2016.

After this tragic event, she went on holiday to Andalucia, where she began to explore writing as a means of expressing her experiences.

Upon returning to London, Michelle decided to take her writing further and enrolled in creative writing courses, transforming her story into "Fools' Paradise".

Set in an inner city London estate, where Michelle grew up, the story explores themes of love, loss, heartbreak, and even a touch of magic. Drawing from her own experiences as an urbanite Michelle has created a relatable and engaging narrative that brings a breath of fresh air to the urban fiction scene.

Michelle's journey is a testament to the transformative power of storytelling. It illustrates how personal experiences, even the most painful, can shape one's creative path.

Despite her newfound passion for writing, Michelle continues to work in the property industry.

ISBN 978-1-3999-7343-4

9 781399 973434 >